PUBLISH

AND

PERISH

D1166494

TOR BOOKS BY PHILLIPA BORNIKOVA

This Case Is Gonna Kill Me

Box Office Poison

PUBLISH
AND
PERISH

phillipa bornikova

TOR

a tom doherty associates book

new york

This is a work of fiction. All of the characters, organizations, and events portrayed in this novel are either products of the author's imagination or are used fictitiously.

PUBLISH AND PERISH

Copyright © 2018 by Melinda Snodgrass

All rights reserved.

A Tor Book
Published by Tom Doherty Associates
175 Fifth Avenue
New York, NY 10010

www.tor-forge.com

Tor® is a registered trademark of Macmillan Publishing Group, LLC.

The Library of Congress Cataloging-in-Publication Data is available upon request.

ISBN 978-0-7653-2684-3 (trade paperback)
ISBN 978-1-4299-4763-3 (ebook)

Our books may be purchased in bulk for promotional, educational, or business use. Please contact your local bookseller or the Macmillan Corporate and Premium Sales Department at 1-800-221-7945, extension 5442, or by email at MacmillanSpecialMarkets@macmillan.com.

First Edition: April 2018

Printed in the United States of America

0 9 8 7 6 5 4 3 2 1

This one is for Christine, who has loved these books, been my cheerleader, and if this ends up as a TV show, it will be all her doing.

Acknowledgments

I couldn't have done this book without the advice and research provided by Dr. Ben Hanelt, professor of biology and parasitology at the University of New Mexico. It was over a dinner with Ben and his wife, Dr. Berkley Chesen, when I was moaning about a particular plot problem I was facing, that Ben said, "You know, there are parasites and bacteria that can switch the gender of their hosts." And I had my answer. So thank you, Ben.

PUBLISH
AND
PERISH

1

It's never a good thing when you go to knock on a person's door at almost ten at night, and it swings open. The full moon gave me enough light to examine the lock and a scar upon the wood. The deadbolt had been ripped out of the jamb, the splinters revealing the pale pine beneath the stain. I had been anticipating this meeting with Jolyon Bryce ever since his mysterious hints that he knew something about my inexplicable power to avoid death and dismemberment at the hands of supernatural creatures such as vampires, werewolves, and Álfar.

My flight from Los Angeles had landed, and I had stopped briefly at a friend's apartment to pick up the cat, and stopped at my apartment, which smelled musty after a nearly two-month absence, to drop off said cat and my luggage. I then headed to Brooklyn for the bracing part. Only to find evidence of forced entry.

I could've been walking into danger, and I wasn't really all that ready to confront danger. My broken rib still hurt. I thought about just backing off and calling the police when a shadow loomed over me. I gave a yelp of fear and swung my purse like a morning star at the figure. There was a grunt of annoyance as the purse found its target and I found myself looking up into my boss, David Sullivan's, aquiline features. As usual, he was frowning at me.

"What are you doing here?" I hissed.

"Keeping an eye on you!"

"You're following me."

"Yes."

"Well, stop it!"

"Well, stop doing stupid stuff."

"I don't do stupid stuff!"

"You absolutely do stupid—"

A sound from inside the house put a stop to our inane conversation. "Shit! There's somebody in there," I said, and I went barging through the door. I had a brief moment where I did think *maybe I actually do do stupid stuff* but by then it was too late and I was inside the house.

The sound that had drawn my attention had stopped and now all I heard was the loud ticking of a clock and very faint music. David laid a warning hand on my shoulder. With a head jerk, he indicated I was to get behind him. This was one order I decided to obey. He was a vampire and far more indestructible than fragile little human me. I slipped around behind him and stepped out of my shoes. We crept forward down the hall. David had stopped pretending to breathe so my breaths seemed very loud as they punctuated the tick-tock of the clock.

The door into the living room was to our left. David pressed himself against the wall and took a quick glance around the corner. I tucked in next to him and took my own peek. We were definitely doing the high/low thing since I'm five feet tall and David tops out at six. My quick glance into the room revealed the face of the grandfather clock staring at me like a startled automaton. Its base was buried in a drift of stuffing torn from the cushions of the floral-print sofa.

In the center of the room, between a battered armchair that had also been cut open and the aforementioned sofa, Jolly's wheelchair lay on its side. There was a huddled form on the floor beside the chair, and a figure with its back to us kneeling over it, hand on the inert body's throat. There was just enough moonlight through the big picture window for me to see the glint of gray-gold hair. It was Jolly lying so still on the floor. I let out a scream that was half horror and half fury and I charged into the room. I didn't make it very far. David grabbed my arm and swung me back behind him. Not only was he male, he was a vampire and far stronger than any human. My back slammed up against the wall of the hallway.

David gave a yell when a slim hand was thrust around the edge of the door, grabbed him by the throat, and yanked him into the living room. I shrieked again. I wanted to run for the front door, but it was clear from the crashes a fight was taking place so instead I ran into the room to help my friend.

And froze. David was locked in a bizarre embrace with a beautiful woman. Long black hair streamed down her back, her skin was the rich cream of old ivory. She wore jeans tucked into knee-high boots, and a shimmering blue silk blouse set a counterpoint to the gray and blue tweed jacket. All of that made a brief impression, but what had frozen me in place were her fangs.

She was a vampire.

My brain was having a stuttering conversation with itself. *She's a vampire.*

She can't be a vampire. There are no women vampires.

AND WHAT PART OF SHE'S A FUCKING VAMPIRE AREN'T YOU GETTING?!

David had also been knocked off balance by this impossible presence. I had seen him fight. That's how he'd gotten the ugly scars that marred one side of his face—fighting a crazed werewolf to protect me. I could easily recall the inhuman scream that had torn from his throat as he'd launched himself at the creature. David had practically bent Deegan into a pretzel, but this woman was strong. She had lifted David off the floor with one hand. Unlike a human, he didn't have to worry about being choked. I watched in horrified fascination as his fingernails elongated until they looked like curved daggers at the ends of his fingers. The effort desiccated his body and he no longer looked handsome. He looked monstrous, and the expression on his now-gaunt face terrified me. I watched those nails drive into the woman's slender throat and began sawing back and forth. He was trying to decapitate her. I saw the fear flash in her dark eyes.

"David! No!" I screamed. "She may know something!" It was a logical argument, but the real reason for my objection was I did *not* want to see a beheading by fingernail.

I needn't have worried. The woman literally flung David away from her. His etiolated body crashed against the far wall, leaving a large dent in the drywall. Blood dripped off the tips of those horrifying nails. It was echoed by the pale and almost translucent blood that coursed down the woman's neck and stained the beautiful blouse. Her eyes flicked across me, and she seemed about to speak, but then David launched himself at her once again. She whirled, racing toward the big picture window that looked out across the small pasture at this Brooklyn riding stable. The glass exploded outward as she jumped through the window. The shards glittered diamond-like in the moonlight. David was at her heels. Apparently escape was not an option for this impossible conundrum. David was going to kill her.

I had a bigger worry. Jolly. I ran to his side, and dropped down on my knees next to him. Blood coursed down the side of his head and there seemed to be a dent in his skull. I wanted to cradle him, but was terrified I might drive a bit of bone into his skull. I lifted one limp hand and felt for a pulse in his wrist. It was there but very faint and very rapid. I grabbed my phone and dialed 911.

I had just finished giving the dispatcher the address, and she assured me the police were on the way, when there was a thud. I jerked and looked up in fear. It was David, who had just jumped back in through the broken window. He looked shaken.

"Is he alive?" my boss asked.

"Barely. Ambulance is on its way. Did you catch her?"

He shook his head. "She turned into mist. Vapor. Vanished in the trees. I didn't know we could do that. I can't do that. I don't know any vampire who can do that." He was babbling, the words tumbling over each other like frightened weasels. I had never before seen him lose his cool this way.

I looked pointedly at his disturbing nails. "I didn't know you could do that either."

He looked embarrassed, and the nails began to retract. "We don't advertise it."

"Probably a good thing." I paused and added, "I thought there weren't any female vampires."

"There aren't," he said automatically.

"Then what the hell was that? A shared hallucination that was able to throw you into a wall?"

"I don't know." He wiped a hand across his brow leaving a smear of vampire blood from his nails and hand. "Jesus, Mary, and Joseph, I've got to tell somebody. I just don't know who. Maybe the Convocation." He headed for the door.

"You're leaving?"

"I've got to. Don't tell the police about . . . her."

"I can't *not* tell them."

"A vampire attacking a human. That's not good. Undermines everything we've tried to build—"

"But she did attack him!"

"Okay, fine. Well, at least don't mention it was a woman. Just say it was a vampire." He broke off and gave me an odd look. "I just don't want that information out there until I have a chance to—"

"To what?"

"Think about what it means . . . might mean." He walked out, then stuck his head back around the door. "And leave me out of it too. The firm doesn't need any more notoriety."

"You want me to lie to the cops? I'm an officer of the court," but I was talking to air because he was gone. I heard the engine roar to life and headlights flared briefly in the windows. I was alone and on my own. "And what if she comes back?" I muttered as I once more dropped down next to Jolly.

A few minutes later the ululating cry of a siren drew closer and closer. A few seconds after that EMTs rushed in, a young woman and an older man. The man did a quick examination, and ordered, "Backboard."

The young woman ran out of the room. "How is he?" I asked.

"Next of kin?" the EMT asked.

"His lawyer."

"Guess I can tell you a little. Not good. Blunt force trauma. His skull's depressed, pressing on the brain. He's going to need surgery." The girl returned with the backboard, and they got Jolly onto the board and his head immobilized.

"Where are you taking him?" They gave me the name of the hospital, and I gave Jolly's limp hand one final squeeze as they wheeled him out.

More sirens, and the room got a lot more crowded as a bunch of police rushed in. Among the Brooklyn police was an officer I knew well, Detective Lucius Washington. Washington was a handsome African American in his mid-thirties and he'd been the cop who'd investigated when back in August my then boss at the law firm had been torn apart by a werewolf. He also wasn't a cop in Brooklyn.

He placed his hands on his hips and revolved slowly to take in the mess in the living room and the broken window. "So, where's the trail of bodies?"

I thought it was churlish of him to bring up the events in New Jersey when I'd been attacked by five werewolves and five werewolves ended up dead. That had happened last year. Ancient history. I gave him a hostile look. "You're *way* out of your jurisdiction, Detective. This is Brooklyn. You're assigned to the Nineteenth. Up. By. Central. Park." I punched each word to make my point. "So, what? You just happened to be in the area? Visiting your grandmother or something?" I challenged.

"I heard it was you and I just had to see what had happened this time."

I glared harder. "Look, I need to go to the hospital with Jolly."

A uniformed Brooklyn officer stepped in. "We need a statement first, Miss . . ."

"Ellery. Linnet Ellery. I'm Mr. Bryce's lawyer."

"At ten o'clock at night?" Lucius broke in. The Brooklyn cop nodded in agreement.

"I also train a horse for Mr. Bryce. The horse was with me in California and I needed to discuss getting him back to New York." Cognizant of David's instructions, I told half the truth. "There was a vampire here when I arrived." I temporized a bit more. "It ran when I came in."

"Given your history with Powers, that was probably a good call on his part," Washington said dryly.

"How did it get in?" the Brooklyn cop asked.

"I'm not sure." My eyes slid to the broken window.

"The glass is broken outward, Linnet," Washington said gently. He walked away and looked at the blood staining the carpet. "This is vampire blood. You want to tell us what actually happened?" His brown eyes drifted pointedly to the damaged wall.

"Must have happened during the attack," I blurted.

"I guess a crippled guy would end up with a lot of upper-body strength," Washington mused in that fake tone that tells you how stupid you just sounded. I had a moment where I did a mental Homer Simpson *Doh!* I felt terrible. I was horribly worried about Jolyon, angry at David for abandoning me, freaked out about the female vampire, and now I was lying to the cops and doing a really shitty job of it as evidenced by the detective's expression.

"The place was all torn up like this?" the Brooklyn cop asked.

"Yes."

The cops exchanged glances. "Like they were looking for something?" the uniform asked Lucius.

"That's what it looks like to me. We should search the rest of the house."

"I'm coming with you," I broke in.

"No, you're not."

"In my capacity as Mr. Bryce's lawyer, I damn well am."

Lucius looked to the cop, who shrugged. I took it for acquiescence and gestured for them to preceed me. We moved through the rest of the old farmhouse. I noted the accommodations that had been made for a man in a wheelchair. In the study, the big desk had been pulled into the center of the room so Jolly could maneuver his chair behind it. The desk drawers were pulled out and dumped, the books pulled off the shelves. It was a man's room, a feeling intensified by the smell of leather and pipe tobacco. I wondered if this really was Jolyon or a role he played of the tweedy English gentleman? The walls were filled with photos of horses at competitions, and the ribbons and silver trophies won by said horses. We also found the source of the music, a flat-screen TV set into a bookcase was on and the DVD player was playing a video of a dressage horse doing a freestyle ride. The other plastic DVD cases had been opened, and the discs flung aside. They were strewn like metallic snowflakes across the floor.

We went into the kitchen. It was like the Vandals and the Visigoths had stopped in for a snack. Sugar gritted under the soles of my shoes as we crossed the linoleum floor, and flour rose in puffs at each footfall. Every cabinet was open, and all the dishes removed and smashed. Spilled milk, orange juice, and broken eggs formed a gelatinous sludge at the foot of the refrigerator.

We moved into the more private living areas of the house and noted the growing trail of destruction. Mirrors had been smashed, the flat-screen television in the bedroom kicked in, even the clothes in the closet had been ripped off their hangers and flung onto the floor.

"If you were searching for something it's logical that you'd pull off the mattress and cut it open, and pull out the drawers and dump their contents, but this?" I said.

"Frustration leading to wanton vandalism," Lucius said.

The bathroom smelled of spilled shampoo and broken bottles of aftershave. Glass crunched against the stone tile floor, and pills of various sorts and colors topped the mess like Christmas sprinkles on sugar cookies. I noted the roll-in shower, the handholds, and the plastic chair placed beneath the nozzle.

We returned to the living room where evidence techs were fluffing fingerprint powder across various surfaces. "Any idea what they might have been looking for?" the Brooklyn cop asked me.

I shook my head. I couldn't say what I really suspected. That more people than just David were watching me, and that they had attacked Jolly before he could reveal something about me and the strange power that had kept me alive for the past half year. The local cop folded up his notebook and handed me his card.

"Well, call if you think of anything," he said.

A few minutes later the evidence techs and the Brooklyn cops trooped out. Washington was still lingering. "You need a ride home?" he asked. I shook my head. Washington studied me for a long moment then added gently, "I wish you would trust me, Linnet. I'm not your enemy."

In a sudden flash of candor, I said, "I can't. There's too much weird shit going on, and I don't want to involve you."

"That's what I do." I didn't answer. "Trust me, I can handle weird." I still said nothing. He sighed. "Okay, just know I'm here when you're ready or able to talk."

After one final look, he left. I returned to Jolly's study and went through the strewn papers around the desk looking for an address book, anything to indicate a family contact. I came up empty and sat on the arm of a ripped-up chair trying to think through the steps to figure out how to deal with a man in a medical emergency with no apparent next of kin available. As I sat pondering I noticed the cable box on a lower shelf. It was probably grasping at straws, but I found the controls, switched from DVD to cable, and brought up a list of the recordings on the DVR. Most were television show or movies, a couple of news shows, and a local New York public access station. I clicked on each show, more in an effort to be thorough than with any real hope it would yield returns. Then I hit the public access station. It was a show called *Mysteries!* hosted by Emmet Rice. It sounded like the kind of show where people came on and talked about Big Foot, or ancient aliens, or Nazis on the moon. The prompt on the television asked if I would like to *resume*. I did.

Seated at a small table was a tweedy professorial type in his fifties and a young Asian man dressed in blue jeans, a sweater, and a leather jacket. The younger man wore heavy, black-rimmed glasses, and his glossy black hair brushed the collar of his sweater. He was talking when the recording began again.

"All of my research indicates this is a parasite."

"But the legends—" Tweedy Man began, only to be interrupted.

"I'm a scientist not a folklorist. The idea that some sort of Godzilla thing is going to be unleashed and stomp around and kill all the Powers is just . . . well, ludicrous."

I had this sudden vision of Godzilla ripping the roof off the sky-scraper that housed the law firm of Ishmael, McGillary and Gold, plucking vampires out like a man pulling sardines from a can and tossing them down its throat. I gave a hollow laugh, switched off the television, and pulled out my phone. It was time to call for a cab and head to the hospital.

By the time the cab dropped me off at the Lutheran Medical Center it was past midnight and my eyeballs felt scratchy. A young couple was huddled in the waiting room, their arms wrapped around each other. I wondered if it was a parent or a child that had brought them out this late at night. A TV hung on the wall, the sound turned very low. On the screen, a man was trying to sell some amazing cleaning product. I went to the desk and explained the situation to a woman who looked as tired as I felt.

"I haven't located any next of kin, but I'm his attorney, and I called for the ambulance. Can you at least tell me his current situation?"

"He's in surgery. That's really all I can say."

"But he's not dead?"

"Not to my knowledge."

"Oh, thank God. Look, he's English so I doubt he's got private insurance—"

"That's been handled."

"Excuse me?"

"A man and a woman turned up and gave us a prepaid credit card. There was twenty thousand dollars on the card."

"The woman, what did she look like?"

"Long dark hair. Sort of foreign looking. The man was Japanese."

"As in Japanese Japanese?"

"Yeah, he had an accent." The woman looked less tired and suddenly concerned and compassionate. "You're very pale. Are you all right? Do you want to sit down?"

"Yeah, I do."

She came out from behind the desk and walked me over to a chair. I sank down onto the cheap vinyl seat. "I don't understand any of this." I looked up at the woman. "Did they say anything?"

"Just that this was money for Mr. Bryce's care and that they would check back on him."

"No! You've got to keep them away from him! Mr. Bryce was attacked, and she was the one who did it. I walked in on her, but she got away."

The receptionist was frowning. "Then why give us the money for his care?"

"I don't know." I pressed a hand against my aching head. "Maybe to lull us? Get close to him and finish the job? We can't take the chance. We need to tell the police." Agitated, I stood and groped for my phone in my purse. "Look, I'm going to stay here until he's out of surgery. I know the doctors can't tell me anything, but I just want to make sure he comes through the surgery okay."

"Of course," the woman said gently.

I called the number the Brooklyn policeman had given me and reported this latest wrinkle. They promised to keep an eye on things. I had my doubts. Despite the uncompromising angle of the chairs I fell asleep. A gentle touch to my shoulder brought me bolt upright. I forced my gummy eyelids apart. An older doctor in blue surgical scrubs stood by my chair. I looked around the room. The young couple was gone. According to the wall clock it was 5:15.

"I'm Dr. Kapur. You're Mr. Bryce's attorney?"

"Yes."

"He's out of surgery. He's in intensive care so—"

"I can't see him. I understand. I know you can't give me any details, but can you give me a general prognosis?"

"Cautiously optimistic. We'll know more when . . . if he regains consciousness."

"So he's in a coma? Sorry, I know you're limited in what you can tell me."

"Let's just say he's unable to speak right now, and until he wakes we won't know the extent of the damage."

I fished out a business card and handed it to him. "Thank you. If he does wake could someone let me know? Also, there may be a woman or a man and a woman who will try to see him. Please alert the nursing staff to call security if they see either of them. She's the one who attacked Mr. Bryce. The man may be working with her."

"I will warn the staff immediately."

"Thank you. Okay, then I guess I'll head home."

2

Later that day I was seated in a trendy café near the Metropolitan Opera House having lunch with my fellow associate at Ishmael, Mc-Gillary and Gold, Caroline Despopolis. Outside the windows was a gray March day with the wind trying to peep up women's skirts and tugging urgently at coat hems. I felt lightheaded from lack of sleep and gnawed with worry.

Caroline noticed. "You're being very quiet. It's not like you."

"I can't figure out if there's a barb in there or not," I said.

Caroline, her perfectly coiffed blond hair falling like spun gilt over her left shoulder, set aside her grilled eggplant sandwich and gave me a *look*. Caroline and I had started as rivals in the vampire-owned law firm of Ishmael, McGillary and Gold. We had moved cautiously into frenemy territory, and finally graduated to actual friends, but there was still an edge to all our dealings. She proved it by saying,

"Little bit. So what's wrong?"

"A friend of mine got assaulted last night. He's in the hospital."

"That's awful. I'm sorry."

I hesitated and then said, "And I think I might be a superhero."

"Okay, I know going to the Academy Awards, and wearing a designer gown, and hanging around with a famous movie star might go to your head, but—"

"I also stopped a massacre, and cleared two Álfar of murder . . . and nearly got murdered myself—"

"Which sort of disproves your theory, doesn't it?" Caroline drawled.

I stared down into the depths of my potato leek soup and gave the contents a stir. "Not if my super powers only work on . . . well Powers. You know, werewolves, vampires, and elves."

"Oh my!" Caroline said sarcastically.

"I'm serious. I mean, think about it. My very first case at IMG had me battling murderous werewolves. Then I go to California and get attacked by murderous Álfar. And the score so far? Linnet one, werewolves and Álfar zero."

"Proving that you are just very lucky." Caroline's tone was dismissive.

"You are a very unusual human, Linnet Ellery." The words of the elderly Álfar who had tried and failed to ensorcel me and force me to commit suicide returned to haunt me. I had puzzled over Qwendar's words and now with Jolly incapacitated I had no hope of an explanation for what made me so unusual.

Caroline's voice pulled me back to the present. "So, how do you intend to use these newfound powers? For good, I hope."

I didn't miss the sarcasm, but decided to give her a straight answer. "Actually, I was sort of thinking I might go into Fey and get John."

"He's that Álfar private detective who used to work for the firm, right?" I nodded. She cast her eyes heavenward. "And are you utterly out of your mind?"

"Oh, probably." I sighed.

She eyed my almost-untouched soup. "Are we done or are you going to eat?"

I pushed away the bowl and shook my head. "Not really hungry, I guess."

We divided the bill and tossed down money. Just inside the door I pulled a hat over my ears, gritted my teeth, and faced the weather. The weather for the last few days in LA had been beautiful, and I just wasn't prepared to face the rump end of an East Coast winter.

Back in my office I called the hospital, and finally got to the nursing station in intensive care. They wouldn't tell me anything beyond the fact that Jolly was still there. Next, I called the barn manager and told Kim what had happened to Jolly. At that point, I had no more excuses for not working so I began reading through a stack of case files, but found I couldn't concentrate. All the cases revolved around people who had money wanting more of it, and it just felt pointless right now. A friend was lying in a coma and I feared it had something to do with me, and another man I cared about in a complicated, undefined way was a prisoner in Fey again thanks to me. I couldn't do anything for or about Jolly right now, but I might have the power to free John. Both of those things seemed way more important than the cases on my desk.

Since I couldn't do anything about Jolly, I decided to concentrate on the John problem. I also had the excuse that John was a trained investigator. If I got him back I could hire him to investigate the attack on Jolly. Grabbing a legal pad, I made notes about how I would approach the rescue I was contemplating. Once I had it down on paper I studied the list. One notation in particular leaped out at me.

Have at least a fig leaf of legality.

There was only one way to get that. I spun to face the computer and typed in the train schedules between New York and Philadelphia. It turned out there was a train leaving from Penn Station within the hour. Grabbing my hat and coat I headed out, only pausing by her desk to tell my assistant, Norma, "I might be late getting in tomorrow."

Norma was an older woman whose perfectly coiffed silver hair had all the softness of a knight's steel helmet. I had inherited her along with my office when my previous boss had been torn apart by a werewolf. I had a feeling she did not approve of the substitution.

She proved it again when she cranked her head around to look at me and muttered, "Like this is a surprise."

It hurt, and I found myself defensively saying, "The firm sent me to LA. I wasn't exactly vacationing in California." I forced a smile and added, "And hey, look at it this way, less for you to do."

Suddenly Norma gave me one of her rare smiles. "Linnet, honey, you almost got there, but you needed to drop the whiny justification, and add *not that you do much anyway*." Bland contempt dripped off her tongue as she demonstrated the proper delivery.

I suddenly realized that Norma might actually like me, and I smiled back at her. "I didn't know how to supply the rim shot," I said and headed to the elevator.

Two hours later a taxi dropped me in front of the narrow blue-sided, three-story house in a suburban Philly neighborhood. The snowmen that had been there—God, had it only been a week ago—still stood in frozen immortality in front yards. The streetlights made the ice crystals glitter, and the sunken stone eyes seemed faintly ominous.

I shook off the unease, climbed the front steps, and rang the bell. Big Red O'Shea, a great bear of a man with a shock of graying red hair, threw open the door, gazed down at me from his six-foot-three height, gave a bellow of pleasure, and enfolded me in a rib-crushing hug.

"Meg, honey! Linnet is here," he shouted as he led me into the hall and took my hat and coat.

Meg O'Shea, a plump little woman with a smile that was sheer sunlight, emerged from the kitchen. There was a smear of flour on her nose and her husband tenderly wiped it away with his thumb and gave the tip of her upturned nose a quick kiss.

From the other side of the hall a middle-aged man appeared in a doorway. He was a smaller version of Big Red—same red hair, but there was only gray at his temples. Unlike the older man his hair hung below his shoulders. Big Red glared and Parlan quickly gathered the loose tresses into a ponytail and confined it with an elaborate silver clip in the shape of a butterfly.

Meg looked nervously between the men, then hurried into speech. "Oh, Linnet, it's so lovely to see you. I'm making an apple pie. You'll stay to dinner, won't you?"

"Yes, happily," I said.

"You here about John?" Red asked.

"Indirectly," I hedged.

"So, no word," Meg said sadly.

I shook my head. "The various branches of government just keep passing it back and forth. State says it's a problem for customs, customs says the FBI ought to handle it. The FBI says it's technically not a kidnapping since John wasn't carried across state lines and they send me back to State."

"So we've lost our son forever," Red said. A dull flush rose in Parlan's cheeks. He spun on his heel and went back into the den.

"We have our son back," Meg said softly and gripped Red's upper arm. Her husband's jaw worked but he said nothing.

I looked away, uncomfortable at being a witness to their pain. Technically, Meg was right—Parlan was their child, bound by ties of blood and DNA, but also a stranger. Because the day they'd brought the infant son home from the hospital a powerful Álfar queen had stolen the human child and left her own son in his place.

It seemed odd now, almost fifty years after the Powers had revealed themselves to humans that nothing had been done about a kidnapped child, but back in 1972 no one exactly knew how to deal with the fact that vampires, werewolves, and Álfar had crashed into our consciousness and our world. Since the mid-1960s we had been living in a world where your lawyer or history professor was likely to be a vampire, your stock broker a werewolf, and your weekends would be spent watching gorgeous Álfar actors on the screen at your neighborhood gigaplex, but it took a while for society to adjust. In 1972 no one knew how to react or what to do about a child stolen away by elves. The government and the legal profession had ultimately told the grieving parents that there was nothing they could do and to just be glad the queen had left a substitute. So the O'Sheas had given this new son their old son's name—John—and raised him as their own.

John O'Shea had followed in his human father's footsteps. He'd become a cop, put in his twenty years, retired, and opened a detective agency in Manhattan. He had been hired to conduct investigations for Ismael, McGillary and Gold, which was how we met. While being pursued by murderous werewolves and to keep me and my clients safe, John had called on his Álfar powers and taken us out of human reality and into the Fey. Where his real mother had decided that she'd like to have him stay. She gave him a hideous choice—his freedom or ours. Of course John had stayed. Some might have found that act of gallantry quaint, even laughable, but Meg and Big Red O'Shea had instilled all their essential decency in their exotic child, and John lived up to what his parents would have expected of him.

That left the queen with two sons, one Álfar and one human.

Having lost interest in the human child, she dumped him back where she'd found him. But Parlan wasn't a child any longer. He was a forty-four-year-old man who had never lived in the human world. Instead he had lived as a pampered Álfar prince, had no education to speak of, and didn't have a single useful skill.

"Look, I've got an idea. It's a little crazy . . ." I paused. "Okay, it's totally off the wall, but it might just work to get John back. But I need your help to make it work."

"We'll do it," Red said.

I held up a restraining hand. "Wait until you hear what I'm planning. You were a cop and this is . . . dodgy."

"I need to get that pie in the oven," Meg said. "Give me five minutes."

"I'll help," Red said. "And how about we order a couple pizza pies rather than cook that roast? Faster that way."

She nodded and they went into the kitchen. I went into the den in search of Parlan. He was slumped on the couch frowning at the television. I was startled to see he was watching *Bridezillas*.

My unruly tongue once again took control. "You watch crap television?"

He raised aquamarine eyes to meet my gaze and gave a small nod. Then shrugged. "It's the closest thing to Álfar behavior I can find. You're all so controlled and subtle. I have a hard time understanding what humans want or mean."

"Wow, so the extremes of human behavior are the norm for the Álfar?"

"Yes, I suppose that is true."

"How are you doing?" I asked.

"After the excitement at the Academy Awards it was hard to come back to this." He gestured around the room.

It had a comfortable lived-in look. There was a toy saddle on one worn arm of the sofa ready for when a grandchild came by and wanted to play cowboy. Pictures of Meg and Red's four human children, one changeling, and five grandchildren lined the walls. I stared at a photo of John in his PPD dress uniform. His hair was cut short, but it couldn't disguise the tri-part colors that streaked the underlying blond or the unearthly green of his eyes and the pointed features and upturned eyes and brows that marked him as *other*.

Parlan followed my gaze to his changeling brother. "Yes, my nemesis. The man against whom all others are measured and found wanting. Even Brian, Marie, Patrick, and Sean cannot measure up," he said, referring to the human children Red and Meg had had after the loss of their firstborn.

"John couldn't help it. You know how the Álfar throw glamours on humans whether they want to or not." I changed the subject. "You're unhappy."

"Yes. Very."

"So do something about it. Have you thought anymore about my suggestion?"

"Opening an Álfar restaurant?" Parlan asked. I nodded. "I've begun looking into cooking schools," he said, and it didn't sound like it had been a good experience.

The wind was moaning around the eaves of the house, and snow began pecking at the window like nervous fingers. I hoped I was going to be able to get back to New York and my apartment tonight. If I didn't, John's cat, which I had adopted, was going to be really pissed.

"I thought you'd made a hobby of cooking in Fey," I said.

"I did, but you humans make everything complicated. I can't just open a restaurant. There are permits and leases and liquor licenses, all of which require money, which, since I have none, means I must find investors. I have no idea how one accomplishes such a thing."

"The firm I work for represents a lot of very wealthy people. I can ask around." I paused then added gently, "And you're human too."

His fingers convulsed on his thigh, closing into a fist. "My body maybe, but my mind . . ." He shook his head. "As for the cooking school, I realized having a few credentials would probably help me find these investors, and I wanted to know something about human cooking and how I could meld the two styles. Most important, it gets me out of Philly."

The slang name for the city set an odd, almost charming contrast with his very formal speech patterns.

"And away from Meg and Big Red," I said softly.

"Yes. They seem like nice people, but I don't know them and they're not my parents. And I'm certainly not the son Big Red would have wanted."

"How does he feel about the restaurant, the cooking thing?"

"He doesn't understand. And it just adds to his sense that I'm not . . . manly." He reached back and flipped his long hair over his shoulder. He gave me a rueful smile. "I could tell him how many females I have bedded, but I'm not certain that would redound to my credit or mollify him."

Meg and Red came into the den carrying a bottle of red wine and four glasses. Wine was poured. Red offered a toast.

"To absent friends."

The tension was back in the room, and Meg stared down at her tightly clasped hands. I hurried into speech.

"Well, that's why I'm here." I gave both Red and Parlan a smile. "And I need something from both of you O'Shea men. Red opened his mouth to object, but thought better of it. Meg gave me a grateful smile. "What I'm going to say here has to be kept in absolute confidence, okay?" They all nodded.

I drew in a deep breath and began. "I seem to be a somewhat indestructible human. When any of the Powers attack me, weird things happen."

Red was frowning. "What do you mean, weird things?"

"A jar of marbles falls off a shelf, breaks on the stairs. The were-wolf slips on the marbles, falls through the bannister, and impales himself. An Álfar tries to shoot me and a giant movie camera on a track goes nuts and runs over her."

"It's true," Parlan said. "I witnessed it at the Academy Awards. When that Álfar actress attacked you the Oscar statue fell so you could escape and while it held your weight she fell through."

Red's frown deepened. "I don't buy it."

I took another deep breath. "There's more. When I was in LA that old Álfar who got arrested . . . well, he tried to put a whammy on me and make me commit suicide." Meg gave a gasp and Parlan uttered an Álfar oath. "Obviously it didn't work. Which got me to thinking. If no Power can touch me then I could conceivably go into Fey and bring John back out."

"You're human. You can't cross without Álfar help," Parlan said bluntly.

"Which is why I'm here. I need you to talk to your friends and former bodyguards who helped us in LA. See if any of them would be willing to go up against an Álfar queen and commit a bit of sedition."

Parlan sank back against the sofa and tugged at his upper lip. His expression was very thoughtful.

"Would they do that?" Meg asked her stranger/son.

I waited, but Parlan didn't respond so I spoke up. "John had made it pretty clear that the Álfar tend to live as if they're all starring in their own private operas. The bigger and more dramatic they can make an event the better, so it just might work."

Parlan stirred. "While insulting, that is an essentially accurate statement. We all like to preen, but there is a vast distance between attacking an Álfar traitor and going up against a powerful queen in her own stronghold."

"So, you're saying no one will help me?"

"No, I didn't say that." He tipped a bit more wine into his glass. "There is significant restlessness among the young. I think there will be some Álfar who would help us. Unfortunately most of them stayed in California," Parlan concluded.

I noted the use of the plural, but didn't remark on it. Just took a moment to feel the glow that comes from knowing you have an ally.

"What about Ladlaw?" I asked. "He came back to New York with us to report to Queenie."

"And the very fact of his reporting to my mother probably means he would not be sympathetic to your goals."

I darted a surreptitious glance at Meg to see how she reacted to her son discussing *his mother* while his actual mother sat not three feet away from him. I saw the slight flinch and the tightening of the lines around her mouth, and I supposed that the bonds of biology and labor were stronger than years.

Red jumped into the conversation. "You're talking about kidnapping here." His frown was Jovian in its intensity.

"Which is why I need you and Meg to hire me and my new company, which specializes in freeing people from cults, to go in and *rescue* John."

"And does this company actually exist?" Red asked, but he was starting to smile.

"I'm a lawyer. You think I couldn't whip up a corporation in a flash?" I said with a grin. "And yes, the company will exist by the end of the day tomorrow. I prepared all the paperwork on the train down."

"I will get a message to Tulan, Aalet, Cildar, Donnal, and Zevra," Parlan said.

Meg suddenly spoke up. "This could be dangerous. You say you can't be hurt, but what about John?" Her eyes slid toward Parlan. "Or anyone else who helps you? I don't want either of my boys hurt."

A sudden memory returned. Of a werewolf literally tearing my boss, Chip Westin, in half. My strange power had saved me via a broken high heel, a weakened elevator door, and a long plunge down an elevator shaft for the werewolf, but it had done jack shit to protect Chip. I considered lying, but I couldn't, not to these people.

"There is a risk—"

"I'll take the risk," Parlan interrupted.

Red cranked around to stare at him. "It's clear you're signing up for this crazy scheme, but why? You don't know John from the pope. He doesn't mean a damn thing to you," he grated.

Parlan stood and looked down into his father's red and irate face. "He was loved by you, you are proud of him, you miss him, and I'm clearly a poor substitute. I'd like to not always be compared and found wanting."

Red looked away, and his cheeks turned an even deeper shade of brick red. Meg gave Parlan a pitying look, then stood, crossed to him, and gave him a brief hug. For a moment he looked like a vulnerable little boy, then the Álfar mask was back in place. Parlan studied his nails.

"And if *she* wants him it would give me infinite pleasure to take him away from her," he added, and his tone was ugly.

I caught a late train back to New York City after accepting a retainer check from the O'Sheas in the amount of one hundred dollars, dated the day after tomorrow. During the journey I called the kid who was subletting John's apartment and told him he needed to be out in the next two days. He wasn't happy and I felt a bit like a jerk. If this didn't work I'd have to find someone else to move in. Or maybe I should just give up at that point and assume that John was lost for good. I also called the hospital. There had been no change in Jolly's condition, but the police had placed a guard on the ICU. That made me feel a bit better.

I was beyond exhausted by the time I got home, and Gadzooks, John's big orange tabby cat, was indignant over our brief reunion after my long absence in California. It was past midnight and he hadn't had his customary evening snack. Food reduced the piercing yowls to twerting grumbles, and he deigned to join me in bed. I stood for a moment contemplating the foot of my pretty four-poster bed, remembering how a few days after John had stayed behind in his mother's realm I had awakened to find a small branch from a flowering tree resting on the comforter and filling the air with floral perfume. That hadn't been the last contact I had with John, but I didn't like to remember the last time. He had been cruel.

So why, exactly, are you doing this?

Since I didn't have an answer I went to bed.

3

I came padding out of the bedroom at eight a.m. the next morning.
I needed coffee and instead I found an Álfar standing in my living
room. He was tall and willowy with long black hair that held a tinge of
green and deep green eyes. His features were preternaturally perfect,
chiseled and refined, and he was dressed like a prince from a Viennese
operetta, all braid and lace and knee-high boots and very tight pants.

"Oh, holy shit!" I yelled. "Jesus, Ladlaw! What if I slept in the
nude?"

He shrugged one shoulder. "Then you would have been embarrassed." He gave me a suggestive smile. "And I would have enjoyed
the view."

"Jerk. Would you like some coffee?"

"Yes, please, and by the way, that is a singularly ugly nightgown.
It would be better if you did sleep nude."

I looked down at the faded-yellow-flannel, floor-length nightie
with the pink roses and gave him an exasperated look. "It's cold,
okay? And not only do I have to put up with strange Álfar in my
apartment, I also get shit from the Álfar fashion police too?"

"Yes, because it is exceedingly ugly."

I gave up, made a disgusted noise, and marched into the kitchen to pour out two cups of coffee. As expected, Ladlaw loaded his down with sugar. I had recently learned that Álfar all had a weakness for sweets. And yet I had never seen a fat Álfar, which made everything about the unnaturally beautiful creatures even more unfair.

"You want some breakfast?"

He looked surprised by the question, glanced around my small apartment as if looking for something, and finally nodded. I realized what he was looking for, and laughed.

"No, I don't have a cook, a maid, a butler, or any other kind of help."

"Is it difficult to live so . . . roughly?" he asked as he leaned against the counter and watched me pull bacon, eggs, and bread out of the fridge.

"No. You adjust. When I was growing up I was fostered in a vampire household, and Mr. Bainbridge had servants, but then I went away to college and learned how to fend for myself. Basically it's a tradeoff—time versus money." Ladlaw cocked his head questioningly. "You either spend the money to hire help or you spend the time to do it yourself." I laid out bacon on a jelly-roll pan. "Each person has to figure out which is more valuable for them."

"I had never thought of time as money."

"That's actually a human saying, but you Álfar live a long, long time so time is probably less meaningful to you."

"Interesting. I should talk more with humans."

"Speaking of which—why are you talking to this one right now?" The bacon went into the oven and I asked, "How do you like your eggs?"

"Scrambled." I started cracking eggs into a bowl. Ladlaw studied the backs of his hands for a moment then said, "Cildar was contacted by Parlan, and then he contacted me."

My stomach filled with lead and I dropped the whisk into the bowl. "And you told the queen," I said dully.

"No." Surprised, I whirled to face him. "Zevra has a theory that perhaps senility is not solely a condition which afflicts humans. Certainly her majesty's behavior toward me was . . . most uncivil when I returned from California."

"So, she was pissed that you all helped me stop Qwendar from killing humans at the Oscars, and you were the only one she could get her hands on because the others stayed out West."

"You have apprehended the situation most accurately."

"So, what? Why are you here?"

"I have come to offer you my services. I will accompany you and Parlan when you assault Fey."

"Assault? Ugh, that makes it sound so . . . I was more picturing *The Matrix*. You know, me walking serenely through the guards while they struggle to touch me."

"I am unfamiliar with this Matrix, and while I have seen your unusual ability at work, the building is large. Having a guide to lead you to the Prince's quarters will be of help to you. If you take too long they may move him."

"Good point. A question. Is it smart for us to enter Fey right where she lives? Would it be better if we went in someplace else? Made our way to the Fey version of the Dakota?"

"No. While we can enter our realm from anywhere, our presence will not go unnoticed and that will give them more time to prepare their defenses."

"Last question. Any ideas on how to get that ice sliver out of John's eye?"

"I am not a magic wielder, and that's deep magic."

"Well, we'll figure it out. One problem at a time, right?" I stuck out my hand. "So, welcome to the Scooby Gang, Ladlaw." He looked confused. "You don't know Scooby-Doo?" He shook his head. "Well, after breakfast we have to fix that," I said.

After breakfast I dumped Ladlaw in front of the TV and

downloaded a number of episodes of *Scooby-Doo*. While he stared, rapt, at the screen I took a quick shower, then called Parlan and told him to get up to New York and over to my apartment as soon as possible.

I waved a hand in front of Ladlaw's face. "Look, I've got to go to work. When Parlan gets here tell him to call me." I scribbled down my office number on a notepad, and just to be sure I pointed out the phone. You never knew how much an Álfar knew about human technology.

Returning to the bedroom I dressed in my Professional Woman Uniform. A glance out the window had shown me a gray day that was trying to spit snow at the long-suffering commuters who, with turned-up collars, were rushing toward subway and bus stops. I dressed in a white wool knee-length skirt, a rolled-neck sweater in twinning shades of gray and lavender, and knee-high black boots.

I stepped back into the living room and Ladlaw gave me an approving look. "Much better," he said.

" 'Cause your approval is so important to me," I snarked.

He looked startled and I realized that they weren't used to getting any kind of push back from humans. The Álfar threw out attraction without consideration or effort. Humans went weak-kneed over them. *But not me.* I really did need to figure out why, but that was yet another problem for another day.

Once at the office I asked Norma to see if Mr. Ishmael had time for a brief meeting. Since Shade was a senior partner and had his name on the firm's letterhead, I could only hope that the fact I was sort of his protégé would actually get me in to see him.

I closed the door to my office and worked for several hours drafting a particularly knotty brief for the Federal court. Norma stuck her head in the door.

"Mr. Ishmael will see you now."

I saved my work and headed for the stairs. Two steps and my cracked ribs decided to make themselves known. I made a U-turn and headed to the elevator instead.

The seventy-third floor was the preserve of the partners. The only humans on that floor were assistants and the very handsome receptionist, Bruce. I stepped out of the stairwell and into a hushed vision of teak, marble, and the heavily glazed windows that protected the vampires from direct sunlight. I actually got a friendly smile from Bruce because I had managed to get through to him that just being gorgeous wasn't going to be enough to get him Made by a vampire. In fact, he waved me over, looked around in a furtive fashion, and whispered.

"I'm almost done with my novel. Would you be willing to read it for me, Linnet?"

I was surprised and a bit dubious. I wondered what a rather self-centered twenty-year-old might have to say, but I nodded.

"Sure. I didn't know you wrote."

"I've been scribbling since I was a kid. I put it aside, but what you said to me about accomplishing something made me realize I really missed it."

"Good for you, Bruce. But I better go before Shade takes a call or something."

I went down a hallway to my mentor's office. It was elegant and rather austere and it even sported a prie-dieu. Whenever Shade had been Made and whoever he might have been, one thing was clear—Shade had been devout. The senior partner, his hands clasped behind his back, was gazing out the window at the thickening snow.

"I find myself trying to remember the touch of snow," he said thoughtfully.

I was surprised. "You can't feel it?"

Shade turned to face me. He had chiseled features and silver-flecked dark hair. The bespoke suit accentuated his broad shoulders and narrow hips. "It's too subtle a touch."

As usual my unruly tongue took control and I said exactly what I was thinking. "I think that's sad."

"So do I. The feel of a baby's skin, the soft flutter of a lover's sleeping breaths." He broke off. "I'm sorry, Linnet, I am being maudlin." He moved to his desk and indicated the chair across the polished wood expanse. "So, I understand you have formed a company."

"Can I never put anything past you?" I complained as I sat down.

His lips quirked in a small, closed-lip smile. "No, it's how we vampires keep our mystique."

"Then you know what I'm planning."

"I can suspect. And I suppose you wouldn't listen if I asked you not to?"

I shook my head. "John deserves a chance to actually decide who he wants to be and where he wants to be."

Shade drummed his nails on the desk and frowned into the distance. "I suppose since he was an employee of the firm we do have some responsibility. So IMG will also pay to undertake this endeavor, but we insist on having one of our own along to observe."

There was a click and the door to the office opened. "And let me guess, it's going to be David," I said without looking around.

"I can't let you go careening off on your own," came the voice of David Sullivan from over my shoulder. "You'll just end up in the soup if I'm not around to bail you out."

Shade was sporting what would be a grin on anyone who wasn't a vampire. Vampires were too elegant to actually grin. I cranked around to look at David.

"Well, I hope you're not going to assault fairyland in a Canali suit," I said, but I couldn't help noticing how beautifully the material fit his body.

"How are the ribs?" David asked.

"Fine," I said shortly, not wanting to admit that they still hurt. I looked back at Shade. "May I have a few days off?"

He nodded gravely and gestured toward the door with the air of a medieval pope bestowing a blessing. David and I left. Outside the office I looked up at David and gave him a frown.

"I do not need a babysitter."

"You so totally need a babysitter."

"You do modern slang really poorly."

He glanced around then leaned in closer. "What's the word about your friend?"

"He's in a coma."

"I'm sorry."

"And the female—" David looked alarmed and I broke off. "Uh. The *person*, you know. Anyway, she and some guy turned up at the hospital with a prepaid credit card."

"That would suggest she's not the individual who attacked your friend."

"She's was kneeling over his body. This might be a way to try and get to him. And thanks for ditching me, by the way. So, who did you report to?"

He looked away. "I haven't actually. I wasn't exactly sure who to tell, and it raised an interesting issue for me. But enough of that," he snapped. "Back to your latest harebrained scheme . . . What's the plan?"

"We go to my apartment and create the plan."

He forced extra air out of his lungs to create a sigh. "I was afraid of that. I'll meet you there. I need to gather a few items."

Parlan was at the apartment when I got home. He and Ladlaw were slouched on the couch still watching *Scooby-Doo* and sharing a bag of potato chips I'd hidden away for a snack-attack moment. For once I had thought ahead and picked up Chinese takeout for dinner. David was going to be on his own. I didn't know what kind of blood he preferred and vampires were as snotty as wine snobs about their preferred blood type. Some vamps wanted fat-saturated blood. Others something highly oxygenated. It was rumored that some more dissipated vampires liked the blood from a drunken host for the buzz it provided.

The two couch potatoes bestirred themselves and went to get plates and utensils while I unloaded the white and red boxes from the big paper bag. We tucked in, and both Parlan and Ladlaw were fascinated watching me wield chopsticks. They insisted on trying and Ladlaw caught on right away. Not surprising given the grace and quickness of the Álfar. It took Parlan a bit longer but he was fairly adept by the time we had finished.

There was a knock at the door. I ran to open it and as expected it was David. He had his left hand hidden under his long overcoat, and once he reached the table he revealed why. Concealed beneath the coat was a gun about two feet long with a snubbed-off barrel and an extremely truncated wooden stock. It landed on the table with a solid thud.

"Dear God, what is that thing? It looks like something that would have been carried by gangsters back in the roaring twenties," I said.

"It's a cut-down BAR." Parlan and Ladlaw looked lost. "Browning automatic rifle," David explained and then looked down at me. "And yes, a gangster did use one like this. Clyde Barrow carried one," David answered.

"As in Bonny and Clyde?" I asked.

"Yes."

"You weren't Clyde Barrow, were you?"

His voice caught on a laugh. "No. My body isn't riddled with bullet holes." He touched his chest. "Well, aside from that one I got in California." He rightly interpreted my expression. "Oh, don't feel guilty about that too."

"I haven't been very good for you," I said.

"Not true."

There was an awkward silence, then I said, "Seriously, we want to avoid any deaths."

"And you may not get what you want, Linnet. We are assaulting the realm of a powerful individual who can use magic to steal away her son. We're going to meet resistance," David said, and his tone was grim.

My stomach lurched and I wished I hadn't eaten quite so much kung pao chicken. I turned to Parlan and Ladlaw. "Have the Álfar adopted guns?"

Ladlaw looked down his nose and Parlan laughed and said, "We use bows when we hunt."

"And swords to settle arguments," Ladlaw added.

"These noisy contraptions . . ." Ladlaw gestured at the gun.

"Aren't sporting," the two men concluded in chorus.

"Well, I'm not a damn bit interested in playing fair," David said. "I want us to get in and get out without anybody getting hurt."

"On either side," I added.

"No, on *our* side," David corrected.

I planted my hands on my hips and glared up at him. "I repeat—I don't want anybody killed."

"Linnet, five werewolves attacked you and they all ended up dead." My guilt must have shown in my face because David added more gently, "Not that you actually killed any of them, I'm not saying that, but nonetheless they died. And if Álfar start dying they're going to fight back. I want to be able to counter that."

Ladlaw had been looking increasingly grim. "No one died in

California. I had not heard of these other deaths. I can't be party to this if deaths are likely." The tall Álfar bowed gravely. "I thank you for the meal." He headed toward the door.

"You're going to warn her now, aren't you?" I called after him.

"I feel I must. I am torn between loyalty to my people and my friendship with Parlan, but . . ." He shook his head and walked out the door.

I sank down on the couch and tried not to cry. To know that John was only a few short miles away, that I might have freed him, and then to have it all collapse was a crushing blow. Silence hung like cobwebs in the room.

David picked up the sawed-off BAR. He had a smile that was grimly satisfied. "Well, good, this nonsense has been laid to rest."

My head jerked up and I glared at him. "If it was so stupid why did you sign on?"

He stared down his nose at me. "To try and keep you out of trouble, of course." He pulled on his overcoat and slipped the gun beneath it. The door shut with a sound like endings.

"Arrogant bastard!" I said.

Parlan looked at me for a long moment. "He's in love with you, you know."

The complete idiocy of the comment, and also the undeniable truth of it, stole away my breath. The only thing I could think to say was a totally inadequate, "Oh . . . shit."

Because the risks to a vampire and a human woman who got involved were pretty significant—as in end-up-dead significant—there was an absolute prohibition against vampires—all male—ever Making a woman. Same went for werewolves. The problem for vampires was if you actually loved someone and knew you were going to live virtually forever and they were going to die after a few short years the temptation to keep them with you would inevitably lead to a Making. Which would end the love affair real fast since a female Making was punishable by death for both parties.

David loved me. I tried to analyze my emotions and found only tangled confusion. There was only one thing I knew and I knew it with a razor's clarity. I would have to leave the firm. For David's sake, the temptation had to be removed.

My world was in ashes—career, John, Jolly, everything. I stood, gathered up the printouts I had made of the Dakota off Google Earth and started to toss them into the trash.

Parlan gripped my wrist and held me back. "Wait. There may be another way to enter Fey."

A green shoot had appeared in a landscape of nuclear winter. "Okay. How?"

"My mother herself brings you in."

"And she'd do that . . . why, exactly?"

"Because you will challenge her for her place."

"You want me to fight an Álfar queen so I can become a pseudo-Álfar queen?"

"Yes."

"Just me against Queenie? Nobody else involved?"

"Yes."

"You're nuts." Parlan looked crestfallen, then brightened when he saw my grin. "I love it," I said. "What do I have to do?"

4

Parlan wrote the formal challenge using a thick-nib fountain pen and expensive watermarked paper from a stationery store. It also wasn't in English and that's when it struck me yet again that I was naive. The Álfar were aliens. Not human. A different species with a different language living in a different world.

After studying the delicate swirls and twists I gave Parlan a suspicious look. "Okay, what does it say? You're not talking smack are you?"

"I don't know what that means."

"Are you being rude?"

"A little." He gave me a quick grin that made him look younger. "But very elegantly."

"Well, thank heaven for that." I paused and added, "Is there a spoken version of this language?" I asked.

"Of course." Parlan said something that sounded more like a bubbling fountain than discrete words.

"So, how do you come to know English?"

"We study it. We are, in a manner of speaking, in your country and English has become the international language. But I can't write it worth a damn. Frankly, it's an absurd tongue. Why do you have so many words that sound the same but are spelled differently and mean different things? *Bear* and *bare*. *There* and *their*. *Dear* and *deer*. And not the least—*right* and *write*. Ridiculous."

"And we did that just to inconvenience you," I drawled, amused by his princely sense of offended privilege. "Now, what does it actually say?"

Lifting the page off the table, Parlan declaimed, "Whereas the most Puissant and Supreme Queen has taken from me my vassal and servant without recompense or substitute and offered insult to the person of This Most Noble Human and Friend of the Lifeless, This Human therefore calls challenge against the Queen and demands the right of combat upon acceptance of this challenge to ascertain authority in all realms and all principalities until the stars burn dark and worlds ends."

"Forget the cooking school. You should become a lawyer," I said.

Parlan smiled. "I shall make ten copies, have you sign them, and leave them at the intersection of ley lines. And make sure your signature is impressive. Lots of flourishes."

The letters were signed and deposited and I went meekly back to work the next day. I knew I needed to quit, had to quit, but I couldn't do it until after Parlan and I pulled off our caper. Leaving one of the most prestigious law firms in the country was going to draw attention, and I couldn't withstand the scrutiny right now. The best I could manage was to avoid David. He probably assumed I was sulking over his refusal to help, but I'd live with that if it would keep him away until I could quit. I kept my office door closed and arranged for a deposition to be held at an opposing council's office rather than our own so I could get out of office.

I also kept calling the Brooklyn police, who wouldn't tell me anything even when I forcefully pointed out that I was Mr. Bryce's attorney, and the hospital, who also wouldn't tell me anything beyond the fact that Mr. Bryce was still in intensive care. I was just about to call the barn manager when she called me. Kim didn't waste any time.

"Linnet, have you heard anything about Mr. Bryce?"

"Nothing beyond the fact he's still in the hospital."

"Look, I was authorized to pay the bills for the management of the stable, deposit board checks and so on, but you know what's it's like at a barn—you're always a dollar short and a day late when it comes to horses. Jolly left a pretty good cushion in the account, and there's the board checks, but I don't know how long we can keep operating. We've got five horses here that are school horses so their costs are all on Jolly's tab. It's pretty clear Rikki needs to have his hocks injected, and that's five hundred bucks, and . . ." Her voice faded. "What happens if he . . . well, you know?"

"First, we're not going to think like that. Jolly's a fighter and he has good doctors. He'll be okay." *I hope.* "Next, how much cushion do you have?"

"We can probably go for at least three months, four if I stretch, and that only works if we don't have any unexpected expenses."

I exhaled and leaned back in my chair. "Well, I hate to do this to you, but I'm about to create an unexpected expense. We need to get Vento home."

"I know. Jolly had me make arrangements as soon as it was clear you were coming home. They'll be picking him up in LA on Thursday. With layovers and so forth he'll probably get here in six or seven days."

"Great, that's one problem dealt with."

"Keep me posted? I'm really fond of Jolyon."

"Believe me, I will."

I hung up and went back to work, but it was hard to focus. I wondered if the energy I was spending on John should have been directed toward Jolly. Why had he been attacked? I was pretty sure it was about me, but I'd like to know for sure. Was the female vampire behind it? Did he have a will? Relatives? I needed to find them. Well, if I got John back I could put him to work doing what he did best—investigating.

The next day the queen's reply came back. She had accepted the challenge. I rushed out of the office and bought a pepperoni pizza on my way home. The changeling was perusing her letter when I arrived. He looked up as I came in.

"She's set the date for two days hence and she's settled on swords . . . that smells good . . . you know how to use a sword of course."

"Not a clue," I said with a serenity that I hoped came across as real. I dropped the pizza box on the table.

Parlan goggled at me. "You don't . . . then why—"

"I gotta trust the super power."

"*Hilal*."

"Is that an Álfar cuss word?"

"Yes."

"And it means . . . ?"

"It roughly translates as *oh holy shit*." Parlan sighed and dropped his face into his hands. "You are putting a great deal of faith in this mysterious ability."

I opened the box, pulled out a slice of pie, and started eating. "It hasn't failed me yet," I mumbled past a mouthful of hot, gooey pie. "And I got the basics—keep the pointy end aimed in her direction."

"Well, I can't teach you swordplay in two days," Parlan said grumpily, but the lure of pizza trumped his annoyance and he fished out a slice. "We're to meet in the courtyard. I went by the human building," he mumbled around another huge bite. "It is heavily guarded."

"Yes."

"So how are we getting in?"

"I've got a plan for that."

The next day I went out and rented a panel van. Which totally made me feel like a serial killer. I then had a magnetic sign for a fake florist shop made up, and I stuck that on the driver's door. Next up, research on the residents so I could pick my mark. It wasn't easy because the residents of this exclusive real estate jealously guarded their privacy. Which had a certain piquant irony since these wealthy humans were literally living on top of another version of the Dakota that existed in Fey and they had roommates they didn't even know about.

I settled on the wife of a hedge fund manager who had just made a million-dollar donation to the Metropolitan Opera Company, so it wasn't inconceivable that the opera guild would send her a thank-you bouquet.

I actually cooked a dinner the night before, and Parlan and I engaged in nervous conversation until I could gracefully retire to the bedroom and worry by myself. Gadzooks abandoned me to sleep with Parlan on the couch, the ungrateful little shit. I comforted myself with the thought that maybe he was just a man's cat.

The appointed day dawned, the clouds were gone, and the sun was shining. I decided to take it as a good omen. I dressed in a pair of riding breeches and paddock boots that had rubber soles with a good grip. I topped it off with a sweater and a tweed jacket my folks had bought me in Scotland. Studying my image in the mirror I thought I looked very Lara Croft or Indiana Jones. I almost added a hat, but realized my playing dress up was just to cover my growing nervousness.

I left the bedroom with Gadzooks twining and purring around my ankles and threatening to trip me with every step. Parlan was already up and dressed—in all his Álfar finery.

I sighed. "Well, let's hope you can fit the coveralls on over all that froufrou." I held up a plain white coverall with the logo of my fake florist shop. Parlan reared back and his nose pinched and turned white as he gazed down at the offending garment.

"I am going to wear that?"

"I'm wearing one too. We can ditch them once we're in Fey," I added to mollify him.

He grunted a grudging assent and removed his coat and boots to pull on the coveralls. A new thought struck me. One that should have struck me a long time ago. "You do know how to drive, right?"

"No, I've always preferred horses. I know I will need to learn if I'm going to obtain that pizza delivery job." He tried to keep it light, but there was real anger and real pain beneath the bantering tone.

I gave him a hug. "There is going to be more in your future than that. Believe me." He closed his eyes and gave a sharp nod.

Down the stairs and into the van. We stopped at a florist's shop to pick up the elaborate floral arrangement of roses and gardenias that I had ordered the day before. Fortunately, the bored girl behind the counter didn't notice the supposed florist van parked out front.

The trees of Central Park hove into view burnished with a pale green that gave us hope that spring was at last arriving. At the corner of Seventy-second Street and Central Park West the stone bulk of the Dakota loomed up on our right. The high gables, deep roofs, and dormers gave it a Germanic quality. Behind it towered an aggressively modern skyscraper. The incongruity was perfect given the reality of the two worlds existing side-by-side.

We rolled past the main entrance with its guard and gate and around to the service entrance. I hopped out, gathered up the bouquet, and approached the guard on that door.

"Delivery for Mrs. Mascheroni."

"I'll take it," said the guard. His square cleft chin showed blue where five o'clock shadow was already forming despite it being just a bit before nine a.m.

"I need to get a signature."

"Nice try. No."

I gave him my most limpid grey-eyed look. "But my boss—"

"No. *My* boss will have my ass."

I stood there feeling stupid and cursing movies that made this kind of thing seem easy and routine. Parlan climbed out of the van and joined me. The guard stiffened warily at his approach.

Parlan pulled out an elaborate pocket watch. "We must resolve this quickly. If you are late you will have forfeited."

I turned and headed back for the van. "Hey," the guard yelled after us. "What . . . ?"

The slamming of our doors cut off the rest of his sentence. I rested my arms on the steering wheel.

"Well?" Parlan asked. "What now?"

"Just how Álfar are you in your attitudes?"

"Very."

"Shall we go through that front gate?"

"Will your firm get us out of jail?"

"Maybe."

"Good enough for me."

We pulled back into traffic and went around the block. As we approached the main entrance I saw the older, heavy-set guard walk into the guard shack and pick up the telephone. I had a feeling Blue Jaw had just made a call about the suspicious people in the van. I glanced down at my watch. We had five minutes.

There was a small sign in front of the art nouveau iron gates that read AUTHORIZED PERSONS ONLY BEYOND THIS POINT. I spun the wheel, floored the accelerator, and sent us toward the gates. One was half open, so with luck we wouldn't do too much damage. Parlan braced himself against the dashboard, and I had a brief flash of the guard rushing out of the guard shack with his mouth working frantically. The little sign bounced off the hood of the van and we careened into the gates. The open one swung back. The other was bolted, and there was a shriek of abused metal from both the car and the gate. The bolt sheared off, the gate flew open, and we were through the narrow tunnel and in the central courtyard.

I had a memory of this space when I, along with John and two of my clients, had been pulled into that courtyard by the queen's guards. That time the guards had pulled us into Fey when we were still out in the street. This time we remained in the human world, and humans were reacting . . . badly.

Guards were converging from all directions. An older couple just emerging from the building stared at us with shock and some fear. Parlan jumped out, tore off his coveralls, and reached behind the driver's seat to pull out a sword. His entire affect changed. He was no longer a rather stocky middle-aged man. He was an Álfar prince and it showed in his stance and the disdainful expression.

"God, don't stab anybody! Don't make this worse than it already is!" I screamed in warning as I climbed out.

The guards were almost on us when the humans found themselves no longer alone. Álfar guards, tall, willowy, and exotically attired, were among them. The human guards recoiled in shock. The older couple scurried back into the building.

Several of the Álfar bowed to Parlan, who deigned to give them a regal nod. He then lost his noble demeanor and gripped one of the Álfar by the shoulder, which soon became an enthusiastic man hug. Then they were both speaking that mellifluous language. I shimmied out of the coveralls and donned my jacket.

Human words grated and rattled like falling pebbles among the euphonious cadence of Álfar. Especially when you added in a strong Brooklyn accent. "Hey! Lady! What's with the costume party?"

Other human voices added to the confusion. *"We've called the cops." "These guys gotta get outa here."*

Assuming my best courtroom manner I held up my hands and

began. "You see, the Álfar also live here, but in an alternate reality that lies side-by-side with ours, and I had an appointment that I had to keep . . ." My voice trailed away at their expressions. "Oh, forget it," I sighed. "If it's any help I suspect we're going to be gone soon. Or at least you'll *think* we're gone."

As if summoned by my words John's mother emerged from the building. This time she wasn't dressed like an Erté figure in a shimmering dress, but in an outfit oddly reminiscent of my own attire—tight-fitting pants, a laced and frogged coat, high boots above the knee. Her long black and white hair was confined and her green eyes were glittering. I couldn't tell if she was outraged or eagerly anticipating skewering me like a pincushion. Suddenly my reliance on my unknown power seemed really, really stupid.

The human male guards were stunned into silence. I couldn't blame them. She was exquisitely, breath-stoppingly beautiful. I, who had never managed more than cute, felt like a small toad as I looked up into her chiseled face. Now that she was this close I could tell—she was really, really pissed.

"You dare to challenge me with one pathetic follower who is not really one of us?" The strange eyes raked across Parlan. "Merely a pet."

I glanced at the human changeling, but the insult hadn't seemed to faze him. He was staring into the face of the only mother he had ever known with an amused smile.

"You challenge me for my place, but who will follow you?" the queen continued.

I stopped paying a lot of attention because I saw John walking out of the building. His white, blond, and black hair had grown so it now fell to his shoulders. I realized with some shock and guilt that eight months had passed. I should have done something sooner to end his gilded captivity.

I glanced over at Parlan. The two men couldn't have been more different. John was preternaturally handsome and slim with extravagant cheekbones and a pointed chin. Parlan was a bit taller than John, but he had his father's robust build. Parlan looked like a youngish forty-four-year-old man. John looked to be in his mid-twenties even though they were the exact same age.

Once he was close enough I could see John had the same sneering yet oddly disinterested expression he had worn when I had seen him the one and only time since his capture. He took up a position at his mother's right shoulder. I stared at him. I couldn't help it. I remembered the taste of his lips and the feel of those slender hands on my body. Better to remember that night rather than the cruel things he had said on another night at the Château Montmartre.

He gave me one brief glance. One eye was still green, the other milky white since his mother had driven that sliver of ice into his eye, blinding him. Almost worse than the mutilation was how the action had suppressed all emotion in John. He turned his attention to his mother, which brought me back to the moment. And yep, she was still droning on. I forced my attention away from John and back to her.

"We reject you, and I refuse to debase myself by answering this challenge. You have no standing—"

I knew she didn't mean it that way but now she was speaking my language. Standing was a legal concept. Without standing a person could not go before a court and request relief from a particular situation. Only a person with a sufficient interest in the case could seek redress. It wasn't exactly on point, but it gave me an opening.

"I am the person who proved the innocence of two of your citizens. *My* actions saved your people in the human world from threat and suspicion. And you're holding one of *my* employees. I have plenty of standing to be here."

"And yet you stand alone with only a mongrel," her eyes flicked to Parlan, "at your side."

Parlan cleared his throat. "Not quite alone."

He gestured and Kerrinan and Jondin walked in through the gate. They were marquee idols in the human world and pure Álfar with jewel-bright eyes, parti-colored hair, and exquisite features. They had also fully embraced the human world, as evidenced by their modern street attire rather than the operetta style favored by most of their kind. They had both committed heinous murders in Los Angeles, but while under the total control of a murderous Álfar elder who was angry that so many of his kind were abandoning Fey in favor of the human world. I had proved they were not actually responsible and won their freedom. They took up positions just behind me.

As to why they were here? I had a suspicion and turned to Parlan. He gave me a shrug and a self-conscious grin. "Your doing?" I asked.

"I thought she might try to declare you unworthy and avoid the duel. And they owed you a *geas*." At my look of confusion he added, "*Geas*: an obligation magically imposed on a person."

"Yeah, you really should be a lawyer. Preferably a litigator," I said. "Talk about a Perry Mason moment."

"I don't understand."

"Old television show. You'll come across it at some point if you keep watching Nick at Nite."

Then my attention was drawn back to the gate, where five of the Álfar who had come to help me at the Academy Awards were entering. Tulan, his brother Aalet, Cildar, Donnal, and last was Zevra, who gave me an elaborate wink and a leer as he sauntered past.

Ladlaw, who had been the sixth member of our merry band, was among the guards surrounding the queen. I could see him struggling, but he finally cast his eyes heavenward, stepped out from behind the queen, and joined us. The look she gave him was absolutely poisonous.

But there was worse to come for the woman because John, moving like an automaton fighting against programming, stepped away from his mother and came over to our side. As he passed I could see beads of sweat running down into his sideburns, and he was trembling as if he was pushing against a heavy weight.

Parlan let out a woof of surprise and we exchanged startled glances. I glared at the queen. "That enough to make me worthy, you bitch?"

"Preach it, sister," exclaimed one of the human guards and he gave me a high five.

That little act of human gaucherie snapped the queen's patience. The world shimmered and shifted and suddenly the crumpled van and the human guards were gone and we were in the Fey version of the Dakota.

5

Oddly there were more cars parked in the Fey version of the court-yard than there had been in the human world. Twenties' style touring cars with long hoods, bud vases holding flowers on dashboards, elaborate hood ornaments. There were also a couple of small carriages drawn by glossy pairs of high-steppers and a few saddled horses. One horse was being put through his paces by his Álfar rider while a human groom looked on with worshipful approval. There were a few Álfar servants, but most of the people handling horses and strapping picnic baskets onto the backs of cars or serving as chauffeurs were male humans dressed in livery.

I wondered again what kind of person would prefer a life of servitude in an alternate reality with creatures whose lives are measured in centuries? And were the humans there willingly? A new question to be answered and perhaps another legal wedge to force comity between the Fey and the human world. Yes, the Powers were . . . well . . . powerful, but maybe it was past time to use the force of law to demand greater equality and accountability between humans and the vampires, werewolves and Álfar. My firm might be in a unique position to broker this new power sharing.

Then I remembered that I had to leave IMG. That was depressing and I didn't need any distracting thoughts right now because the queen was accepting a rapier from one of her entourage.

"And now I remember why I left," Jondin said. "All this medieval bullshit."

I realized that I had never heard her speak. Well, I had heard her voice on the screen, but not in person. The one time I'd interacted with her she had been in a virtual trance and was trying to kill me and a lot of other people on a soundstage on the Warner Bros. lot.

"Wish I had brought you a gun," Kerrinan said. "That would end this in a big damn hurry."

"I'm betting that would be considered cheating," I said as lightly as I could manage given my jumping heart. I held out my hand to Parlan for his sword.

There was a sudden babble as the six members of my Álfar entourage offered their blades too. Kerrinan and Jondin rolled their eyes. Then everyone fell silent when John said in a bored tone, "Do take mine. It will be interesting to see what odd thing you will do next." He offered me the rapier hilt first.

He was a prince so everyone stepped back and bowed. I took the hilt, and he looked irritated. "Mary, Joseph, and Jesus," he snapped and he sounded much more like Big Red and Meg's son, who had been raised Roman Catholic. "Don't you even know how to hold it?"

I shook my head. With a put-upon sigh, he stepped behind me and reached around to show me how my fingers were supposed to grip the hilt. His body seemed to radiate heat and I gave a sudden shiver. With his cheek next to mine I could smell the spicy scent of his cologne, and his breath puffed against my ear. The skin of his hands was much softer then when he'd been a PI, and his nails were buffed and manicured.

"Like you're an expert after eight months," I razzed. But the new position was more comfortable and the sword felt better balanced in my hand. I nodded my thanks and stepped away.

Everyone moved back, leaving the queen and me in the center of a ring of interested watchers. The mounted Álfar leaped off his horse and threw the reins to his human groom so he could join the circle of observers. The groom led the horse over to the side of the building, well out of the way.

Okay super power, you can kick in any old time now, I thought.

I had a mad insight that maybe I needed to be under attack from a Power. Every other time this had happened I hadn't initiated the attack. I decided to keep to the same pattern so I waited, watching the Álfar woman.

Seconds crawled by. I risked a glance at my watch. Almost two minutes had passed. I shrugged. "Okay, guess we'll all be going then. Parlan, grab John and—"

The queen moved, preternaturally fast, leaping toward me. I stumbled back, my heel slipping in a pile of manure and I went down hard, and landed painfully on my tailbone. A flare of pain shot through my chest from the cracked ribs. I also felt squishy wet dampening the seat of my breeches.

I had fallen in the horse shit. Because of course I had.

There was a brief instant to reflect that the mysterious protection never seemed to worry about my dignity. Then the sword that should have pierced my heart cut across my shoulder, giving me a shallow cut. It stung and the blood was warm against my skin. I yelped, scrambled crab-like to the side, and used the hood ornament on a parked car to regain my feet. As I clambered up, the ornament— consisting of five prancing horses and made of pearlescent glass— broke off in my left hand.

A collective gasp from the assembled watchers gave me a second's warning. I spun, and the ornament clanged against the blade of the queen's sword, shoving it aside. The glass shattered and some of the slivers peppered her face, drawing blood. There was a combination of moans and cheers.

She retreated and pulled a sleeve across her face to wipe away the blood. We circled each other like cats preparing to pounce. I was beginning to see how this worked. Whatever mysterious power was protecting me it helped if it had things to work with. I edged closer to the encircling crowd, hoping that might offer it more opportunity.

The queen lunged at me. I awkwardly lifted the sword and caught her blade on mine. The blow landed close to the hilt and sent a concussive wave up my arm and into my sore chest. My fingers went momentarily numb. I retreated with more haste than grace. My opponent's blade was weaving an intricate pattern in the air in front of me that was almost mesmerizing. Feeling that I ought to do something, I thrust out my blade to disturb that movement.

The Álfar woman's mouth stretched in a vicious grin, and my stomach felt hollow as I realized I had done just what she wanted. My sword was pushed aside, and she was lunging for my chest. An errant gust of wind danced through the courtyard, ripped a delicate scarf from the neck of an Álfar lady, and wrapped it around the queen's face. I spun to the side, and the Queen, blinded, failed to compensate. The blade passed harmlessly behind me.

I tried to turn around and capitalize on the moment, but I was too slow, and by the time I was facing her she had pulled away the scarf. Did I only imagine the sense of irritation and frustration that briefly flooded my mind? I shook my head and tried to focus on that deadly point.

I heard Parlan bellow, "Don't watch the sword! Watch her eyes!"

I jerked up my gaze to those emerald eyes. They told me nothing. "What am I looking for?" I screamed at Parlan.

"Her intent."

"It's to kill me," I shouted back as I danced away from another lightning-fast lunge.

By now I was no longer trying to fight. I was just running, trying to keep out of her reach. The cold air clawed at my lungs as I panted and gasped, and the pain from my ribs pounded in time to my heartbeats. There was that subtle shivering in my leg muscles, the precursor to muscle fatigue and ultimately collapse. My super power had so far proved to be pretty damn wimpy. It was possible that I had bet my life on a fantasy.

The crowd had gone unnaturally quiet, anticipating the inevitable conclusion. A sharp *crack* split the silence, and a lone icicle, nestled on the shaded north side of the building and protected from the first touch of spring, fell. It landed point first like a frozen spear on the rump of the saddled horse.

The animal squealed, bucked, broke free from the human groom, and bolted across the courtyard, the steel shoes beating like hammers against the stones. Its speed and panic had it slipping a bit, which put my heart in my throat. Seeing a horse break its leg would make this day even more craptastic.

The frightened animal plowed into the encircling crowd, and they split apart like a school of startled fish. The queen whirled, the horse's shoulder grazed her shoulder, and she started to fall. I ran forward, ready to take advantage when she hit the ground. Unfortunately, Álfar coordination saved her. She managed to tangle a hand in the flying mane and, using the horse's momentum, she swung up into the saddle.

She was a good rider, controlling the horse with her legs and only one hand on the reins. Her expression was both twisted and joyful as she prepared to ride me down. She raised the rapier with the motion of a picador going for a bull.

I didn't wait for the power to take a hand. I had this one under control, for I had seen how the rider handled this animal and I knew how it had been trained. I faced the charging horse, threw up my hand, palm out, and shouted,

"HALT!"

At almost the same moment, Parlan snapped out a single word in the Álfar language. The horse planted its front feet and went into a hard-sliding stop. The queen, balanced to spit me and perched lightly in the saddle, somersaulted over the horse's head and landed hard on her back, right at my feet. The sword flew out of her hand. I planted my foot on her chest and placed the point of the sword at her throat.

"Give up?"

"The proper term is *yield*," John drawled from the sidelines.

"Okay. Yield." For an instant it hung in the balance. *Please, yield, please*, I prayed, because I knew I couldn't actually drive that blade into her delicate white throat and kill her.

She nodded a tight, barely perceptible gesture. My Scoobies burst out cheering, and suddenly I was getting hugged and my cheek was being kissed.

"You're like the dog with the proverbial car. You've caught the damn thing. Question is, what the hell are you going to do with it now?"

Parlan, John, and I were all gathered in the Queen's personal quarters in the Álfar Dakota. The art deco furnishings made me feel like I was in a BBC production of some 1920s mystery. It was John who had spoken. I glanced over at him and tried to reconcile the modern speech patterns out of someone dressed like an operetta prince. What I hated to acknowledge was that he had raised a valid point, and Parlan supported him by saying, "He speaks truth. With your victory, you are the ruler of this principality."

I studied the two men. The one so clearly human and so clearly comfortable in his Álfar finery. The other clearly Álfar and not so comfortable. They were like funhouse mirror images of each other even down to their speech patterns. I didn't answer. Instead I wandered into the bedroom to try and quell my agitation. Both men trailed after me.

I studied the elaborate sleigh bed, which seemed to be carved from mother-of-pearl. Our entry set the fragile draperies around the bed to swaying. I stopped and stared at the jewels that were overflowing a silver box on a dressing table. A quick check of the closet cemented my conclusion.

I turned back to the men. "She left everything." I knew the queen, with her remaining loyal followers, had decamped the premises within minutes of her defeat, but this was just crazy.

"Yes. To the victor go the spoils," Parlan said quietly. I wondered if his rage against the woman was now colliding with the reality that she owed her downfall to him.

"So what? She's like an Álfar bag lady now?"

Parlan looked confused, but John got it. "No, someone will take her in. Maybe even my father."

"Your dad's alive?" John nodded. "So why wasn't he around?" I asked.

"He runs some other place. And they don't get along. Actually, I don't think he likes her very much."

"Gee, *quelle* surprise." I moved to the jewel box and picked up a heavy emerald necklace. I set it aside with a clunk. I twined a long rope of pearls through my fingers. "I didn't want this," I finally said when the silence became too uncomfortable.

"What did you want?" John asked in that cold tone.

"You know the answer to that. I was hoping to just grab you and bring you home . . ." I shrugged. "That didn't work out so well."

"Instead you've thrown all of Fey into a tailspin," John said. We went back into the living room. John went to the elaborate liquor cabinet. "Anyone want a drink?"

Both Parlan and I nodded. He handed out brandy. I settled on the white leather sofa, squeezed a pillow against my aching ribs with an elbow, and rolled the snifter between my palms. The cut on my shoulder was stinging, and I hated that my beautiful coat had gotten torn. I pinned John with a hard look.

"So, are you staying or are you going?"

John spread his arms. "I am yours to command." The mocking, nasty tone was back.

"Oh, cut the crap. If I *am* in charge I can tell you that you can do whatever the hell you want. Stay. Leave. Whatever. It's up to you if you want to keep living like a mushroom while dressed up like the dictator of some tinpot banana republic."

My tone rocked John back a bit. He covered by taking a sip of his brandy. Parlan gave me a faintly hurt look. "You think our attire is silly?"

"Very."

"Oh." He plucked at the lace at his cuff and frowned.

"I don't want to stay here," John said. Parlan gave his sort-of-brother an incredulous look.

And that's when the solution came to me. I looked at Parlan. "But you *do* want to stay here, right?"

"Yes. It's my home."

"And am I totally in charge here?"

Parlan nodded. "Yes."

"I can do anything I want?"

"Within reason. If you did something too outlandish the council would . . . well, they might intervene."

John gave a snort. "It would have to be pretty damn outlandish."

I looked from Parlan to John and back again. "All righty then. Parlan, I'm making you regent . . . or prime minister or something. I'll draw up a power of attorney that puts you in charge, something you can wave at people. And it's time, probably past time, we started to get a little full faith and credit going between our world and Fey."

I glanced at John and decided not to say what I had been going to say in front of him. "And could I talk to you privately, Parlan?"

He nodded and we went into the kitchen of the elaborate suite. We realized that the abrupt decampment had extended to here as well. There was a half-chopped carrot on a cutting board, a skillet with half-melted butter on the stove. Parlan looked around. "Well, I'm going to need new servants."

"Just make sure you pay them and don't enthrall them."

"You know me better than that, Linnet. And besides, I cannot throw a glamour."

"Well, speaking of that. You made a study of Álfar magic. I need you to use your authority and new position to find somebody who knows how to take the spell off John. Get that damn ice splinter out of his eye."

"Of course."

"Okay." I held out my hand. We shook on it, and Parlan threw his arms around me and gave me a quick hug.

"You'll explain to Red and Meg? Though they probably won't care with John back."

"I don't think that's true. And I hope you'll visit them. You've got a second family now. That's not a bad thing."

He seemed struck by that. "No, you're right, it's not. May I be magnanimous to my mother?"

"I'd think less of you if you weren't. But don't forget. You're in charge now."

"I won't."

We returned to the living room, and I crossed to John. "Are you ready to get out of here?"

Since John was a real Álfar we didn't need any help getting home. I braced to be hassled by the Dakota guards, but everyone gave us a wide berth. Maybe it was the torn and bloody coat and shirt I wore, or the fact they were still in shock over discovering the world was not what it seemed. A tow truck was hooking up the crumpled van. It took some fast talking, but the tow truck guy agreed to just take some money for his time and let me drive the van out of the courtyard.

"Have I still got an apartment?" John asked as we drove.

"Yeah. It was rent controlled so I didn't want to let it go. I've been subletting it to a student at NYU. I told him he had to move out."

"You were that confident."

I bowed my head and considered that for a moment. "I suppose I was. The things that have happened over the past few months have given me . . . well, let's just say the sense I can do more than I thought I could."

"So why are we going to your apartment?"

"I thought you might like to get your cat."

"You took him in?"

"Of course."

There was a parking space on the street right in front of the building's door. I had seen this happen with John over and over again so I had to assume it was some weird Álfar power that he didn't even know he was using. My building didn't have an elevator, and I kept having to stop at each landing to breathe and give my ribs a rest. I really hoped the universe would give me a chance to heal before it threw some other weird crap at me.

I unlocked the door and we stepped inside. Gadzooks was curled up sleeping on the sofa. The golden eyes opened, and he blinked at me, then the ginger cat spotted John, gave a yowl like a boiling tea kettle, and launched himself into the air. He hit John's chest, and John instinctively caught him. For the briefest moment there was a flicker of reaction on the frozen face.

He ran his fingers through the thick fur on Gadzooks's back then set the cat aside. Suddenly uncomfortable, I gave him a quick grin. "Look, I'm sore and dirty. I'm going to soak in hot water for a little while. Help yourself to anything in the kitchen." I headed for the bedroom door. "Oh, and I kept some clothes here for you. If you want to change."

"Oh yes, I want to change." There was something in the way he said it that made me wonder if it referred to more than just clothing.

"Your folks came and packed up most of your personal items and took them back to Philly."

"I wonder if they'd ship them to me," John mused.

"You need to go down and get them and see your folks."

"I suppose it can't be avoided."

I found the reluctance to see his family disturbing, but I didn't want to argue about it right then. I retreated to the bathroom and emerged forty minutes later wrapped in a heavy fluffy robe and with the skin on my fingers and toes completely wrinkled from the long bath. John had changed into blue jeans and a turtleneck sweater. He lounged on the sofa with Gadzooks purring on his chest. The smell of freshly brewed coffee twined through the apartment. I poured myself a cup and settled in the armchair across from John. We stared at each other for a long time.

With a sigh he set aside the cat, who evinced his displeasure. John leaned forward, hands clasped between his knees. Eventually he looked up. I searched his features for some hint of emotion and didn't find much.

"I remember the things we did together." I blushed as I remembered that one night of amazing sex we had shared. "Objectively I know I had feelings for you. I just want you to understand that—"

"You don't have those feelings any longer. Yeah, I know." I hoped it came out as matter-of-fact and not whiney.

"It's not just you. I don't have any feelings. Well, that's not quite true. I've got this low level of pissed off going all the time."

"Maybe because you were violated in a really fundamental way," I said softly.

He stood and crossed to me. Stared down into my face. Gadzooks wound through his legs purring and meowing. Something flickered in his good eye, and he tentatively started to reach out.

There was a fierce hammering on my front door. I jumped and John yanked back his hand. The brief flash of warmth was gone. I hurried to the door and used the peephole. David was standing in the hall. I had a momentary flare of cowardice, a desire to pretend I wasn't home, but I pushed it aside and undid the chain and the lock.

"You did it anyway!" he snapped as he pushed past me and entered the apartment. "And you didn't tell me."

He grabbed me by the shoulders and gave me a shake. It hurt my cut and I cried out. Also, deep in my chest *something* seemed to turn over, sit up, and take notice. All of it was terrifying.

"Didn't take me—" He broke off abruptly when he saw John, released, me and stepped back very carefully.

I stood between them, tension crackling through the room. David visibly pulled himself together. "Ah, Mr. O'Shea. Welcome back."

"Thanks."

"Will you be returning to work?"

"That's the plan."

"Well, I can't stay. Do you need a ride home?" he asked John.

"Yeah, sure."

David inclined his head to me. "Linnet."

John gathered up Gadzooks, and then they were gone. The only sound was the old cast-iron heater on the wall slowly pinging as it sighed into silence.

I was alone. Aside from my increasingly self-aware little super power.

On tomorrow's calendar—quit my job, call about a friend in the hospital. It was not going to be a pleasant day.

6

"I need you to become the attorney of record on my cases," I said as I pulled out the paperwork that would accomplish that task. Caroline and I were at the Seventy-second Street Gourmet Deli having breakfast at seven-thirty a.m.

She tossed her long blond hair back over her shoulder and frowned at me. "Why? What is going on, Linnet?"

"I'm resigning from the firm today, and I'm not going to be giving notice. The letter goes in and I go out."

"Why? What's happened?" Caroline demanded.

"Nothing—"

"Oh bullshit! You don't walk out of a White Fang law firm giving no notice on a *whim*."

"It's personal, and hard to explain. I just have to have everything in order so I can get out. Now." Tears stung my grit-filled eyes.

It had been a long night. After John and David left I had called Meg and Red and reported that we'd succeeded. Meg had wanted to know when John was coming to see them. I mouthed the usual polite lie that I was *sure he'd come to visit real soon* even though I had no idea if that was true or not.

I then sat down in front of my laptop and tried to draft my letter of resignation. I'd type a line, then stand and pace, trying to figure out some way to stay at the firm. Eventually the letter had been completed, but I resisted printing and signing it until nearly four a.m. Ultimately reality smacked me in the face. There was no way out of this. I had to leave the firm for both David's and my own sake. Add to that worry over Jolly, and the insanity of a female vampire, and the unsatisfying way that John and I had parted, and I just gave up on trying to sleep.

A waiter who looked as tired and surly as I felt dumped our bagels in front of us and slouched away. I picked mine up, watched the cream cheese ooze out the sides, put it back down on the plate, and pushed it away.

"Is it because of John?"

"How do you know—"

"He came in late yesterday afternoon. Some of us talked to him. He's . . . changed."

"Yeah," I said bleakly.

"Is that why? Because you can't bear to be around him with him so . . . different," Caroline said softly as if fearful the words themselves could hit me physically.

This romantic explanation seemed totally out of character for the poised woman and I goggled at her. "No, it's not that," I said.

"Then what?" She slammed her fists down on the table.

I reached out and touched one clenched hand. "Be my friend. Trust and accept that this is something that I have to do."

Caroline looked like she was about to cry, which really knocked me off balance. "I thought we were going to leave together and form the Two Tough Bitches Law Firm," she said.

"Caro, you're a brilliant lawyer. You belong in a top-flight firm."

"Like you haven't had some huge wins," she said pointedly.

"Yeah, but you win with panache. Me, I blunder into victory after causing the maximum amount of uproar." I cocked my head and considered that. "Hell, the senior partners may be glad to see me go. I know Gold will."

Shade was not happy to see me go. He held my letter of resignation as if it were coated with anthrax. Not that anthrax would have hurt him. "Dearest Linnet, why? Have you been unhappy here? Have we not treated you well?"

His tone and expression indicated he was honestly upset. Some of that might have been because he actually liked me, but it was more likely he was worried about his standing with the other senior partners. Shade had hired me. He had been my protector when I had become a chaos magnet and all kinds of weird shit had happened all around me and to me. Now, after a mere ten months on the job, I was quitting. It looked bad and called into question his judgment, but I couldn't help that.

"No, it's nothing like that."

"Is it because of Ryan? Does that still affect you? We can transfer him. Perhaps to the LA office."

Ryan was a junior partner and a vampire who had been playing dangerous sex games with the female associates. The other partners had turned a blind eye, and no woman was willing to warn a newcomer. I had broken the pattern and gone public, resulting in Ryan getting demoted down to the human floor.

What was starting to really irritate me was that everyone I had told of my decision assumed it was because of the actions of some male. To be fair, my decision was because of the actions of a male, but so far (mercifully) no one had hit upon the *correct* male.

"Oh, God, no. I never think about Ryan."

"Then why, Linnet?" Shade asked, and he no longer sounded so kind and concerned.

I couldn't give Shade any hint of what was really behind my

decision. "I just feel like corporate law isn't where I want to be," I said, feeling that was safe and nicely vague.

"So you're thinking public defender? DA?" Shade asked.

"I haven't gotten that far. I just feel like I need something a little more . . . down to earth? Working with people whose bank accounts don't extend to buying small countries. Does that make any sense?"

"Actually, it does." He forced out a gusting sigh. "Meredith will be very upset."

The mention of my vampire foster liege added a new source of worry and potential complication. I had been so focused on freeing myself from the firm that I hadn't considered the broader ramifications. The web of connections between vampires was tangled and intricate, and as a "client" family with a foster child we were closely enmeshed in those webs. I had the job at IMG partly because my foster liege, Meredith Bainbridge, had approached Shade on my behalf. My quitting was going to be viewed as an insult to him as well. Which would affect the business relationship that my father had with Meredith, which would infuriate my dad. Oh yeah, I was going to be facing a really pleasant few weeks. I wondered if just running away, changing my name, and assuming a disguise was an option?

"I'm sorry to disappoint him, but I have to do this," I said firmly.

Shade forced a sigh. "I can see you are quite determined on this. We will miss you. When will you leave?"

"Caroline has already taken over my caseload, and she's informing the clients. I'm leaving today."

His expression had been morphing from concern to formality and now he was furious. "It is customary to give an employer a month's notice. I am extremely annoyed."

A million years of evolution screamed that I was on the verge of becoming prey to a monster. I blanched and instinctively made the submissive gesture of cocking my head and offering my neck. It was the first thing I had been taught when I entered the Bainbridge household, and it had been drilled into me through the intervening years. Just as quickly as terror had taken me, it was replaced by outrage.

"Look, I know this isn't being fair to the firm, but you know me well enough to know that I wouldn't do this on a whim. I have reasons and they're good ones. You should trust me on this." I held out my hand. "I hope we can at least part with respect for each other if not friendship."

Once again Shade proved he was one of the good guys. He took my hand and shook it. "I wish you well, Linnet, though you have disappointed me tremendously."

I nodded, turned, and left. I stopped at the receptionist's desk in the elegant and understated waiting room. Bruce gave me a smile. "I started your novel, Bruce. It's good," I said. He blushed and looked very young. "I also wanted to let you know I'm leaving the firm, and I wanted to tell you goodbye. If you ever want to talk . . ." I scribbled down my cell phone number on a message pad. "You can call me anytime."

The young man was goggling at me. "Leaving? But . . . But . . ."

I didn't want to wait around for more questions, or try to decide if I would answer them or not. I headed to the stairwell and went down to my office. I was a little surprised and a bit melancholy over how quickly I could pack up my professional career. I had my diplomas in a banker's box, the few actual dead-tree books that I had brought into the office, my wind-up Godzilla and Gidra toys, and my laptop in its rolling case. I didn't have a Rolodex—everything was on my phone or on the computer. I had no photos of family.

I didn't seem to have left much of an imprint on this space or the firm. Then I realized I was being maudlin and indulging in a pity-party. I had made a big impact on IMG. My investigations of a co-worker's murder had netted a huge payday for the firm. My actions in Los Angeles had certainly made headlines and put IMG in the news. Which was another argument for why I wasn't, ultimately, a good fit at IMG. Notoriety and press, good or bad, were considered unwelcome intrusions and gave vampires hives. They just wanted to drift elegantly behind the scenes, pulling strings and getting results. I had been like a noisy off-key brass band dropped into the middle of a concert by a classical quartet. Frankly, they should be glad to see me go.

I looped the strap of my purse over my shoulder, tucked the box under my arm, grabbed the handle of the laptop case, turned out the light, and left. Norma stood beside her desk, arms folded across her formidable bosom and a Jovian frown on her face. Her hair, teased and sprayed into a frozen gray helmet, didn't move as she gave her head a disgusted shake.

"I can't believe you are doing this."

I set my box on her incredibly clean desk and gave her a hug. "I'll miss you, Norma."

She gave a snort that sounded suspiciously like a sniff and returned the hug. "You take care. You haven't got any more sense than a kitten."

The wheels of my rolling case chattered over the stone tile floor. Associates emerged from their offices to watch as I left. As usual the gossip had flown through the office at light speed. Caroline stepped out and our eyes met. She gave me a sad smile and a nod and went back into her office.

Ryan emerged from his office and stared at me. If vampires really had some of the powers attributed to them I would have been struck dead from the hate that twisted his face. The Legal Eagles Pop Brigade—Cecelia, Nancy, Delia, Juliette, Kathy—surrounded me and we moved as a flying wedge toward the elevators. They were all talking at once. I caught a phrase every now and then.

"How can you?"

"You go, girlfriend!"

"Why?"

"What happened?"

"Where?"

I released the handle on my case, jabbed at the call button, then held up a hand and shouted, "Stop!" They all fell silent. I could hear the elevator rushing up the shaft toward us. "I don't know where I'm going yet. Yes, I'll let you all know. No, I won't tell you why." I gulped a bit. "And I'm going to miss you all. So much."

The elevator arrived with a *ding*. The doors opened and I plunged inside. I didn't turn around. Unfortunately, I could see their expressions reflected in the burnished silver of the elevator's back wall. Juliette and Nancy were crying. The door closed behind me. I let out a sob. Tears were running down my face when I arrived in the lobby. The security guard, looking alarmed, rushed out from behind his desk.

"Are you all right?"

No, I'm not all right. I'm crying, which should have been your first clue. But I didn't say it. He meant well. I brushed away the tears with the back of my hand, forced a smile, and nodded. "Fine. Really. Thanks. If you could get me a taxi."

He nodded and rushed through the front doors. I fished in my purse for a tissue, gave my nose a defiant blow. An elevator gave a ding and I heard the doors open. Hands, unnaturally cold and unnaturally strong, closed on my shoulders and spun me roughly around.

Vampires respect personal space. In fact, their idea of personal space sometimes feels like the length of a football field, but David had us only inches apart. There was a coiling deep in my chest, much stronger than the last time I had experienced the sensation and it hurt, setting my chest to aching and sending a stabbing pain into my throat. It frightened me, and the expression on David's face didn't help with that. A hard twist of my shoulders freed me from his grasp and I stepped away. The coiling sensation faded slowly.

"Would you quit grabbing me! I have a cut on my shoulder."

David didn't try to touch me again. Instead he grated out, "What the hell are you doing?"

I had thought Shade was angry. It had been nothing compared to the fury on David's face as he glared down at me. Once again I started to show submission, and I defaulted to quipping in an effort to defuse the situation.

"Waiting for a taxi."

"You will answer me! Why are you quitting?"

Outrage swept through me, burning away the fear. All thought of showing throat was gone. "*My* business, David. I worked for you. I didn't *belong* to you."

"I never behaved toward you in that way—"

"Oh, bullshit! You were always following me, checking up on me."

"That's because . . . because . . ." His voice faded away, his hands reached out for me but more in supplication. The expression that washed across his face filled me with pain and panic. *Don't give yourself away!* I wanted to scream at him.

I grabbed the handle of the computer case and headed for the front doors. I needed to get out of the office before he said anything more or betrayed himself any further. I was out on the sidewalk making my way through clots of pedestrians. Occasionally my computer bag rolled across someone's toe and I got a glare or a yell of protest. There were running footsteps behind me. I put on a burst of speed trying to reach a subway stop, but I was encumbered by box, purse, and computer. David caught me easily.

"Please, Linnet, for friendship's sake if nothing else. Tell me what I did? How I offended you?"

Tears stung my eyelids. "Oh, David. You haven't done anything.

Well, that's not exactly right. Look, if only it were for friendship's sake." I gave him a level look. His eyes slid away.

We were blocking the entrance to the subway. I sighed, handed him the box, and led him down a less crowded side street. He had forgotten both hat and umbrella and the skin on his cheeks and the backs of his hands was starting to blister from the sun. I led him quickly into a small florist's shop on the bottom floor of a building. The sweet aroma of flowers balanced atop that swamp water scent that seemed to accompany all floral arrangements no matter how fresh or how new. It was kind of gross. The girl behind the desk gave us a weird look then darted into a back room. I guess she could tell we weren't there to buy a bouquet.

I stole a glance up at David. He probably did look fearsome to an ordinary person with the three deep twisting scars across one cheek, the popping blisters, and the parted lips revealing his fangs. What the girl had read as rage I realized was grief.

"It's not what you—"

I cut him off. "Yeah. It is."

David's shoulders slumped. He turned away and began nervously handling every object on the counter. "I told myself it was just a boss's concern for a particularly useful and . . . irritating underling." He spun back to face me. "But it's not." He reached for me. I stepped back, dodging the potential embrace. He dropped his hands to his sides. "So, you don't care for me."

"Not that way. You're my dear, dear friend. Maybe my best friend, but . . ." I shook my head.

"You love the Álfar." It sounded accusatory.

"Why do you men always think everything devolves down to love for women? I'm fond of John, but I don't exactly know him. And maybe if you were human something might have happened between us because there is so much about you that's admirable. You're

handsome and brilliant, and honorable, and even occasionally funny."
I realized this list of virtues was taking us in exactly the wrong direction. "But it cannot be! I don't want to die. I don't want you to
die. For both our sakes I have to leave."

"Why do we even have this idiotic rule?" David cried out. "Why
can't I Make you? Why can't I be with you? We saw a female vampire. Something that supposedly doesn't exist so . . . so . . . none of
this makes any sense."

"Did you report her?"

He hung his head. "I realized I had no idea who to tell. I wanted
to think about it first. What it might mean . . . for us."

"Nothing. It means *nothing* for us. I want children. Dead women
don't have children."

"We could adopt—"

I covered my ears. "You're delusional. David, I'm sorry to hurt
you, but I don't love you."

"You just been conditioned while you were fostered—"

"That might be part of it, but give me a little credit for knowing
my own mind and heart."

His eyes were shadowed and I felt like a brute. He turned away
and gently stroked the petal of a rose in one of the bouquets. "It's
not fair that your life should be derailed so early in your career. I've
had years—"

"No, you are not going to quit."

"It's the gift I can give to you."

"Oh, please don't act like we're in a damn romance novel. And
would you stop with the chivalrous bullshit and think like a hard-
headed lawyer. I'm a woman in a vampire law firm. The chances of
my making partner are slim to none. You're a junior partner. If it's
the flighty human walking away from the plum job there will be
fewer awkward questions. If *you* leave there will be questions, lots

of questions, and we can't survive that. Literally. They will bring in a Hunter and we will be killed. Now tell me I'm wrong."

He hung his head, then gave it a slow shake. "No, I can't." I took back my box, grabbed the handle on the case. "Will I ever see you again?" I didn't look back, just shook my head.

I almost made it to the door before a beautiful bouquet of yellow roses was laid on the top of the box. The water off the stems formed a Rorschach pattern on the cardboard. I wondered what it would say about me if I read it.

7

"Hey, sweetie. How are you?" My father's voice came through the phone warm and happy.

I was seated in my apartment, cell phone under my chin and a pint of Rocky Road ice cream in one hand and a spoon in the other. Ice cream therapy. "I'm . . . I'm good. I was thinking maybe I'd come up to Rhode Island for a few days."

"Taking a couple of days off?" he asked jovially.

"Umm . . . not exactly. I . . . uh . . . I resigned from the firm today."

For a few heartbeats there was silence, then he burst out, "Jesus Christ, Linnet! Are you out of your fucking mind?"

The vitriol in my dad's voice sent me cringing against the back of the couch. My stomach as well as my lower lip was wobbling and the ice cream I'd eaten was threatening to come back up. I dropped the spoon and pulled the cell phone away from my ear. I could still hear him.

"This is a disaster! Goddamn you. How could you do this without discussing it with me first?"

"There were reasons. I had to quit."

"What reasons?"

"My boss was getting too . . . fond of me."

"Shade?" he asked, his tone unbelieving.

"Oh, God, no. Promise you won't say anything. It was David. I made the only prudent choice."

It was as if I hadn't spoken. He certainly wasn't listening to me because he was saying, "I'll talk to Shade. We'll get this guy transferred or fired. You get back over there and tell them you've changed your mind."

I threw aside the ice cream carton. My palm was slick with sweat and I gripped the phone tightly. "*No*. And *no*. You're not going to do that to David. If even a hint of this got back to—"

He cut me off. "You stupid little bitch. You have no idea what you've done!"

Who was this man, I wondered. Then I began to regrow a spine. I leaped to my feet and screamed into the phone, "Stop it! Don't you dare talk to me like this. I'm not a kid. I'm twenty-eight years old. My life is my own now. It's not for you or Meredith or Shade or anybody else to tell me what I have to do."

There was silence at the other end of the call and I realized he had hung up on me. For a long time I just cried. Eventually the sobs subsided. I tottered into the bathroom, blew my nose, and started filling the old claw-footed tub. I added lots of bubble bath, went back to the living room to pick up the discarded ice cream carton, rinse it out, and toss it in the trash. By the time I returned to the bathroom the bubbles were almost overtopping the tub. I stripped and crawled into the hot water.

My mind kept trying to skitter away from thinking about that bizarre and horrifying conversation. Granted, I didn't know my father well. I had left home at eight and, aside from holiday visits back to Rhode Island, I had lived in my vampire foster liege's home. When, at eighteen, I had been released I had headed off to college and then to law school. My memories of a father-daughter relationship were two decades old. Had this angry man always been there and I just hadn't recognized it as a child? But this seemed like the voice of a stranger.

What was so important about IMG and my presence in that particular law firm that my quitting would elicit such fury? I forced myself to remember every word of the exchange. The ache in my throat returned as I replayed the conversation, but a new thought began to intrude. Fury yes, but there had been an undercurrent of fear too. Meredith had once said to me that anger was just fear disguised and that's why he had tried to train me to use anger deliberately, as a weapon and a tool rather than allowing it to dictate to me.

So my dad was afraid. But of what? And why? And how did I fit into all this?

I decided to take my woes and worries off to my friends Ray and Gregory's apartment on the edge of Wall Street. I hadn't seen them since I'd returned from LA and I had a lot to tell them. God, did I have a lot to tell them. Ray threw open the front door and wrapped me in a hug. He was a professional dancer on Broadway, thin and lithe and very cute. His boyfriend, Gregory, was beaming at me from over Ray's shoulder. Gregory was older, a bit heavyset, and far more staid then the effervescent Ray.

I opened my mouth to say something only to have Ray thrust his left hand under my nose and wiggle his ring finger. There was a plain silver band. "Engaged!" he sang out.

I looked to Gregory, who rolled his eyes, but then smiled and held up his own hand, where a matching ring rested. "Congratulations," I said as I hugged Ray. "When's the wedding and do I get to come?"

Ray drew me into the elegantly appointed apartment as Gregory said, "Come? Of course. In fact, we were hoping you'd be in the wedding party."

"You will, won't you?" Ray added.

"I'd be delighted."

They settled onto the couch together while I took a nearby bucket armchair that was actually low enough that my feet reached the floor. Gregory was a trust-fund baby paid by his very conservative Kansas family to stay well away from them, so the couple lived in what was a very large space for Manhattan. The walls held original art and some great photos of Ray dancing, there were lots of bookcases and even a baby grand piano.

"Okay, I want to hear all about the Academy Awards," Ray said. "We were watching." There was again an eye roll from Gregory and Ray dug an elbow into his fiancé's ribs.

"If you were watching then there isn't much to tell," I said. "There was an old Álfar who wanted to separate his people from the lure of the human world so he used magic to cause a couple of Álfar actors to commit brutal murders. Then he made a bunch of Álfar go crazy at the Oscars." I shrugged. "It got sorted out. At some point I'll have to go back to LA to testify at Qwendar's trial."

Gregory chuckled. "It got sorted out because of *you*."

"I had help," I said and remembered that help. *David*. Everything kept coming back to fucking David. Or the threat of actually fucking David that had created havoc in my life. Of course the fact I *had* a life I also owed to him. I sighed.

"Okay, what's wrong?" Ray asked.

"I quit my job today. My father is furious. My boss is furious. A good friend is furious and hurt. Oh, and another friend was attacked and is lying in the hospital in a coma." They goggled at me, which made me glad I hadn't mentioned the female vampire. Of course not being as well versed in vampires they might not fully appreciate just how staggering this was. I shrugged. "You asked."

"Ice cream therapy?" Ray inquired.

"Already done that. Didn't help."

"Anything else you want to share?" Gregory asked.

"I'm technically a queen in Elfland," I offered, feeling this great need to just get it all out there and see if somebody else could make sense of my crazy life.

"Yeah, and how did that happen?" Gregory asked, treating it like a joke.

"Fought a duel with an Álfar queen. Got her territory."

Ray jumped up. "Okay, now you are just making shit up. You're staying for dinner, and then I propose popcorn and trashy movies and lots and lots of booze."

I realized that they weren't going to be a sounding board for me. But they were going to be my friends, support and comfort me, and right at this moment that felt like enough.

The scent of freshly brewed coffee and baking biscuits pulled me awake. For a moment I was disoriented, then I remembered. I was in Ray and Gregory's guest room because somewhere around the third or fourth movie I had lost count of the number of fruit-flavored blended margaritas I had drunk. I sat up, groaned, and grabbed my head. A hot shower later I pulled my rumpled clothes back on and tottered out to the kitchen.

Ray handed me a cup of coffee and guided me into a chair. A plate was deposited in front of me. Bacon, eggs, a biscuit, and something that looked like Cream of Wheat. I cocked an inquiring eye at Gregory.

"Grits," he said. "You can eat them with butter and salt and pepper or butter and sugar."

"They're disgusting," Ray offered.

"What are you up to today?" Gregory asked as we all settled down to eat.

"I don't know. It's weird. I have no place I have to be. First time since I started college that this has happened. I think I'll start by checking with the hospital, and then . . ." I sighed. "I start thinking about finding a job. The bills have to be paid." I cracked open a biscuit and breathed in the aroma of fresh-baked dough, smeared on some jam, and took a bite. "This could be problematic. I doubt I'm going to get a very good recommendation from Ishmael McGillary and Gold."

"So apply where people already know you. Know how good you are," Ray said as he nibbled on a slice of bacon.

The memory of a pugnacious face floated across my mind. I grinned. "Ray, you are a genius. It would be a real change from a White Fang firm, but it might be just what I need."

I jumped up and headed for the door. "What happened to taking a day off?" Gregory called after me.

"I've always been terrible at goofing off."

I had never actually been to Syd Finkelstein's office. On the subway ride from Wall Street back to my apartment I tried to Google the address, but I never could get a connection. It wasn't until I was trudging up the stairs to my apartment that I got a chance to type in his name. I paused to put a key in the lock, stepped into my apartment, let out a yell, and dropped my phone.

Once again there was an Álfar standing in the middle of my living room. It was John. Since I'd last seen him he'd cut his hair and was back to looking more like himself.

"Feel free to walk right in," I said acidly as I picked up my phone. I was pleased to see it hadn't been damaged. "Did you come in through Fey?"

"No, I picked the lock." I opened my mouth to object that that made it even worse when he floored me by adding, "Somebody else had already picked it and come in."

"Somebody else?" I repeated witlessly. "And how could you know that?"

John shrugged. "They weren't very good. They left scratches on the lock. I let myself in to see if they were still here."

I raced around the apartment checking my desk for my checkbook. It was there. My jewelry box was in the bedroom. Everything was in place. I stopped in the middle of the living room and glanced around, frowning. "Nothing's missing."

"Which would indicate it wasn't a robbery," John said.

"So why break in . . . Oh."

He voiced my unspoken thought. "They were looking for you."

"Okay, officially creeped out now."

"You might want to stay someplace else for a while. Maybe think about a new apartment."

"That would really suck. I like this apartment and I'd have to break the lease."

"Getting kidnapped or murdered would suck too. So, any idea who might be behind this?"

I paced and thought about who else had been kidnapped and it hit me with blinding clarity. "Oh, God, the female vampire. The one that attacked Jolly. It has to be."

"I could be more help if you'd stop talking in fragments and brought me up to speed." It was delivered in a flat, unemotional tone, and his features remained still, giving away nothing.

"Okay, but this is going to take a while. You may as well get comfortable. Coffee?" I threw back over my shoulder as I went into the kitchen.

"Yeah. Please."

Once we were settled at the small dining table with our hands cupped around gently steaming mugs I gave him a speculative look. The man I'd known before his capture I would have trusted with anything, up to and including my life. But since he'd lost his emotions he was much harder to read and therefore trust. There were no expressions to clue me.

"Where to start."

"At the beginning," he suggested. I searched for humor, irony, something, but there was nothing. This, I reflected, was probably what it would be like to talk to an android.

"I've got to go way back. Back to when I first went to work for IMG. There was that werewolf that killed Chip and then tried to kill me except the heel on my shoe broke, I fell down, and he took a header down an elevator shaft—"

John interrupted. "I know that. I also know about the five werewolf mercenaries who tried to kill you except they all ended up dead in various absurd and silly ways."

"Well, while you were being a prince in Fairyland you probably missed the Álfar actress who shot up the movie set, so shut up and listen. Anyway, I didn't get shot because she got flattened by a camera on a dolly that spontaneously took off and ran over her."

"And I watched that duel with the queen—the convenient scarf, the icicle. So what are you saying?"

"That this is crazy, right? Nobody should have had this many narrow and improbable escapes—except I did." I sucked in a deep breath. "And here's the pièce de résistance. There was the old Álfar guy who tried to put a spell on me except he couldn't. It didn't work. He even said there was something weird about me."

"So what's your explanation?" John asked.

"I don't have one, but I think Jolyon Bryce did—"

"That's the gentleman with the horse stable? I picked you up there once."

"Right. He loaned me the horse I ride. He even sent Vento to California when I was out there, and that horse saved my life. But that's another weird story. Anyway, Jolly seemed to know something about why I can dodge danger and survive. It's the reason I was so sure I could rescue you—"

"Don't get sidetracked."

"Sorry. Anyway, I went out to his house to talk to him but the house had been ransacked and he'd been attacked."

"To keep you from talking to him?"

"That's my guess."

"So what did he tell you?"

"Nothing. He got his skull bashed in and he's in a coma. But that wasn't the worst thing—Okay, that didn't come out right. The *weirdest* thing was that there was a female vampire in the house. I'm sure she attacked Jolly, but she got away—"

"Which brings us back to your belief that she's the one who broke into your apartment," John broke in.

"Who else would it be?"

"Are you sure it was a woman? Female vampires—"

"Don't exist," I paused. "Except this one did. And no, it wasn't a guy in drag. David saw her too. Fought with her. You can ask him." I ran agitated hands through my hair.

"So which mystery do you want to tackle first?" John asked "Who broke into your apartment? Why they attacked your friend? Why you seem to have magic powers?"

"I want to start with a simple one," I replied. "Why did you come here?"

Clearly the question had him puzzled. He frowned off into space. Took a few more sips of coffee before he answered. "I wanted to understand why you quit. I assumed something bad had happened or was happening and I want to help. I owe you. You got me out of Fey. Gave me back my life."

"You've got the trappings of your life back. You're still not free. I don't know if you can acknowledge that with that thing in your eye, but you're not really human." If he had been normal my harsh words would have hurt. As it was, he just blinked at me and said simply,

"I never actually was . . . human." He stood up and carried his empty cup into the kitchen.

I followed him. "When are you going to go see your folks?"

"Soon. Eventually."

"Good God, John, you need to get to Philadelphia. They haven't seen you for months. I called to tell them it worked and I got you out of there so they'll be expecting you. How could you not go right away and see the people who raised you?"

He frowned down into the sink. "I had to get a haircut first." A slim hand ran through the thick and exotic hair. "I knew Red wouldn't approve of the long hair." He turned to face me. "And I don't feel anything for them. I know I ought to. I know I used to but I don't anymore."

"They're your family. They accepted a changeling and loved him as if he'd been their own. They'll handle this too."

"No, they'll get upset. Especially my mom. She'll make a scene. Scenes exhaust me." He gave me a sideways glance. "I'm a little surprised you're not making a scene."

"I don't make scenes."

"Well, that's a lie. You made a scene at the firm when you called out Ryan for playing sex games with the female associates. And you made a scene with me in Los Angeles."

"Yeah, because you were being an asshole. Which you kinda still are, but you might notice I'm not making a scene."

He fell silent. "I remember the night we fucked."

"I know saying we made love might be a bridge too far, but can we at least say 'slept together' rather than use the F word?"

"I remember actions of the body."

"But not how you felt."

He shook his head. "No, they seem vague, impossible to grasp."

"Parlan's going to talk to mages or wizards or whatever you guys call them in the Fey. They'll come up with something. We'll fix this, John."

His lips twisted and I realized it was a sort of smile. "Never give up! Never surrender!" the Álfar said, quoting a line from a movie.

"Yeah, something like that."

"So back to *your* problems. Where do you want me to start?"

"I can't pay you. I don't have a job right now."

He shrugged. "Like I said . . . I owe you."

"Okay, start with Jolly. I'd say he's in a way worse spot than me right now."

"At least until your intruders come back."

8

The map function on my phone had guided me to a rather run-down business district in Queens. I was standing in front of a four-story, rather unprepossessing office building. It was small and unworthy of me, but I felt a twinge of regret for the seventy-three stories of glass and steel at the edge of Central Park where I used to work. The building that housed my old firm seemed to scratch at the clouds and it exuded power and authority. This one exuded . . . tired. I pushed through the front doors and found myself in a linoleum-floored lobby. No guard on duty, no signing in. But maybe that wasn't a bad thing if Syd did hire me. The guard on duty the night the werewolf killed Chip had also been murdered. And I did seem to bring trouble wherever I went, so no guard was good.

A plastic-fronted wall plaque held a listing of offices and who rented them. Syd Finkelstein was on the third floor. I opted for the stairs over the elevator. When I reached the office door I realized I had gone about this in a really stupid way. Syd could be in court or at a deposition. I should have called and made an appointment. So why hadn't I? Ambivalence about working for the guy? Then I remembered how Syd had stood up for two powerless women against a multimillion-dollar company. What kind of guy was Syd? A good guy. And I was being a snobby jerk.

I pushed through the door. The assistant behind the desk surprised me. First, she was young. Second, she had studs over one eyebrow and one in her nose. Third, she had spiky electric pink hair. Fourth, she was dressed in a baggy sweater and, from what I could see beneath the desk, jeans and hiking boots. There were a few cheap chairs clustered around a coffee table loaded with old *People* magazines and *Ladies' Home Journal*s. Filing cabinets lined the walls. A coffeemaker sat on top of a small fridge, the pot half empty. Next to the fridge was a big water cooler.

"Hi. You don't look like somebody who'd be one of our clients," she said. She had a bright, almost chirpy voice.

"You're right. I'm not."

"Lawyer, right?"

"Uh-huh. Is Syd in?"

"Yep. Who should I say is calling?"

"Linnet Ellery."

She sent her chair rolling away from the desk and over to the closed office door. Grabbing the door knob, the young receptionist yanked it open and called, "Hey, Syd, there's a Linnet Ellery here to see you."

An instant later Syd himself came trundling out of his office. He was short, barely taller than me, and chubby. The fluorescent lights gleamed on his bald pate, which was surrounded by a rim of graying black hair. He was in shirtsleeves. "Linnet!" He thrust out his right hand and I looked at the black and chrome prosthetic. "That's right, you haven't seen my Terminator arm." He unhooked the overly large and gaudy cufflink and rolled up his sleeve to reveal the entire length of the artificial arm replacing the arm lost to a ravening werewolf. We shook, and I noted how delicately the metal and plastic hand gripped my own.

"What brings you slumming in my part of town?" he asked.

I glanced at the neon-haired assistant. "Maybe in your office?"

"Oh, it's that kind of meeting. Hope it's as lucrative as the last time you had a tip for me."

I studied the round bulldog face looking for some hint of irony or snark and didn't find it. I shook my head. "Syd, the last time I gave you a tip I inadvertently sicced a werewolf on you. You were mauled and you lost your arm."

"Yeah, and you also found the will and helped me win the case and a fucking big payday. Now get your ass in here, and tell me what's going on," he added, swinging his arm toward his office.

"You guys want anything?" the receptionist asked. Syd cocked an eye in my direction. I shook my head.

"Nah, Belinda, we're good."

His office was very well organized. Files neatly stacked, a few books out, his computer screen showed he was linked to FindLaw. He took his chair and gestured to the one across the desk from him.

I sank down and fiddled with the clasp on my purse. "How's your family?"

"Fine. Lovely weather we've been having too. What's with the small talk, Linnet?"

"I'm nervous, okay?"

"Because of this?" He raised the artificial arm.

"Partly. I never really did apologize to you."

"What are you apologizing for? Not knowing that we had to act like fucking secret agents? No one could have predicted how nuts Deegan actually was. So, if it will make you feel better—apology accepted. Now, why are you here?"

I lifted my chin, sucked in a deep breath, and said, "I was hoping you would hire me."

The dark eyes blinked at me for several seconds. "Yale Law School, right?"

"Yeah."

"*Law Review*, right?"

"Yeah."

"Magna cum laude, I believe."

"Your point?" I asked, starting to feel both embarrassed and irritated.

"White Fang law firm versus . . ." He waved his arms, indicating the office and maybe all of Queens. "Bottom-feeding, ambulance-chasing, one-man law firm. Why the fuck would you want to work here?"

"A, because I need a job. B, because you are a really decent person who fights for justice, and C . . . well, I don't really have a C."

"You get canned?"

"No, I quit."

"May I ask why?"

"You can ask. I'm not going to answer. It's private and personal."

Syd leaned back in his battered chair until the springs squeaked and shrugged. "Okay."

"So?"

"No, I won't hire you." It hurt way more than I expected, and for the first time since I left IMG I started to feel a flutter of panic. I took a deep breath and reminded myself that I could just hang out my shingle and hope I brought in enough work to pay the rent on an office, keep a roof over my head and food on the table. Syd was talking again and I realized I had missed the first few words.

". . . for you to be working for me. You're recently out of law school with great credentials. You worked for a prestige law firm. It's crazy that I'd be ordering *you* around. No, what you can do is go buy a desk and chair, some filing cabinets, and move into the extra office and we'll work together. We can share Belinda. You're going to have to put a little skin into this game—pay half the rent and half her salary. So, is that something you think you might want to do?"

Nobody bossing me around. Assigning me cases. Peering over my shoulder. It would all be on me. I was terrified and elated.

"Yes. Oh, yes."

Back out on the street I went into overdrive. First up—find an office furniture store. A perusal of the net garnered me something even better. A *used* office furniture store. I headed over there and picked out a desk, three chairs, filing cabinets, and a bookcase. The cute salesmen told me they were from a startup internet company that went belly-up. There was a moment of suspicious dread that failure could seep into wood or fabric, but I shook it off, handed over my credit card, and arranged to have the furniture delivered.

I stopped at a FedEx and quickly had business cards designed and printed. The cards with IMG's elegant logo were pulled out of my card case. I held them over a trash can and wavered. Gritting my teeth, I forced my fingers to relax and let the cards flutter into the trash.

By now it was past one and I was starving. I found a deli and went in for a sandwich. While I munched on egg salad on a bagel I thought back over the number of subways I'd had to ride to get from my apartment at the far north end of Manhattan Island to Queens. It was an ugly commute. It had ended up cheaper to buy the fake florist van I had used in the John rescue then to repair it, so I now owned a car, but driving in New York was nightmarish, street parking was worse, and I really couldn't afford to pay for a space in a parking garage on my now much reduced (as in no) salary. I needed to sell the van and find an apartment in Queens.

I sipped at my ginger beer and considered if I really wanted to add a move on top of a new job where I had to hustle for clients? There was also John's warning that I ought to clear out of my place. So, who did I know who might let me couch surf for a few days or a week?

I thought about John's apartment in Greenwich Village, and my heart lifted briefly at the thought of seeing him over the breakfast dishes. There was also the lure of a cat. I missed Gadzooks's warm, purring presence, but John only had one bedroom and, given our past history, and his present situation, it only took a moment of reflection to decide that was a terrible idea.

I ran through the women I worked with . . . *used to work with* . . . at IMG. Caroline would probably take me in, but did I really need that constant reminder of what I'd given up? And if David found out, he'd be able to keep tabs on me through Caroline, and I wanted to be as far out of his orbit as possible.

Finally, I thought about Queens in relation to Ray and Gregory's apartment. It would only require two subway rides and a quick hop on a bus to get to Syd's. They had a guest room, and there was also the lure of Gregory's great cooking. A committed, engaged gay couple so no sexual pressure. No career rivalry with a former associate. It was perfect, and I was sure they would say yes.

It was also, if I was honest with myself, a fear of totally upending my life. Buying the furniture for my office had felt more like playacting. If I also gave up my apartment all the sudden and wrenching changes became very real and very permanent. So I'd punted.

"The Scarlett O'Hara solution," I muttered at the surface of the table. "Tomorrow. I'll think about that tomorrow."

A phone call later I had an enthusiastic assent from Ray and Gregory to my plan, and I began the long trek back to my apartment to pack up enough clothes for a couple of weeks. By then I thought— hoped—I'd have a better handle on my life.

By four o'clock I was ensconced in the guest room. Ray went off to take class, Gregory was hunched over his computer doing something with bonds or derivatives or something on various Asian stock markets. At loose ends, I decided to check in with John. A quick check on Google revealed that he already had a new office on the edge of Times Square. Given the rents in that area I figured he'd gotten a hefty bonus from IMG since he'd been kidnapped while helping with a case that ultimately netted them several million dollars in fees.

The previous office had been in an old brownstone with a frosted door and his name stenciled on the glass. Inside there had been a sagging old couch, a battered desk, and even a hat rack—all very Sam Spade. This building was newer, and when I walked into the office, accompanied by a loud and very unpleasant buzzer, I was startled by the sparse modern look, lots of chrome and black leather with a metal desk that looked like a twisted jungle gym. The walls were completely bare.

"Love what you've done with the place," I said dryly.

"It requires nothing from me," he said slowly. "It doesn't demand any kind of emotional reaction."

"I'm sorry you're so damaged," I said before I thought better of it. "Wow, that was rude. I'm sorry."

"Stop apologizing. It is what it is. You can't change it so don't feel guilty about it. Now why are you here?"

"Wondering if you had anything on Jolly yet?"

He didn't answer, just turned and walked to the desk. I hesitated. "Uh, do you want me to sit down or are you blowing me off?"

He looked back with that flat stare. "Of course I want you to sit down. I've got things to tell you."

He settled behind the desk. I took one of the tubular chrome chairs. It was as uncomfortable as it looked. John spun around in his chair and pulled out a drawer on the dull gray filing cabinet behind him. He spun back and tossed a cell phone at me.

Taken by surprise, I fumbled my dexterity and the phone hit the floor. I snatched it up to find the cheap plastic cover had cracked. I flipped it open. It was what I had suspected, a burner phone.

"Okay. I'll bite." I raised my eyebrows in interrogation and gave a perplexed shrug.

"This is prepaid for thirty days. The minutes are in my name, so no one will know you're using it and they won't be able to trace you. Leave it on at all times so I can trace you. Don't call anybody but me on this phone. I'll put your phone in a safety deposit box at a bank across town. They can trace the damn things even when they're turned off. So they can trace it to a bank."

"And how am I supposed to call other people, my clients?"

"There isn't a landline?"

"Well, there is at Syd's office. He's sort of old-fashioned that way, but Gregory and Ray don't have a phone."

"Tell them to get one. Or find a pay phone."

"And why are we playing spy games?" I asked.

John didn't answer, just riffled through some papers and skimmed one sheet across to me. I stared down at the names printed out on the page.

Sheldon Brashton

Charles Beachamp

Martin Bevis

I looked up and gave another puzzled shrug. "Meet all of the other Jolyon Bryce identities." A hollow appeared where I used to have a stomach. John went on. "We can be sure of one thing. His real last name probably begins with a B. He was Bevis in Australia, and Brashton when he lived in Rome and Beachamp when he was in Cairo. Each identity seems to run for five to seven years, then the new person appears. He's got money, but I haven't been able to trace where it comes from. Whoever is funding him has a shitload of money because each new identity appears very well-heeled."

I thought about the prepaid credit card. "Then what the hell is he doing managing a riding stable in Brooklyn?" I broke in. "And what was he doing . . ." I glanced back at the page. "In Australia and Italy and Egypt?"

"Brashton was doing research for a history of the Vatican. He had access to some of the archives. Beachamp was funding archeological digs, and Bevis . . . well, I'm not sure, but it was during his stint in Australia that he was crippled. Happened deep in the Outback."

"He said it was a car accident," I murmured past lips stiff with shock and anger.

I remembered the warm expression in Jolly . . . or Martin or Charles or Sheldon's . . . eyes. The way he smiled and applauded when I put Vento through his dressage paces, the serious note in his voice when I had called him from LA to demand how he knew that I was on the verge of being murdered. He seemed so decent and caring. And it had all been a lie.

"I haven't told the police any of this," John said. "I was waiting to talk to you."

"Do you think they'll find it?"

The hands with their long, tapered fingers lifted, straightened, and aligned the papers on the desk. "No, the cops in Brooklyn are faced with a break-in and assault. They're not going to assume that person is anything other than what he seems to be."

"So why did you dig deeper?"

"Because he took such an abnormal interest in *you*, and you're weird."

A shiver fluttered down my back. *"You're a very strange human, Linnet."*

"Be careful, Linnet, it feels like there's a lot of moving parts here, and a lot of unknown players all moving in the shadows."

9

Three days later I sat in my new office putting the final touches on Ray and Gregory's inter vivos trust. Now that they were getting married I could clear away the thicket of documents that had been in place to make certain they could care for each other in sickness and inherit each other's assets in death. My furniture had arrived the same day I ordered it, and Syd hadn't let me ease into the job. He had shoved a couple of small cases my way on my first full day. He had worked the cases and all that remained were the court appearances, so I found myself racing between courthouses to make the final arguments.

I was one for one on my scorecard. I had successfully gotten a family's money returned when a breeder had sold them a sick and dying puppy. I'd lost the hearing for the deadbeat dad who hadn't been paying his child support. Not one of my finest moments, but such was the life of a sole practitioner. I needed more cases, but Ray and Gregory had promised to ask among their friends, and Ray would see if any of his fellow dancers, stagehands, etc., needed legal help.

Whatever the shortcomings of the building, my new office was great. I had a big window that looked out across the street toward a postage-stamp-size park. I could watch mothers playing with children in that speck of greenery, an older couple walking arm-in-arm, folks walking their dogs. Not professional dog walkers like in Manhattan, but the actual owners of said dogs spending time with their pets. At IMG I'd had a tiny window, but from the seventieth floor you couldn't really see anything except a bit of sky and the occasional cloud. Here, life was parading past.

My evenings were quiet because Ray was not only dancing, he had a small speaking role in a show that was in tryouts up in Boston, and Gregory had gone up to watch. There was now a landline in the apartment. I had offered to pay for it, but Gregory had waved off the offer. I now had a way to communicate that couldn't be easily traced, but I hadn't availed myself of that option. I felt very cut off from friends and family alike, but that was self-inflicted. I couldn't bring myself to call Caroline or any of the other women from Ismael, McGillary and Gold and tell them where I was working. Syd was a great guy, but it really was a huge step down, and I was embarrassed. Which proved that I was not a very good person. I had several times reached for the phone to call my father, but when I remembered our last conversation I got angry and hurt all over again and couldn't bring myself to do it. I hoped he was worried sick about me, and I took perverse pleasure in picturing my cell phone, now locked in a safety deposit box, filling up with increasingly frantic messages from my dad.

I sighed and banged my forehead lightly on the edge of my desk. Yeah, I really was a terrible human being. I needed to get it over with and just call him. I reached for the phone, but before I could lift the handset out of its cradle Belinda came into my office.

"Hey, you got a client looking for you."

I frowned at the calendar on my laptop. "I don't have it on my schedule."

"He's a walk-in, but asking for you specifically."

"Cool," I said as I came around from behind my desk and followed her back into the waiting room.

There was a young Asian man, slender and handsome. He wore his jet-black hair in a ponytail, and his eyes were a tawny brown behind heavy black-rimmed glasses. He was looking around with a puzzled frown. He seemed vaguely familiar to me, but I couldn't place him. I walked over and extended my hand.

"Hello, I'm Linnet Ellery. What can I do for you?"

We shook as he said, "I'm Dr. Kenneth Zhèng. Jolyon Bryce told me I should hire you." Memory clicked in. This was the scientist who had been on that silly television show. The show that Jolyon had recorded. Zhèng continued. "I went first to your old firm, but they told me you had quit. I figured one lawyer was pretty much like another, and it seemed like a big firm so I hired somebody there." A frown darkened his brow. "Then I get a call today that they won't represent me after all. Just dropped me flat without any explanation."

"Who did you retain over there?" I asked.

"Doug McCallister," he said.

That killed any chance of finding out why the good doctor's case had been dropped. Doug was not a member of my fan club. Well, his loss my gain. I had just been thinking how I needed more clients.

"I tried to call Mr. Bryce to see if he knew where you went, but he's not answering."

"I'm sorry to tell you that Mr. Bryce is in the hospital."

"Oh, shit."

"Please come into my office."

He preceded me into the office and I closed the door as I indicated a chair and took my place behind my desk. I folded my hands on a stack of pleadings and gave him an inquiring look. "So, how *did* you track me down? I've only been in the office three days."

"I went over to the office to get a refund on my retainer, and this Álfar guy caught me in the lobby and told me where to find you."

My lack of a poker face was a real trial to me. I wondered what Zhèng was reading off me because what I was feeling was a complex stew of emotions. Gratitude that John had sent a client in my direction. Unease that he appeared to be keeping tabs on me. A sense of comfort that he was keeping tabs on me. I pushed all that aside and tried to focus.

"So, how can I help you?" For a long moment there was silence.

People in lawyers' offices come in two varieties. The ones who are so outraged over what is happening to them that they can't wait to pour out their problems, and the ones who seem embarrassed to find themselves in a lawyer's office. It looked like Zhèng was falling into the latter category. I waited. My almost one year as a practicing attorney had taught me that leading questions were never good, no matter the setting.

He pushed his glasses up his nose and finally mumbled, "I'm . . . I'm an assistant professor at NYU." He lapsed once more into silence.

I nudged. "What do you teach?"

"Parasitology."

I was surprised and very disappointed by our institutions of higher learning. "They teach that at universities?"

The professor looked exasperated. "Not parapsychology . . . *paraSITology.*" This time he really enunciated the *T* so I heard it correctly.

"Ah, okay, got it. Parasites. That sounds . . . interesting," I lied. It actually sounded sort of gross.

It was like I had opened a floodgate. The words came tumbling out. "It is. It's fascinating. I study how parasites interact with their hosts, their life cycles, and how to break those cycles since parasites can cause so much suffering. I'm a biologist by training but parasitology is very interdisciplinary. I only teach one class. Mostly I do research. Write grants to fund my research."

"And the problem that has you seeking legal help is what?"

The frown was back. "The administration is blocking publication of my research paper. A paper I've been working on for the past three years, and if it doesn't get published I won't get promoted to associate and get tenure. And also, this needs to be out in the scientific community." Now the outrage had arrived and his voice had risen.

I pulled out a yellow legal pad, grabbed a pen, and began making notes. "Have they given you any reason for blocking publication?"

"About ten different reasons. Everybody I talk to has another excuse and none of them make any sense. Nobody has challenged my methodology or the foundational aspects of the paper. Personally, I think one of the big donors is leaning on them."

I looked up at that. "Usually donors are only interested in a university's football team—"

Zhèng interrupted. "NYU doesn't have a football team."

"Oh, okay, point is, they put money in what interests them, if not football then a medical school working on a cure for cancer. They don't usually go for esoteric scientific work."

The frown was back. "That's so true."

"So, what are you researching?"

"The Hunters and their relationship to the predator, though it should more properly be referred to as a parasite. I think the Hunters were designed to break the life cycle of that parasite."

Stunned didn't begin to cover it. I sat for a few seconds thinking back over all I knew about these creatures that had given rise to the legends of zombies. Hunters were grotesque, shambling creatures with pale white skin and no discernible features on their pale oval faces aside from a red wet *O* of a mouth out of which a long, mucus-covered tongue would emerge. The fingers on their elongated hands were like worms, but it was said they could stiffen into blades capable of stabbing through a person's chest or cutting off a vampire's head. It was said they stank like rotting meat, which was one reason even vampires didn't want them around even though vampires had created them. The legend was that the Hunters were created to locate a mysterious predator that if released would destroy all the vampires and werewolves in the world. But here was a seemingly sane scientist, hired by a major university, who was telling me the predator was real.

"By analyzing the Hunters, I think we can begin to postulate the attributes of the parasite, attributes that the Hunters have been created to sense and eradicate."

"So, you don't think the predator is just a legend?"

"Absolutely not. I've only had access to one badly decayed Hunter body before it was whisked away by the Powers, but the surface of its skin appears to be covered with pheromone-sensing receptacles."

"So the predator is a creature like the Hunters?"

"No, I think it's much smaller, a true parasite that needs a host. I think it's carried in a host body until circumstances are right for it to propagate. The Hunters are designed to destroy the host body before that gestation is complete."

"So the Hunters are like bloodhounds, Dr. Zhèng?" I asked.

Zhèng nodded enthusiastically, which sent the glasses sliding down his nose. He pushed them up again. "That's a really good analogy. Oh, and call me Ken. Zhèng is kinda hard to say."

"What kind of host are we talking about?" I had stopped looking at this like a lawyer. As someone who had been fostered in a vampire household and who had worked in a vampire law firm, this was fascinating.

"I've studied documents dating back to the Middle Ages and even one from the Roman era that came out of the Villa of the Papari in Herculaneum. All of which, together with my exam and tests of samples of the Hunter body lead me to believe that the predator can only survive and mature in an XX environment—"

"What does that mean?" I asked.

"Women have two X chromosomes, which means the parasite can only be hosted by a human woman, and that fact has led to the absolute prohibition on female Making. It has defined the very structure of Powers society."

I leaned back in my chair and sat with that for a few moments. "So, you're saying the ban on female vampires or werewolves is because of this parasite?"

"Exactly. Yes." He was nodding enthusiastically with the expected slide and forefinger push between each nod to restore the glasses to the bridge of his nose.

Unable to sit still I stood up and took two short steps and two steps back. "So, what would this parasite do?"

"Given the severity of the punishment for turning a woman into a vampire or werewolf—death to both parties—one can only assume that the effect of the parasite would be calamitous to the Powers." The pedantic delivery left no doubt that Ken was an academic.

But I saw a female vampire.

My world was slowly turning upside down. I took a deep breath. "Okay. So how does Jolly—Mr. Bryce—come into all this?"

"Several months ago he approached me about my research. Then when all this trouble started he said he and his organization could privately fund my research, but I want tenure."

"What's his organization?" I asked faintly.

"I don't know. He never said and I didn't ask because I want to do it under the auspices of NYU and my research grant."

"So you were funded to do this research?"

"Well, sort of. It started because werewolves are so much tougher than normal humans. I wanted to see what diseases might affect them, but then I found this trail and I followed it, and then all the craziness started when I turned in my first draft for peer review. So," he added hesitantly, "are you going to take my case?"

"I will absolutely take your case, Doctor." I leaned across the desk and we shook hands.

"Would you like to read my paper?"

"Uh, sure. I'm not certain how much I'll understand if it's written in science talk, but send it along."

"Great. I'll shoot a copy over to you."

I gulped. This was the part I hated. "My hourly rate is two hundred and twenty-five an hour. I pro-rate in fifteen-minute increments, and I have a timer on my computer. You are entitled to see that report to verify the time I spend working on your case. You're responsible for all court and filing costs. Is that acceptable?" I braced myself.

"Wow." The brace became a whole-body muscle clench. "That's really cheap. The rate for that guy at your old firm was five hundred an hour."

I slumped with relief. "Well, this isn't a giant white-fang law firm. I'm a sole practitioner and I've only been at this a few days."

"Hey, works for me," Ken said as he stood up. I followed suit and we shook hands again. "So, what's our first move? You sue 'em?" he added eagerly.

"No." I reacted to his evident disappointment. "Look, it's never good when things actually make it all the way to court. It means you've spent a ton of money and we're down to our final moves. What we do is, I contact the university, tell them I've been retained, and ask for a meeting. With luck, we can handle this before it ever reaches a courtroom."

"That would be great." Then he frowned. "Though I'd kind of like to stick it to these guys."

"Not if you want to keep working at NYU you don't," I said rather dryly.

"Good point."

He left and I sat frowning off into space while I nervously tapped a pen on my desk. So Jolly had approached an obscure researcher in an esoteric field, and then told him to hire me? Why? I grabbed the phone and called the hospital again. The nurses' station reported no change. I had to hope John could find some answers and not more questions.

After Ken left I wandered over to Syd's office and stuck my head around the door. He was speaking slowly and carefully at his computer. "Therefore plaintiff requests a full and timely—son of a bitch! *Timely, timely.* Not *tiny*—" He broke off and looked up at me.

"Sorry, damn word-recognition program." He held up his artificial arm. "I can do a lot, but I still can't type worth a damn. What do you need?"

"I'm going to take off a little early—"

"Linnet. You don't work for me. You're your own boss. You set your own hours. You don't need my permission. Taste the freedom, baby."

"Yeah, right. Okay."

"Oh, one thing." I leaned back into the office. "I need a number where I can reach you."

"Yeah, I guess that would be good. I'm staying with friends." I gave him Ray and Gregory's home number, and added the address as well. "Eventually I've got to find an apartment closer to the office."

"It's nice out here. Prices are way better than Manhattan too," Syd said.

I paused to load up my computer case and the laptop. I wasn't sure there was anything for me to ride back out at the stable, but I needed to get on a horse to clear my head. I also needed to check in with Kim and get an update on Vento. The big trucks crisscrossed the country going coast to coast loaded with expensive show horses and racehorses and the occasional family horse, and the carriers were always kind and professional, but Vento was special and I wanted to track his progress. I knew Kim would have done the same and could give me an update.

After a few subway rides and a bus ride I stood at the top of the long driveway that led to the old stable. It was crisp and a bit cold, but a number of early spring robins were putting up a twittering racket in the trees that lined the drive. Spring cleaning and remolding-the-nest day, I thought as I watched one of the birds swoop past with a clot of shredded horse hair in its beak. It was hard slogging, dragging the rolling computer case down the gravel drive. The strap of the duffel was digging into my shoulder. The tires of a car crunched on the rocks and stopped. I glanced back. An older woman rolled down the window and smiled at me. There were three little girls some-where between five and ten years old giggling in the backseat.

"Would you like a ride?" the woman offered.

"Oh yeah," I breathed. She leaned down and released the catch on the truck. I loaded in my computer and duffel and climbed in the front seat next to her.

"Hi, I'm Dorinda," she said as she put the car in gear and drove on.

"Linnet."

"I know, my daughter, Jessica, and her friends come home and talk about watching you ride. They're in the jump class with Kim, but they sure do like to watch you and that white horse work. I do too, and I don't know anything about horses."

"But you drive them," I jerked my head toward the giggling trio, "out here to ride."

"Absolutely. Friend of mine got both her girls all the way into college before they even noticed there were boys. She swore it was the horses that did it."

"She's right," I said.

We nattered other meaningless pleasantries until we reached the barn and parked. Jessica and her two friends boiled out of the car and ran toward the barn only to be stopped by Kim's barked command,

"No running in the barn!" They slowed to a sedate walk and entered the dimness of the breezeway. "Jessica, you're riding Rosi today, Merl, you're on Martini, and Gretchen, you get Larry. Now go get tacked up."

By now I had retrieved my belongings and reached the entrance. Kim was in her mid-thirties, red-haired, a pretty South Carolinian with a rich treacle accent. She usually had a cheerful smile, but I could see the shadows in her eyes and the frown between her brows.

"Oh, Linnet. I don't know if we have anything for you to ride. Now that the weather is getting nice everybody wants to come back," Kim said.

"That's all right. I knew there was only a small chance, and I'm out here more as Jolly's attorney."

She glanced toward the house, which was surrounded by yellow crime scene tape. "Any word?"

I shook my head. "No change."

She sighed. "Let's go in the office while the kids get tacked up. I got questions for you."

There was a cluttered and comfortable lounge that abutted the small indoor arena that hung off one end of the barn. A tiny office had been carved out of the lounge space.

"Did Jolly ever tell you anything about his people?" Kim asked. I wasn't exactly sure what she was asking. She sensed my confusion. "Sorry, I'm Southern. Family, kin. Anybody we should be contacting?"

"No. No, he never said anything to me," I answered and felt that coil of discomfort in the belly that comes from telling fibs. I didn't think the barn manager needed to know that Jolly had a number of aliases. A new thought occurred. "Is this just your office, or did Jolly do any work down here?"

"He used it too."

"Mind if I look around?"

"Be my guest. I better go check on the kids and get teaching."

She left and I moved to take the chair behind the messy desk. I began going through the piles and scraps of paper, which brought on a momentary flashback of going through my boss's cluttered office after he'd been killed by a werewolf. Was my life always to be paper, paper, and more paper? *You decided to become a lawyer,* I reminded myself. I sorted through receipts for stall shavings, grain, hay, and farriers' bills, setting them in discreet piles. There were telephone numbers scribbled in the margins of bills; inexplicable sentence fragments in two different hands. I created a new pile to accommodate the pages with notes, however brief and cryptic.

A few papers were in the well under the desk. I rolled back the chair, dropped to my knees, and crawled in after them. One had a note on it and it leaped out at me because I saw my name. I scrambled back out to where I had better light.

Linnet/Hattie=good?

It had been dug into the paper and traced over several times as if Jolly hadn't been sure or had been thinking about it during a conversation. I had certainly done the same thing more than a few times. I eyed the landline phone on the desk. I couldn't get a list of numbers that had been called on that phone. But I knew someone who could.

10

By six o'clock I was sitting at Detective Lucius Washington's desk at the 19th Precinct. The smell of stale, day-old coffee was very strong in the bullpen. He held the piece of paper with the barn telephone number on it and eyed me.

"As you rightly pointed out, this case is way out of my jurisdiction. So, why should I contact Frontier Communications and give you this information instead of passing this on to the Brooklyn PD?"

"You could do both," and opting for total honesty I added, "But if you just give it to them *they* won't tell me what they find."

Lucius gave a snort and shook his head. "You've got some chutzpah, that's for damn sure."

"I'm not saying you shouldn't tell them. I was just hoping you would check too, and give me those numbers. I might notice something they would miss."

"And why is that?"

My eyes slid away from his piercing gaze. I noticed he had a bulging satchel next to his desk. "I'm sorry, I'm keeping you from going home."

"It's okay. I'd just heat up a frozen dinner and watch TV. And you haven't answered my question."

"It's . . . um . . . complicated. How about I buy you dinner and try to explain," I offered.

Lucius stood and grabbed his satchel. "That's sounds like a hell of a deal. Do I get to pick the place?"

"Absolutely."

I had expected a steakhouse, but he'd picked a sushi restaurant in the area. Since this was roughly the neighborhood where my old office stood I was familiar with the place. It was good, relatively inexpensive, and had small and private tatami rooms. I was curled up on a pillow in one of those rooms. Across the low table Lucius was watching me closely as I concluded, ". . . so I think Jolly was attacked to prevent him from telling me what's going on with . . . well, me and my crazy sort of super power." I then stirred a tiny dollop of wasabi mustard into the small bowl of soy sauce, clacked my chopsticks together, and grabbed up another piece of my spider roll. The mustard hit the back of my nose and set my eyes to watering. Coughing, I grabbed for my glass of water.

Lucius didn't respond. Instead he scooped up a giant amount of the evil green substance, added it to his sauce, carefully dipped a piece of salmon, slowly masticated it.

"I can't tell if you're taking this so calmly because you accept it, or if you're trying to decide whether to call for men in white coats to come and take me away," I said finally.

"In a world where we have vampires, werewolves, and Álfar, why would I be surprised by anything? And in a weird way this makes me feel better. I desperately needed an explanation for how you survived all those werewolf attacks. Especially since I'm a werewolf, and I wasn't sure whether to be nervous or not." He gave me a smile. "Apparently if I don't attack you I'll be fine."

"You're a . . . you're a . . . Why didn't you tell me?"

He shrugged. "Didn't seem relevant, and it's not something you just plop into a conversation."

"When did— How did it happen?"

"My brother was a marine. Fought in Iraq. He got taken down by some of Saddam's elite werewolf guards. I was close to my brother. I wanted to give it back to those bastards courtesy of an American wolf. I enlisted. Found a mentor. Ended up in a Ranger division. We called ourselves the Pack." He paused and leaned over to refill my tea cup from the steaming iron pot. "You've intrigued me. Watching a five-foot-nothing girl take down a pack of hounds? I wanted to know more. There's something about you . . ." His voice trailed away.

"We still don't have an explanation for how I can do that," I pointed out. "We have somebody who *claims* to have an explanation but who can't tell us since he's in a coma, which is why—well, one of the reasons why—I need to learn everything about him."

"You know you probably saved your friend's life. If they really wanted to silence him before he talked to you they meant to kill him."

A parade of people marched past. People I had hurt—Chip, Syd, John, David, Jolly.

Lucius reacted to my expression. "What? What's wrong?"

"I may have survived, but the people around me . . ." I shook my head and swallowed hard several times. "So, are you going to get the phone numbers? And tell me what you find?"

"Yeah, I'll do it, but you have to keep me in the loop too. This is not a one-way street," Lucius said.

"Okay."

"So, have you told me everything?" he asked, pinning me with an all-too-knowing look. There was a reason he was an NYPD homicide detective; he was no dumb bunny.

I squirmed then decided *in for a penny in for a pound*. "There was a female vampire in Jolly's house that night."

"They're not supposed to exist. Any more than female wolves

exist." He gave me a stern look. "You didn't think that was a detail you needed to mention?"

"I think it's an incredibly dangerous detail, which is why I initially told you I didn't want to get you involved."

"Well, I'm involved now, but if I'm going to help you, you don't hold back anything. Deal?"

"Deal."

We ate in silence for a few moments. "How did your family take your . . . change?"

"Pretty well. I was mostly worried about my granddad. He's a Baptist minister and I wasn't sure he wouldn't tell me I was damned to Hell, but he just said God don't make mistakes and he figured even the Spooks were God's creatures too. Yeah, he talks that way, but you make allowances."

"He sounds like a good guy."

"He is." Lucius pulled out his smartphone. "Give me the number you want me to research and let me give you my personal numbers." He held it out, obviously intending to have the numbers beamed over.

I shook my head. "I'm using a dumb phone right now. I'll have to actually type."

"Do I want to know why?"

"John wanted me off the grid, or going dark, or however you want to put it."

"Why?"

"Somebody broke into my apartment. It's one of the reasons I'm not staying there right now."

"Another little detail you neglected to mention?"

"I just forgot, okay?"

Lucius frowned. "Okay, this is starting to sound dangerous."

"You hadn't gotten that before now?"

"I'm starting to."

I gave him the office number and Ray and Gregory's home phone number. "Now, let's talk about something other than weird and scary shit. Tell me more about yourself," I said.

When the phone rang at my office the next day I had hoped it would be Lucius with the info about the phone, but it was John. "Dinner. The folks. Tonight. Come to my apartment, we'll go by the Dakota and get Parlan and head down."

"We could take the train to Philadelphia."

"If I have a car I can escape Philadelphia."

"It's not going to be that bad."

"Famous last words," he muttered and hung up.

The phone rang again, but it again wasn't Lucius, it was the legal department at NYU. I'd sent them an email and followed up with a phone call only yesterday informing them that I was now counsel for Dr. Kenneth Zhèng. I hadn't requested a meeting. I didn't want to look too eager, but now I had the assistant to their chief counsel telling me they wanted to discuss a "settlement" and could my client and I come in tomorrow? I agreed, and called Ken.

"This is good, right? It means they know they were wrong, right?"

I untangled the garbled sentence. "I don't know, Ken. Let's see what they're going to offer. Try not to stress tonight, okay?"

"Okay, I'll try. I still think this is good."

I hung up and finished off the adoption form I was preparing for a new client, packed up the computer, said goodbye to Syd and Belinda, and made my way to the Village. John was waiting and I barely had time to pet Gadzooks before he hustled me back out the door. A quick walk and we were at the garage where he kept his car. I was surprised to see the Toyota Camry had been replaced by a big black Buick Lacrosse.

"New car."

"Yep."

"Guess you did get a good settlement from the firm."

"Yep."

"And so you buy a staid daddy car? You're a hot Álfar private detective living in New York City. You didn't think a sports car might be in order?"

"I like this car. Reminds me of my police cruiser back in Philly, and I like to feel there's a lot of metal between me and bad guys."

"It still seems kind of boring," I muttered as I snapped the seatbelt shut.

We headed uptown to the Dakota. Just before we reached the building I asked, "Do you need me to grab hold of you?"

"No, I got a lot better at making the transition while I was living in Fey."

And sure enough, the world shimmered, the traffic jam around us vanished, and we slipped into that alternate reality where Central Park was a whole lot bigger and there were fewer cars and more carriages and people mounted on horses. We turned through the gates into the courtyard of the Dakota.

Parlan was waiting for us, and he was wearing modern human attire: khaki slacks, a sweater, sports jacket. It was a wise choice. Big Red took a very dubious view of Álfar finery. Ladlaw opened the door for Parlan and bowed him into the backseat.

"Are you sure you wish to dispense with your guard, sir?" Ladlaw asked.

"Trust me, it's better this way," Parlan drawled.

I quickly seconded that, and Ladlaw shut the door. Parlan leaned over the seat and gave me a hug. "Linnet, how's the shoulder?" he asked.

I rotated it. "Pretty good. How's my principality?" I quipped.

"Getting sorted out," Parlan answered.

John gave a snort. "Can't believe you actually want to be here."

They matched looks, bucks measuring their racks, and I gave an eye roll.

"Fasten your seat belt," John ordered.

Parlan leaned back and John took us through the gates and back into our world.

"You know there's a lot less traffic in Fey. We could get there faster if we stayed out of—"

"I'm not spending any more time in Fey then I have to," John shot back.

"Fine. Have it your way." Parlan sounded sulky.

"Think about it. We're probably both on Mommy Dearest's fecal roster," John said impatiently.

"I said all right!"

I rested my head in my hand. "I guess it doesn't matter that you're different species and raised apart, you are like the poster children for sibling rivalry."

Parlan gave a sniff and leaned back with his arms folded across his chest. John gave a snort and snapped on the radio, indicating that conversation would not be occurring during the drive. I sighed. It was going to be a long two hours.

"Come in! Come in!" Big Red's voice boomed out, excited and maybe just a little bit forced.

We stepped into the entry hall. The house smelled of roasting meat and freshly baked bread. Meg emerged from the kitchen. She gazed at John, then a sob burst out and she ran to him and hugged him tightly. He stood stiffly, looked to me. I mimed hugging, but he didn't take the hint. It was awkward and Meg released him and stepped back. She looked hurt.

I hustled my way to her side, slipped an arm around her waist, and said in a too-bright tone, "Can I help? What needs to get done?" I started moving her toward the kitchen.

"Let's go in the living room and have a drink before dinner," Red suggested to the two younger men.

As Meg and I went into the kitchen I reflected that we were like a cliché on a 1950s TV sitcom. The men were all off talking manly stuff while the women were in the kitchen. It brought home to me that the O'Sheas had a very traditional marriage. Had it affected John's attitudes? What did he really think about career women? Meg had stayed home and raised the kids. Would he expect the same from his wife? Not that John and I could have kids. Humans and Álfar couldn't crossbreed.

I decided I was being silly. First, even thinking about marriage right now and assuming that kids were always going to repeat the pattern set by their parents. My parents had the exact same marriage, and it hadn't stopped me from picking a different path. It had probably been a heavier lift for the O'Sheas to keep Meg at home on Big Red's policeman's paycheck than it had been for my upper-middle-class family, but it had clearly been worth the sacrifice. She'd raised five great kids. I wondered for a moment how my family would measure up. In some ways I didn't count, I hadn't actually been raised by my real parents. My mother was a bit of a horror, so maybe it would have been better for Charlie if she hadn't stayed home, though he seemed to have survived and had come out okay. I found myself wondering how the Álfar queen had been as a mother. I'd have to ask Parlan, but maybe not tonight.

Meg snatched a Kleenex out of a box on the counter and gave her nose a defiant blow. "Sorry. I knew what to expect. You'd warned me, but I still wasn't prepared." She busied herself turning the potato pancakes that were frying on the stove. "Does he hate us now?"

"No, he doesn't feel anything. He knows he used to, but he can't remember the emotions so he gets even more frozen and rigid, which makes it worse."

"How are *you* coping? I know you two were . . ."

"I wanted to free him. Beyond that . . . I don't think or at least I hope I didn't have any expectations." I shook my head. "Maybe I shouldn't have forced this visit. I just felt like—"

"No, I wanted to see him. He's my son. It's going to be all right."

I had my doubts, but I kept those to myself. Meg and I made a small hors d'oeuvre plate with cheese and crackers and went into the living room. Silence greeted us. The brother's held tumblers with splashes of whisky. Red was drinking a beer. The tension in the room had me writhing.

"Okay," I chirped. "Meg has made a feast. You guys are in for a treat."

Nothing from John. Parlan proved he had been trained as a courtier. He stood, took the plate from Meg, and escorted her to the chair he'd just vacated.

"You are a wonderful cook, Meg. I do hope you made those potato pancakes. I remember them fondly from my stay." Of course he knew she had prepared them from the aroma filling the house, but it helped bridge the moment.

"Drink, Lynnie?" Red asked.

"Yes, please."

"We've got wine." He cast a fond look at his wife. "Meg made me buy a bottle that didn't come with a screw cap."

It fell flat because Parlan had no idea what that meant and John sat sphinxlike in his chair. I hurried into speech. "Hey, that doesn't mean much anymore. Turns out screw caps actually preserve the wine better." No one volleyed back the conversational ball so I plowed on. "And there's been this fungus that's affecting cork oaks. The fungus wrecks the wine. So everybody's going to . . . screw . . . tops."

"I'll go open the bottle," Red said.

"I'll help bring glasses," Meg added. They left the room.

John bolted to his feet. "This won't work. I'm leaving."

"Sit down!" Parlan snapped. "I lived in this house long enough to know they raised you to be better than this."

"This isn't helping them. This . . . me . . . I'm hurting them," John said. "I don't need emotions to know that."

"Then tell them that," I said. "We're all trying to pretend things are normal, that nothing's changed, but it has. We all need to face that."

And me most of all, I thought as I remembered on that horrible conversation with my dad. Hiding from it was the wrong way to handle things. I needed to face him. Find out why my presence at IMG had been so important to him. Find out what he feared.

For a moment it hung in the balance, then John sat down and tossed back the rest of his whisky. The O'Sheas came back into the room and looked from one uncomfortable face to the next.

"You three got it hashed out?" Red asked.

John stood. "I'll start." He looked at Meg. "Yes, I'm blind in this eye." He rested a forefinger beneath that milk-white orb. "Can it be fixed?" John shrugged and looked to Parlan, who shook his head and said,

"My guess is no. There is a cost to magic. My mother . . . Our mother . . . your mother," the human changeling stuttered. "Exacted it from you rather than paying the price herself."

"Typical," John said.

Parlan shrugged. "She has always been practical that way."

"Is that ice sliver still embedded in his eye?" I asked.

Parlan pulled his long ponytail over his shoulder and tugged at the hair. "I don't know. Has it melted and spread the spell through his entire body? An interesting question."

"If it is still in there could it be detected with an MRI or something?" Meg asked.

Parlan looked confused. "It's a medical test," I explained. "And it's worth trying. If it's still in there maybe it can be grabbed and removed."

"Touching Álfar magic with something from this world might have dangerous consequences," Parlan warned. "I think it would be safer to use our methods."

"And you got any ideas about those methods?" Red asked.

"Not as yet. But I will search for an answer now that I have access to books and magicians again."

Meg looked at Parlan. "Are you coming home?"

"Linnet has given me suzerainty over the principality."

"Is that a fancy way of saying she put you in charge?" Red asked. Parlan nodded.

Meg turned to John. "Are you going to come home?"

"I have a job in New York. And neither one of us are kids who need to come home to Mom and Dad."

"Maybe Mom and Dad need that," Meg said with a touch of her old spirit.

"And that's why I can't do it. Your need is like . . . well it's like you're bludgeoning me."

Meg took the verbal blow better than I expected. Red however, not so much. His face now matched his hair. Meg laid a calming hand against her husband's chest, holding him back. "He can't help it," she said.

"He, by God, better help it!" Red said.

"I'm going," John announced and he walked out of the living room.

"He's your ride, isn't he?" Meg asked.

Parlan and I exchanged glances. "We can take the train," I said.

"Yes," Parlan agreed. "We'll stay."

"This is tearing the family apart," Red said.

"Only if we let it," Parlan said. "And we won't."

The maturity and wisdom in his response put me to shame. I had done the same thing as John. Walked away, made no effort to understand or help. I'd get past the meeting with the university and then I was going to go to Rhode Island and confront my father.

11

I had considered walking from the boys' apartment up to my meeting at NYU. At least for the day, spring had arrived and there was a softness in the air. Regretfully, I decided against it because I needed to be in Legal Chic and I didn't love walking in high heels. I had bagged the rolling computer bag and instead carried a smart leather flip case. It made me look less like a geek and more like a high-powered attorney. That was the theory, at least.

I emerged from the subway at Eighth Street. Washington Square Park, where I was to meet Ken, beckoned. The limbs of the trees waved in a gentle breeze, green banners against a blue sky. It was warm enough that the fountains in the big central pool were running again, adding their silver glint to the riot of colors so welcome after a long, gray winter. The sound of the water falling into the pool struggled to make itself known against the roar of traffic, the blare of horns, the frenetic sirens, and the deep bone-shaking rumble of the subways far below.

All around the park were the buildings that constituted NYU. Ken was waiting on the far side of the fountain, the lenses of his glasses faintly misted by the spraying water. He jumped up when he saw me, rushed to my side, and fell into step with me.

"So, what are you going to say?" he asked as he dried off his glasses on the tail of his shirt.

"Depends on what they say, and I'm not going to say much. The best thing we can do is keep quiet, let them make their pitch, and not give them anything in return."

"Have you read my paper?" Ken asked.

"Not yet. I was reading over your employment contract first. My guess is that's going to be more relevant today."

"Oh, God, what if they fire me?"

"Then we'll sue them for wrongful termination." I stopped walking and laid a hand on his upper arm. "Look, Ken, don't go borrowing trouble. Let's see what they're offering. Remember, they asked for this meeting. We're in the stronger position."

"I hope so."

The administrative offices were housed in a large red building that also held the Elmer Holmes Library. Ken and I left the park, crossed the street, and entered. There was a young man in a nice suit standing in the lobby. My lawyer sense tingled and I walked up to him and held out my hand.

"I'm Linnet Ellery, with Dr. Zhèng."

"Marshall Grayson. Let me take you upstairs. They're waiting."

I sensed a criticism and bristled a bit. "We're actually early."

"Oh, I know. I think they had a meeting beforehand." He led us to an elevator.

The conference room was an aggressively modern space. Fancy electronic shades had been drawn across the windows, leaving the room in dimness and shadows. A tingling between my shoulder blades warned me, and sure enough we were in the presence of vampires. Two vampires I really hadn't expected to see—one of the senior partners, Avery Gold, and David. David was seated in a chair against the wall, clearly the junior in this meeting. His eyes rested on me for one long moment, then he returned his attention to the legal pad balanced on his knee.

Gold was at the head of an oval table with a phalanx of humans, four to a side. It seemed like an overwhelming force to confront one assistant professor and his sole practitioner lawyer.

What the hell was in that research paper? And I promised myself I would read it that night.

Introductions were made. I allowed most of the names to slide right out of my head. Most of the men and the two women were just intimidating window dressing. Only Gold and Mr. Roger Figge, chief counsel for NYU, really mattered. Ken and I took the only two available seats at the foot of the table. I snapped open my case and pulled out a yellow legal pad and a pen. I left the employment contract safely hidden away. I didn't even want to suggest that this was about Ken's job. I then folded my hands on the pad and looked at them inquiringly but didn't speak.

The silence dragged on and on. The humans started to fidget. First a small cough there. Then a nervous handling of a pen from the woman on my right. A squeak as someone adjusted their position in a chair. Even Figge reached out and straightened the edge of his papers. He was armed with Ken's employment contract. I kept looking at Gold. I hadn't been fostered by vampires for nothing. I knew this game. Figge broke first.

Clearing his throat, he said, "Well . . ." His voice trailed off as he caught Gold's annoyed expression.

Having made my point, I spoke up. "You requested this meeting. We're here." I went silent again. There was a small choking sound out of David. I knew him well enough to recognize the sound; it was a quickly suppressed laugh.

Figge took over. "We understand Dr. Zhèng's dismay over having his research blocked, but both the medical school and senior staff in the biology department feel the paper is poorly sourced and badly researched."

I wasn't quick enough and Ken jumped out of his chair before I could grab his wrist and restrain him. "That's just bullshit! My paper is solid. My research, impeccable."

"Ken!" I snapped. He clamped his mouth shut. I stood up and started repacking my case. "Then I guess we'll see you in court."

A flicker of emotion crossed Gold's face. "If I may, Mr. Figge. That was perhaps a bit baldly presented. Whatever the strictures on Dr. Zhèng's paper might be, everyone in his department agrees he is a talented young man with great research skills and if properly guided and mentored will do great work. Therefore the university is prepared to offer him an associate professorship if he will drop this unproductive line of research and agree to never take it up at any other institution."

I risked a glance at Ken. A series of complex emotions seemed to grip him. His expression went from one of joyful surprise to devastation.

"That's an interesting proposition. My client and I will discuss it and get back to you," I said.

As we left I couldn't help it, I looked at David. He gave me sad eyes, and I hurried out of the conference room with Ken in tow. He started to talk, but I held up a hand to forestall that. We stayed silent during the elevator ride, and once we were back on the street I headed off in search of a café. It didn't take long to find one. This was Greenwich Village.

"Holy shit," Ken said as he sank into a chair at a corner table. "Associate professor. They can't really give me that title without giving me tenure. But . . ." Agitated, he ran a hand through his hair, pulling wisps free from his ponytail. "I spent three years on this paper."

"They're buying you off." He reacted to my word choice and I elaborated. "There's nothing wrong with that. We do it all the time. Sometimes it's cheaper to pay a settlement than to keep fighting. Other times you do it because you really want something to go away. This feels like the latter to me. But it's your call, and that was just their opening offer. I can probably get them to throw in a monetary settlement to compensate you for lost time."

He rubbed the back of his neck. "Some money would be nice. Help pay off some student loans." He stared down at the surface of the table.

I stood. "What do you want? I'll go order."

"Is this a way to give me time to think about my decision?" he asked.

"No, I don't think you should decide right now. Sleep on it. They won't expect an answer today."

"You got a recommendation?"

"Not my job. They've made you an offer. Promotion and the promise that you are on the tenure track in exchange for you setting aside three years of work and making a promise never to return to that area of research. I can't make that decision for you. So, do you want something to drink?"

Ken lurched to his feet. "Thanks for the offer, but I kinda want to just take a walk and think, okay?"

"Sure. Let me know what you decide."

He dug his hands into his pockets, hunched his shoulders, and slouched away. I checked my phone. It was nearly two thirty and it seemed silly to go all the way back to Queens. I headed for the subway and Ray and Gregory's apartment.

Belinda looked up, the light flashing on her silver studs as I walked into the office the next morning. "Your bug guy has been calling and calling."

"Parasitologist," I corrected.

"Yeah, bug guy."

I sighed. "Thank you."

Once I got settled in my office I called Ken.

"I didn't sleep last night. I just thought and thought," he said. "I can't do it. I can't just erase three years of my life and all that work. And this is important research. It deserves to be out there. Tell them no."

"All right. I'll let them know."

"Thanks, Linnet. So, what happens now?"

"We'll see what they come back with, but I expect I'll be drafting a complaint."

"So, we go to court?"

"Probably."

"Have you read my paper yet?"

I cringed with guilt, but decided to own up. "No, not yet. I will. I promise."

There was no reason to delay. I put in a call to IMG, and asked for Gold's assistant. She told me he was in court. I hung up and debated. Finally I picked up the phone again and called David's line. His assistant put me right through.

"It was good to see you yesterday," he said by way of greeting.

I really wanted to say, *yeah, it was.* Instead I said tersely, "Don't."

Long silence on the other end of the line, then David said, "So, why did you call?"

"My client says no deal. He wants his research published."

"I'll let our client know."

I was holding a disconnected line. The harsh buzz felt like a rebuke and a rejection and it hurt. I wanted to call back and somehow make it all better. But I couldn't. I mustn't. I grabbed my notes on a pending bankruptcy I was handling and went to work.

A few hours later Belinda buzzed me. "Mr. Ishmael calling for you."

That was surprising. I had thought I might hear from Gold, but not my old mentor at the firm. "Put it through." A second later and we were connected. "Hi, Shade, what's—"

"Linnet, I say this as one who has stood as a friend to you. Drop this case."

"But . . . wait . . . why?"

"No good can come of this research, and we will not permit it to go forward. Drop the case." Once again I heard the strident buzz of a disconnected line.

It felt like one of Ken's parasites had scuttled down my back. Shuddering, I hung up the phone. We *will not permit it to go forward*. Who the hell was *we*? The vampires at IMG? Or all vampires everywhere?

What the hell was in that paper?

I had just pulled a Trader Joe's asparagus and shells dinner out of the microwave when the doorbell rang. Tension tightened my shoulders and I eased my way to the foyer. Another ring followed by an insistent knock. I stretched up on tiptoes and peered through the peephole. Syd and Ken stood in the hallway of the building. Ken's expression was furious. Syd looked inscrutable. Both were bad. There was a fluttering in my stomach as I undid the chain, unlocked the door, and threw it open.

"Jesus, thought you'd died in here," Syd said as he marched through the door.

"Hello to you too," I said.

"They locked my office and confiscated my office computer," Ken burst out. "And somebody ransacked my apartment. Took my home computer, every thumb drive, and all my notes, drafts, and source material!"

I threw up a hand. "Whoa. Slow down. Come into the living room and sit down." They did and Syd took a chair. Ken continued to pace, long furious steps that had his glasses slipping over and over again. "You look like you could use a drink," I said to Ken. I didn't think Gregory would mind.

The scientist stopped, ran a hand through his hair. "Yeah, I could."

"Syd?"

The little lawyer held up a hand and shook his head. "I'm good."

I splashed the amber liquid into a cut-crystal highball glass and handed it to Ken. "You had to expect some reaction from the university when you turned down their offer, and they have a right to lock you out and reclaim equipment that they own." Ken gulped down a mouthful of scotch. "I'm more concerned about the break-in at your apartment."

"Sounds like somebody is trying to make sure no copies of this paper are floatin' around," Syd said.

"But it had been sent out for peer review—"

Ken interrupted me. "I never did send out the paper. That was what started all this crap in the first place. I'd shown bits and pieces of it to some other biologists in the department and over at the med school, but it hadn't been formally reviewed."

"But this is just stupid," I said. "You're a savvy scientist guy. I presume you had a backup in Dropbox or the Cloud or some other offsite storage."

"Of course."

I perched on the edge of a big ottoman and nibbled on a hang-nail. "This was a really dumb move. Trying to suppress the information by stealing copies . . . oh, shit, it was vampires."

"What?" the men said in chorus.

"It's the only thing that makes any sense. They're incredibly old-fashioned and they don't handle technological change very well. They knew enough to grab the computers as well as hard copies and somebody had coached them about thumb drives, but it never occurred to them that information floats in the cyber universe now."

"And I emailed you a copy."

"Yeah, that was going to be how I spent my evening. Reading your paper."

Syd jumped in. "Once whoever has taken the computer digs into it they're going to know Linnet has a copy and they'll come after her."

There was a hole where my stomach used to be and I didn't think I felt that empty just because I was hungry. I looked up at Ken. "You can't be the first person who thought of this line of inquiry." And I quickly added, "No offense," at the look on Ken's face.

He swallowed his pride and gave it serious thought. "Yeah, you might be right. I was just so excited because there was nothing out there in the community."

"And now we might know why," Syd said.

"We need help investigating this." I stood and headed to where my purse rested on the side table.

"You got somebody in mind?" Syd asked.

"Absolutely."

12

"Before I hire you I guess I should first ask if you're the guy who broke into my client's apartment," I said when John opened the door.

John stared at me for a long moment. "Would you like to tell me what you are talking about?" Gadzooks, seeing the open door, tried to make a break for it and got grabbed by John.

I outlined the situation while Gadzooks struggled with increasing desperation to escape from John's arms. When I finished, the Álfar gave a disgusted head shake. "You honestly think I'd be that stupid?"

"To do something that illegal or to not understand computers and Cloud data storage?" I shot back.

"The latter," he said. "And why are you still standing in the hall?"

"Because you haven't invited me in."

"When has that ever stopped you? You usually just barge in whether it's Fey, a partner's office, a kidnapping investigation—"

"Hey, I get things done."

"You certainly get things all stirred up," John countered.

"Admit it, you love it."

He just stared at me, shook his head, turned and walked away from the door. I stepped into a small, but neat and nicely furnished apartment. John dropped Gadzooks onto the floor and the big tabby promptly tried to trip me by coiling around my legs.

John headed for the tiny table in the kitchen. "I was just sitting down to eat. There's chili, you want a bowl?"

"Is it hot? I mean chili hot not stove hot."

"Of course."

"No, thanks." The spices coiled through the steam and tempted my nose. My stomach gave a loud growl.

I sat down opposite John and remembered the last time we'd sat companionably across this table from each other. That had been over breakfast after a night of amazing lovemaking. John crumbled crackers on top of his chili, added some grated cheese and a big handful of chopped onions.

"Hope you're not planning on kissing anybody," I said.

"I wasn't."

"Too bad," I said. He gave me a sharp glance and I returned a limpid one. He gave a growl and began eating.

"What do you need?"

"Research. I need to know if any other scientists have undertaken research into the Hunters and the legend of the predator."

"Research the researchers, huh?" John grunted.

"Exactly."

"Okay. Hundred and fifty an hour. Plus expenses, but let's leave this off the books. A vampire law firm is one of my clients. They don't need to know I'm doing research into vampire secrets."

"What happened to 'I owe you'?" I asked.

"This isn't about you. This is about your client. It's business." He took a few more bites and studied me. "Do you want to fuck?" he said abruptly.

The blunt statement unleashed a torrent of conflicting feelings.

Hurt that he could say something that crude to me. What we had shared had been beautiful and now it felt dirty.

Which led me to fury that he could say something that crude to me. I was a person, not an object.

Next up in the emotional merry-go-round—sadness. That he could say something that crude brought home how deeply damaged he actually was.

I grabbed at the whirling maelstrom of emotions and struggled to contain them into something I could channel and actually form into words without ripping his face off. I compressed them into disdain and derision. "Just curious, but how's this approach working out for you?"

He said with some frustration, "I haven't gotten laid once since I got back."

"Imagine that. Here's a few suggestions for pickup lines. You could try—*How bad could it be? How long could it take?*"

"That was mean."

"So was your remark." I rested my hands on the table and leaned in on him. "Look, John, most women need some sort of emotional connection."

"Well, I can't do that."

"I know. And no, I don't want to fuck. Thanks for helping out with this." I started for the front door. John jumped up and followed me.

"I thought you wanted me. Otherwise why the crack about kissing?"

"I shouldn't have said it, and I'm sorry. I want the old John, and I guess I think pushing you is going to make that happen. I'm sorry," I repeated.

"Linnet, what if this is really who I am, who I was all along, and the other me was just a mask?" He seemed uncomfortable.

"It's not. You said yourself the Álfar are all divas and live their own personal operas. This is like the complete opposite of an Álfar. I mean, look at Parlan. He was raised in Fey and he's way overly emotional."

"So maybe between the two of us we might manage to add up to one normal person," John said.

I searched for a hint of irony, but found none. "We'll figure this out, John. I promise."

"So confident."

"I said I'd get you out of Fey and I did. Don't count me out."

The next day I tried to work in between the numerous calls from Ken asking if I'd hired an investigator—yes, and what had they learned—nothing. After the tenth call, I yelled at him. The calls stopped.

After harping at Parlan and John I decided it was past time that I confronted my dad. I picked up and set down the phone several times before I decided that this wasn't a conversation that should be held on the phone. There was a train leaving for Providence, Rhode Island, late that afternoon. I decided to catch it. I got to the station a bit early, bought a ticket, and waited on the platform for the train to arrive. If I'd had my real phone I would have been able to surf the internet to pass the time, but given what had happened to Ken it was probably smart I didn't have it, inconvenient though it might be. I thought about pulling out my laptop, but decided I was too lazy. I was forced to actually look at the real humans occupying space with me. The little burner phone rang. I pulled it out, and finally got the cracked flip cover open.

"Hey, Linnet, Lucius. I got those numbers for you."

"That's great. Thank you."

"I'd love to check them out for you, but I had to hide the request in another case I'm working and I really can't take the time to run them down right now."

"No, no, that's cool, you've done enough. I'll take it from here. Would you email them to me?"

"Only if you promise to call in the experts if you find anything. You won't play girl sleuth."

I sighed. "Okay, but may I call you? Those Brooklyn guys didn't impress me."

"All right. As long as you call someone." I heard the click of a keyboard. "They're on their way."

"Thanks again."

The train pulled in. I got settled into a seat. Not a lot of people seemed to be headed to Providence, so I had my row to myself. The whistle echoed through the station, then a sharp jerk and we were underway. We slid out into the slanting golden light of the sunset. I watched buildings, walls, and graffiti sliding past the window, and tried to think about what I would say when I finally did reach the house, but my mind kept skittering away.

I gave up, pulled out the laptop, and found Lucius's email. As I expected, more than a few of the numbers proved to be suppliers to the barn. I recognized the number for Jolly's farrier and the vet. Those were numbers that didn't need to be checked.

With my laptop balanced on my lap I started dialing. The first number went to voice mail for the Feed Bin. I hung up. The next number had an area code that I recognized as being in Virginia. The number belonged to Elite Hay Haulers. Another number was for the Custom Saddles branch office in Del Mar, California. With the three-hour time difference they were still open, and I ended up having a nice conversation with the woman at their American office. As always happens when horse people start talking, there had to be a discussion of which model I rode and what my horse was like. During the conversation I learned that Jolly had in fact ridden in a Custom before his accident. He had been calling them to discuss putting his saddle on consignment. Which made me feel sad in a really indefinable way. What would I do if I couldn't ever ride again? I pulled my wandering thoughts back to the next number.

It didn't look anything like a number in the States or Canada. It looked like a foreign number. I tried to remember back to my high school graduation trip to Europe and how to make overseas calls. There were country codes, as I recalled, but this one seemed to be missing the code. I went to that source of much knowledge, Google, and brought up a list of country calling codes. I then started dialing. Most of them got me a recorded operator voice speaking French, German, or Spanish. I had to assume the foreign robot operators were telling me *wrong code, try again.* Tired of being told off by robots in languages I didn't understand I dialed the code for Great Britain. Three rings and a man answered.

"*Lux e tenebris,*" he said.

There was a momentary brain freeze at the Latin words. Then the high school Latin that Meredith had insisted I study kicked back in and provided the translation. *Light out of darkness.*

"Hello?" I said tentatively.

"Who is this?" A clipped British accent edged with anger and concern.

"I'm a friend of Jolly's. And who are you?" I shot back.

"Please hold the line."

Silence. It stretched on and on and on. I drummed my nails on the armrest. Irritated, I finally started the hopeless repeat of *hello, hello, hello?* "Goddamn it! This is serious!" The phone went dead, and I had a very polite robot saying *"If you'd like to make a call please hang up. . . ."*

I jabbed furiously at the disconnect button and cussed quietly for a few minutes. I then redialed the number and got a robot. *"We're sorry. This number has been disconnected or is no longer . . ."* I again hung up, this time with more force then was probably good for the buttons on the cheap phone.

Slouching in my seat, I tugged on my lower lip and considered. I stuffed the phone into the pocket of my jacket and turned to the computer. I typed in *lux e tenebris*. I got the expected translation, but another entry in Google caught my attention. It was also a motto of the Scottish Rite Freemasons. Well, that didn't seem that terribly odd. Modern freemasonry began in Britain. *But the number was suddenly disconnected.*

Pushing aside the latest paranoid thought, I moved on to the next number, but the phone gave a disconsolate beep, a low battery warning, and the screen went dark. I fumbled in my computer bag and had a memory flash of the charger plugged into the wall of my office, the connector resting on the edge of my desk. I shut my eyes, furious with myself for forgetting to pack the damn charger. Well, I could always buy a replacement at a Radio Shack in Newport.

I stuck the phone in my purse and looked out the window. About thirty minutes later we were paralleling a two-lane road. There wasn't a lot of traffic, but one car caught my attention by virtue of its speed. It was also weaving in and out of traffic, passing other cars. Even passing some on the right. The whistle began blaring and I remembered there was a train crossing in this area. The road took a sharp bend to the left. I had a brief moment to see the arms on the crossing guard lowering before the racing car crashed through the signal arm and came to a stop on the tracks. A man in a beige raincoat jumped out and ran away.

The whistle became a scream as the engineer held down the horn. The train began to shudder as the brakes were applied. I braced myself just in time before we plowed into the car that was blocking the tracks. The scream of the whistle was joined by the scream of tortured metal and the terrified screams of the passengers. Even though I knew it was coming, I added my scream to theirs.

A few hundred feet farther along and the train came to a stop. People were crying, talking, grabbing at cell phones. I sat frozen for a few minutes. Someone had wanted this train to stop. Because of me? No, I was being completely nuts.

Then I saw a male figure in a beige raincoat through the window of the connecting door. He was a middle-aged man, dark haired, with a neatly trimmed beard, and Japanese. Beneath the coat he wore a suit. His head was turning, clearly searching for something or someone. I remembered the receptionist at the hospital describing the man who had accompanied the female vampire. He had been Asian too. Could this be the same man?

I ducked down below the seat back in front of me. I needed to get off this train and get off now. I looked down at the rolling case and realized I couldn't take it with me. But I had to keep hold of the computer. I had client information on that machine, the telephone numbers Lucius had sent me, and Ben's paper. I tucked the laptop under my arm, slung my purse across my chest, and scuttled out into the aisle.

Fortunately, a lot of my fellow passengers were on their feet, milling around in the aisle too. For once, my lack of height was an advantage. I stayed hunkered over and moved as quickly as I dared to the other end of the car and into the accordion vestibule between the cars.

I yanked open the outer door. It set off an alarm, but I was past caring. I jumped down, my feet slipping on the crushed rock of the trackbed. I ran away from the train and toward the road. I risked one glance behind me and saw the man in the raincoat in one of the broad windows. He was gesticulating and staring right at me. I clutched the computer more tightly and ran all the harder.

I managed to hitch a ride back into Manhattan with a delivery truck driver who kept up an endless stream of conversation about his routes and which towns bought the most different kinds of seafood. I kept nodding and saying "uh-huh" at appropriate moments, and didn't hear a word.

Once we reached Manhattan I thanked my new best friend and had him drop me off in front of a hotel with a taxi stand. It wasn't late, not quite eight o'clock, but enough after work hours that I had the taxi driver take me to John's apartment, only to discover John wasn't there. We went next to his office. He wasn't there either. Date or work? It didn't really matter since I had a dead phone and I couldn't track him down.

"Where to now, Miss Lady?" My driver was a cute young Somali man named Bahdoon. He had warm brown eyes, a nice smile, and, unlike a lot of cabbies, wasn't resentful that I kept sending us in different directions.

I dithered over that for a few minutes. I could have him take me to Ray and Gregory's, but something scary was happening and I didn't want to bring it home to them. We could find a Radio Shack and I could try to buy a charger for my phone. Or I could go back to the office where I had both an old-style phone and my charger.

"Would you be willing to take me to Queens?"

He gave me a bright smile. "Sure. Lots of money for me."

I sighed. "At least one of us is having a good night."

Bahdoon also chatted all the way to Queens, but unlike Rudy, who delivered seafood to points north, Bahdoon was actually interesting. He talked of his home, his family, his dreams now that he had made it to the United States. I appreciated the distraction. Someone had wrecked a car to stop a train and it was pretty damn clear that action had been directed at me. I had no idea what the next escalation would be and I didn't want to find out.

I paid the bill, gave Bahdoon a really good tip, and let myself into the office. Sitting at my desk I plugged in the cheap cell phone, then used the landline to call John. It went to voice mail.

"You've reached John O'Shea. Leave a message."

"Another really weird thing has happened. Need to talk. Call me soonest."

It was stupid, but I checked the little phone. It had only been a few minutes, and it wasn't like my twitching was going to force a charge into the battery any faster. I drummed my nails on the desk, eyed some of the paperwork waiting for my attention. I opened up my laptop intending to read Ken's paper, but what loaded was the email from Lucius.

I stared at that final number on the list. The only one I hadn't tried. I grabbed the receiver out of its cradle and dialed. The phone rang in my ear. I also heard it ringing *right outside my office door*.

When your heart hammers really hard it almost hurts. It was certainly impeding my ability to draw a decent breath. Who was in the outer office? How had they found me? I thought about the long pause when I'd been on the phone to Britain. Had they been tracing my call? Was that even possible? I had a feeling it was.

I had toyed with applying for a license for a gun, but hadn't followed up. I was really regretting that procrastination now. The door to my office didn't lock. I wondered if I could push the desk against the door to block it? And go where? I looked at the window. I jumped up from my chair and went to look out. There was a narrow ledge. I could maybe walk along that ledge and kick in a window in another office. I was also really bad about heights. Sheer terror would probably have me falling off the ledge.

I had to know who was out there. What I was facing. I crept to the door and held my breath. I heard nothing from the other side. I opened the door a crack and peeked out and found myself looking at an expanse of purple silk. My eyes jerked up from the front of a blouse. It was the female vampire from Jolly's house. Our eyes met. She opened her mouth and I slammed shut the office door and put my back against it.

The door began to open, an inexorable force pushing it. I scrabbled, but my bootheels found no purchase on the linoleum floor. Panic constricted my chest, but that feeling I'd had when I fought John's mother in Fey was also present. A sense of something coiling, stretching, moving within my chest. A slim manicured hand reached around and closed on my shoulder. I squeaked and jumped, and lost my footing. My feet shot out from under me, I slid down the door and landed on the floor. The door flew open and the vampire entered the room only to trip over me.

I had a moment to react and I scrabbled on hands and knees into the reception area and jumped to my feet. I ran for the front door as I heard the vampire call, "Please, Linnet, wait! Listen!" Her voice lilted with a curious and unusual accent. "You must come with me."

Fat chance, I thought. I had been vaguely aware of the smell of burned coffee in the office when I'd come in, but I'd been so focused on getting to my phone and the charger that I hadn't checked the coffeemaker. The smell was much stronger now as I ran for the door to the hallway. I heard the woman's footfalls behind me. Suddenly there was a sharp *pop* followed by the sound of shattering glass, and a few shards of glass hit me as the coffeepot, which had clearly burned dry, exploded. The bulk of the glass hit my pursuer. She gave a cry of pain.

Come on, little buddy, I implored my strange super power. *Come up with another one.*

And I promptly tripped over my own feet and went staggering toward the fridge and watercooler. I grabbed for the big blue bottle to try to keep from falling and ended up yanking it off the stand. It hit and rolled away, water gurgling from the neck. The vampire hit the now wet linoleum and slipped. She was falling. Whether she would actually hit the floor was problematic, vampires were very dexterous, but it bought me a few seconds. I reached the outer door of the office and threw it open.

I ran into the hallway. The elevator was out of the question. Taking the interior stairs left me at a disadvantage. She was a vampire, which meant she was both faster and stronger than me. I needed to be outside where there were people who might help me. There was a fire escape off the window at the end of the hall. Balling my fists at my sides, I ran with all I had for that window. A stitch formed in my sides, and my lungs burned with effort. I could hear her closing in on me. There wasn't going to be time to fumble the catch and actually open the window. I hoped it worked in real life the same way it did in the movies. I threw an arm across my eyes and tried to ram through the glass.

It wasn't all cinematic and awesome. There was no shower of glass shards around me. In fact, it didn't work at all. The glass didn't break, but the catch snapped and ripped out of the wood frame, and the window flew open. I fell out onto the metal grating of the fire escape. It flexed and rang beneath me.

This was an old-style escape with a ladder that lowered toward the ground. I grabbed the handholds and swung around, groping for the first rung. My foot hit it, and the ladder went sliding with a violent rattling and shaking toward the pavement in the alley. I clung like a monkey to its mother's back until we hit the end of the slide with a jerk. I was still some three feet above the ground, and the sharp stop meant I lost my grip and fell backward, cracking my head on the pavement, and sending a shout of pain from my not-yet-healed rib.

From my supine position, I could watch the female vampire, long dark hair flying like a pennant, swarming down the ladder. My head hurt from the hard knock and I felt dizzy. I struggled to my feet. She was halfway down the ladder. I started to limp away as the ladder gave a shrill creak and a scream of tortured metal, and the ladder broke free, plunging the vampire to the ground. She was tangled in the rungs, struggling to push the ladder off of her.

I didn't wait to see more. I pushed into a hobbling run and headed for the street. I spotted an out-of-service taxi and took my life in my hands by running out in front of it. The driver slammed on his brakes. I could see his mouth moving, but I couldn't hear what he was saying. That changed when he opened the door and stepped out. Red-faced, he shook a fist at me and shouted in a language that sounded like Russian. I touched the back of my head where I had a cut and showed him the blood on my fingers.

"I'm hurt! Somebody is chasing me," I yelled at him. I looked back over my shoulder, but the vampire wasn't there. "Was chasing me," I amended. "Please, please will you drive me home?"

The taxi driver stopped shouting and looked concerned. "Some punks, huh? Goddamn animals," he said in English. "Where you want to go?" I started to give him Ray and Gregory's address then panicked that I might be followed. I needed help. I gave him John's address in Greenwich Village. "That's a long drive," the driver complained. "I'll only take cash."

"Um . . . well, about that. I don't have my purse or anything. But my friend will pay you. I promise."

He stared hard at me for a long moment. "Okay, I'll take you, but I go with you to get the money. Get in."

I climbed in, closed my eyes to hold back tears, and pressed a hand against my chest. Who were these people and why were they after me?

13

It was pushing ten p.m. before Yuri (I was getting to know so many taxi drivers) and I reached John's apartment. I rang the bell. The door flew open.

"I've been calling and calling. Why didn't you pick up?" he demanded.

"Long story," I said wearily. "Right now I need you to pay the nice man and then give me a ride back to my friend's apartment and make sure I'm not being followed."

"Why? What's happened?"

"First pay Yuri."

"How much?" John asked. The taxi driver told him, and John, grumbling, pulled out his wallet and thumbed through a wad of cash.

Yuri made a big point of counting them. I supposed I couldn't blame him. Neither John nor I were likely to inspire much confidence. After the door closed behind the Russian's broad back John bent a frown on me.

"All right, talk. What happened?"

"First there was the train and then a vampire happened." I sat down on the couch, and Gadzooks landed in my lap. The warm, furry, purring bundle pressed against my stomach eased the knot of tension as I told John everything. I concluded by saying, "I'm broke, I'm tired, and I'm starving. I don't have the skills to make sure I don't bring trouble back home to Ray and Gregory, so are you going to help me or not? Or do I call Detective Washington?"

"Of course I'll take you."

It was a short walk to the garage. I slid into the passenger seat, and then did a face palm. John reacted. "What? What's wrong now?"

"I busted out a window at the office building to get to the fire escape, and the office is unlocked. Well, the fire escape ladder is broken too, so maybe nobody can get in and rob us, but maybe I should tell Syd. May I use your phone?" He handed it over. "I hate to call this late. Wish I knew the name of the building management company."

"You can be rude or get robbed. Take your pick," John said in that cold way that I was trying to wrap my head around and accept.

"Good point. And we have clients' confidential information on file." I gave a sigh and rang Syd at home. It went to voice mail. *"You've reached the after-hours number for Syd Finkelstein, attorney at law. If you need a bail bondsman call Harvey Richard."* The number was provided. *"If you've been in an accident and need to reach me right away press one."*

I pressed one and Syd answered on the first ring. "Syd Finkelstein."

"It's Linnet."

"You okay?"

"Not really." I gave him the *Reader's Digest* version then said, "So we need to inform the management company and get that window and the fire escape fixed." I paused and sighed. "And Syd, I'm really sorry. My brother calls me a chaos magnet and I guess that's true. If you want me out of the office suite I'll understand."

"Don't be an idiot. We've been in the trenches together. You just stay safe. I'll take care of the building."

"Okay, thanks."

That's when I noticed we weren't heading toward the southern tip of Manhattan but rather driving north. "Wait. What are you doing? Where are we going? Ray and Gregory live near Wall Street."

"I'm taking you to the Dakota and Parlan. You'll be safe there."

"Safe from this vampire maybe, but what about your mother's supporters, who are probably pissed?"

"My brother has hot-and-cold running guards and the loyalty of a lot of Álfar that he grew up with. It's the best solution. None of the parties who seem to be breaking and entering various apartments and offices and stopping trains will be able to get at you in Fey."

I noticed the way his good eye flicked between the rearview mirror and the side mirrors. "Are we being followed?"

"No."

We drove in silence for a few minutes. The taillights of the cars ahead of us threw a rosy glow across his face. "You told me the first time I went into Fey when your mom grabbed us that I wasn't supposed to eat or drink anything. Does that still apply?"

"Yes."

"Then please let's stop somewhere and get me something to eat."

"Okay." He spun the wheel and took us off to an all-night Colombian empanada restaurant. As always, he found street parking just a few steps away. I was convinced it was some kind of Álfar magic that John did without realizing he was doing it.

A somewhat dispirited waitress slouched over to our table. I grabbed the menu and ordered a number of small plates: sweet potato and black beans, mushroom and butternut squash, and chicken and chorizo with olives. The chorizo was hotter than I expected, and I went through two glasses of Coke before I had finished it. John had a cherry empanada and a cup of coffee and watched me with his one remaining eye. The blind, milky white eye was disturbing.

As usual, my mouth took on a life of its own. "Have you considered a patch?"

"I'm not going to go around like a damn pirate."

"Nick Fury of S.H.I.E.L.D. wears an eye patch," I countered. John was neither impressed nor amused.

"Are you done?" he snapped.

"Yes."

"Then let's go."

"You have to pay, remember? My purse is back at the office." He gave me another irritated look. I hurried to add, "I'll pay you back for the taxi and the food. I promise."

Eventually the credit card was carried away, and John had signed for my dinner. We got back in the car and drove through Central Park to the Dakota. Just before the entrance John took us into Fey. The press of automobiles was suddenly gone and there were far fewer buildings. There was one 1920s-style touring car with an Álfar couple passionately kissing, and a young Álfar woman dressed for hunting with a bow slung over her back riding through the trees of what was Central Park in our world. We turned through the gates and into the central courtyard. A guard drifted over, but there was no sense of urgency.

"I need to see my brother," John explained.

Somehow the word had gone ahead and servants were roused. Parlan joined us in the living room wearing an elaborate brocade dressing gown.

"What is wrong?" Parlan asked, looking very pointedly at me.

"Why does everybody always go there?" I complained.

"Because it is nearly the witching hour and you are here," Parlan said. John gave a snort of agreement and I glared at them both.

"Okay, yes, I'm in trouble." I once again went through the story, only this time I went further back and added in more details. The break-in at my apartment. The break-in at the university. The break-in at Ken's apartment. Exhaustion snuck up and hit me over the head. I swayed and had a man on either side of me offering support. "Sorry. I guess the day is catching up with me."

"A room has been prepared for you," Parlan said. "Go and sleep." He looked at his changeling brother. "Your old room is available."

"Thanks, but no thanks, I'll go back to my apartment." John turned that single eye on me. "I'll be back in the morning with breakfast—"

"Not necessary. I would not allow her to be ensorceled," Parlan interrupted.

"*You* might not, but it takes a lot of staff to run this joint and some of them may not be too happy about the change in leadership."

"That's me, just making friends and influencing people wherever I go," I quipped in a hollow attempt at humor.

Parlan gave me a serious look. "Actually, that is quite true. My boon companions adore you."

"Oh, don't go encouraging her," John snapped.

I waved at the two men. "'Night, guys. I'll leave you two to argue about whether I'm a curse or a menace." Parlan laughed and even John snorted. "Wait. That didn't come out right."

"Go to bed," John ordered.

Parlan gestured and a servant stepped out of the shadows to lead me to a bedroom.

When I woke it took me a few minutes to remember where I was. Gauzy pale-peach-colored curtains surrounded me. They hung from an elaborate canopy frame like the branches of a tree, but made of crystal. The mattress felt like it was filled with feathers, but as I stirred it released the scent of roses and orange blossoms.

I had vaguely noticed that feature when I'd climbed under the covers. It was nice, and I wished human mattresses could do the same thing.

There was a silk dressing gown tossed across the back of a chair. I slipped it on and headed for the bathroom. A bath had already been drawn, steam etching patterns on the mirror and bubbles threatening to spill over the top of the marble tub. The bubble bath had the same scent as the mattress. I dropped the robe, climbed down the steps into the tub, and sank down to my chin. The hot water found the ache in my arms from when I clung to the fire escape's ladder and stung the healing sword cut on my shoulder.

While I soaked I laid out the plan of action. First: back to Ray and Gregory's for a clean change of clothes. Next: to the office to recover my laptop (please let it still be there) and read this damn paper. Third: start drafting the complaint against NYU. Locking Ken out of his office sure seemed like termination without due process.

An Álfar outfit had been laid out on the now-made bed. There was a lacy scrap that turned out to be underwear. I held it up, shook my head, and went back to my own clothes, stained and dirty though they were. I wasn't going to go through New York dressed like a heroine in an operetta. John and Parlan were seated in the dining room. The yeasty smell of freshly baked bread had my stomach commenting. I stared longingly at the plump strawberries in a bowl and resolutely stuck my hands in the pockets of my jeans. John tossed over a McDonald's bag with an Egg McMuffin inside.

John wiped his mouth and tossed the napkin onto the table. "Okay, I'll get Linnet home, get her packed, and bring her back here." He stood.

"Uh, no," I said. "I have to go to work. I've got a client whose home has been invaded and who may himself be in danger." I looked at John. "Which means *you've* got work to do too. I need that information on other scientists and I needed it yesterday." John opened his mouth, but I rode right over him. "All the chivalry is sweet, and I say this with love, guys, but go fuck yourselves. I'm not some damsel in distress, and I'm not going to be turned into the princess in the tower or—"

I broke off abruptly as something that had been niggling at me all night finally came into focus. John put a hand under my chin and pushed my mouth closed.

"You'll catch flies."

I ignored the snark and instead asked, "Why does Jolly have the cell phone number for the female vampire?" I croaked.

"Interesting question. I was wondering when it was going to occur to you," John said.

The superior tone ticked me off. "You could have said something," I accused.

Parlan patted the air with his hands. "Both of you behave."

John looked mulish and I had a feeling my face held a similar expression, which sort of just confirmed Parlan's opinion. I smoothed out the frown. "Maybe I should try calling her again. From a secure location, of course, and with friends around. See what happens."

"You know poking things with a stick isn't the best investigatory method," John said.

"It gets results," I countered.

"And nearly gets you killed," John shot back.

"I swear. You are worse than children," Parlan complained. "I have a feeling you will get your way about luring this vampire," he continued. "Call upon me at any time so I can help protect you."

"Dr. Stan Mensch, boating accident. Dr. Gillian West, shot and killed during a mugging. Dr. Ibrahim Bahir, fired from his post at

Cairo University; he later committed suicide. Dr. Daniel Fujasaki, heart failure. Dr. Gerhart Rohle, missing persons report filed ten years ago." John frowned down at his notes. "Odd nobody's moved to have him declared dead yet."

It was late afternoon and we were gathered in my office. The space felt too small with John, Ken, me, and another chair added for Syd. He had insisted on being included in the meeting since it was his office suite that had been invaded. I couldn't argue with that. Ken looked queasy. "Bottom line, it's not good for your health to research the Hunters and the predator."

"But . . . but one was a mugging, and there were natural causes, and that Egyptian guy was depressed, and Rohle could have . . ." We all stared at Ken and his voice trailed away.

"If you're that gullible I have got a great deal on a bridge for you," Syd snorted.

"Is it too late for me to take that deal that NYU offered?" Ken asked, his voice small.

"I expect so," John said. "And even if you took the deal I bet I'd be reading about your tragic bicycle accident in the not-too-distant future."

Ken turned a frightened gaze on me. I wished I could offer him comfort, but I couldn't. Instead I said, "I think that John may be right that you're in danger—"

"He's not the only one in danger," John said.

I waved him off impatiently. "As I was saying, we're going to find a way to deal with this."

"How?" Ken asked.

"We read your paper and figure out why this information is so dangerous. Then we use that for leverage."

"Dangerous game," Syd said.

"You have another idea?" I asked.

"Nah, I think it's the only play." Syd stood. "I'll have Belinda make three copies. Sure hope this paper isn't like the tape in that movie *The Ring*. We read the fucker and we all die." He left.

"I'm scared," the scientist said.

"You should be," John said. Ken clapped a hand over his mouth, leaped up, and bolted out the door. "Not what I should have said?" the Álfar asked.

"Not even close. We've got to work on your people skills." I wondered how we would do that with a man who didn't really feel emotions any longer. Maybe the methods used to teach autistic people to read human expressions would help? I was still pondering the John problem when Syd returned with three copies of the paper.

"Where's the doc?" he asked as he handed out the paper.

"Puking," John said.

"Okay."

Ken returned. He had a paper cup of water from the now-replaced dispenser in the lobby and clammy sweat still beaded his forehead. "You guys mind if I stay here while you read? I kinda don't want to be alone."

"You're not going to be," John said. "Though I'm not sure how much help an old short guy with a fake arm and an even shorter girl are going to be to me."

"Yeah, really have to work on the not-being-a-rude-asshole thing," I snapped.

"What did I say that wasn't true?" John asked, and he seemed honestly baffled. I sighed. "Oh, never mind."

"Of course if Ken is attacked by one of the Powers while Linnet's around he'll probably be fine," Syd said.

"Not really," I countered. "It didn't help Chip or that old lawyer or all those folks on the movie set. They all got killed." Ken bolted again.

"Maybe we need to work on your people skills too," John said.

It was as if the gods themselves had interceded to defend her.

She stood among the ravening beasts but none could touch her. In the face of such faith and purity God's very angels enfolded her and the walls did fall to crush them ere they harmed so much as a hair of her head.

I set aside Ken's treatise, spun my chair, and gazed out the office window. Despite the midday sun a chill bit into my bones. I was glad Syd had made hard copies of the paper. Often the rub of paper against skin helped me concentrate on dull legal pleadings, and I had expected this scientific paper to be equally dry and boring. Most of the paper was exactly what I expected, with diagrams of Hunter physiology and discussions of genetic drift. It was the appendices that had me shivering. These were original sources from Ptolemaic Egypt, Rome, medieval Germany, and Moorish Spain. All of them detailed women who had improbably survived attacks by what were clearly werewolves and vampires.

Women just like me.

"You're a very strange human, Linnet."

I set aside the paper with such care that it could have been made of glass. I carefully walked to the door of my office, opened it, and stepped out. John was slouched on the couch reading. Ken was seated at the other end of the battered sofa, head in his hands. Syd's office door was closed. Belinda was busy inputting billable hours into the computer. Everything seemed so normal. Everything except me.

"Belinda, would you go pick up some coffees for us?" I asked.

She glanced over toward the fridge and the now-missing coffee-maker. "Yeah, sure. Guess I better buy a new coffeemaker, huh?"

"Yeah, why don't you do that while you're out too."

"If I do that I could just wait and make coffee when I come back"—she broke off and her frown cleared. "Ah, right, you want me out of here for a while."

"Uh, yeah, please," I said.

"Gotcha." She grabbed her purse and left.

John was looking at me with a speculative expression. I went over and knocked on Syd's door. "Yeah, what?" he called.

"I need to talk to you." I turned back to John and Ken. "To all of you."

Syd emerged. He'd abandoned his suit coat and was in shirt-sleeves. The prosthetic hand was flexing over and over. I wondered if he was aware of what he was doing.

"Yeah, what?" Syd demanded.

I took a deep breath, my gaze flicking between the three men. "I think I'm the predator."

14

The first reaction was stunned silence. Then Syd gave a guffaw. Ken lifted his head and said, "Are you high? That's . . . insane."

I met John's single eye. "I was arriving at that conclusion myself," he said.

There was a duet of "What?" out of Syd and Ken.

"I watched her duel the Álfar queen. She has no training in fencing, but she won. She survived an attack by five werewolves. Attacks by Álfar."

"And I got away from a vampire last night."

The scientist was staring at me like he'd just found the source of the Nile or the Holy Grail. "Really? 'Cause that would be so awesome."

"No, no, it wouldn't," I said firmly. "Hunters. Certain death. Remember? I've got a question," I said. "So if I've got this thing, *how* did I get it? Is it in the water or something? On toilet seats? How the hell do you catch it?" I directed the question to Ken.

"I don't know. That's the one real gap in my research."

"So how do we prove this one way or the other?" Syd asked, bringing us back to the most pressing issue.

"We check Linnet into the hospital. We'll start with blood tests."

Ken was getting very excited. "Then an MRI and a CAT scan. Maybe a bone scan too—"

"There's an easier way," John interrupted. "Show her to a Hunter."

"Yeah, and when it kills me that would be definitive proof. I hate this plan," I said.

"We'll put it in a cage. Or put you in a cage and have it on a leash. Like they do on Shark Week," Ken said enthusiastically.

"Okay, really, really hating this plan. Just sayin'."

"How would we even get ahold of a Hunter?" Syd asked. "The doc here only had a few minutes with a corpse before the vamps took it away."

"What do we know?" John asked. "There's a class of vampire that breed and care for these things. They have to keep them somewhere. We find out where. We go steal one."

Syd looked over at me. "Assuming for the moment we do this crazy thing, we don't take Linnet along."

"Agreed," John said.

"I'm not letting you guys go into danger and not helping," I stated.

John frowned at me. "I thought you hated this plan?"

"I do, but . . . What am I supposed to do? Sit at home twiddling my thumbs and waiting for the menfolk to come back?"

"Yes."

I wasn't giving up yet. I marshaled another argument in favor of my going even though I totally didn't want to go. "There will be vampires there. You'll need me to keep them off you."

"And how the hell would you do that?" Syd asked skeptically.

"If she were to come it would probably involve banana peels, falling pianos, and random flying anvils," John said. "But she's not coming," the Álfar concluded. He tugged thoughtfully at his lower lip. "We need somebody to drive the police van."

"We're going to have a police van?" I asked faintly.

"We want this thing in a cage." The good eye swiveled over to

Syd. "How about you? You're too old and fat to be part of the snatch team."

"Running up against that people-skills thing again," I muttered.

"Oh. Sorry if I was rude," John said to Syd.

"You were, but I take your point. How are you boys going to get in? We have to assume this place is guarded."

"We'll park nearby and go in through Fey. That should get us past any security." Ken held up a hand as if he were a student. "What?" John snapped.

"If we're going through Fey why do we need a car . . . van . . . can't we just . . . I don't know . . . blip between places?"

"You watch too much TV," John said. "Geography is geography. We have to assume these facilities are in isolated locations and not in Soho. We still have to cover the same number of miles in or out of Fey."

"Weird," Ken muttered. He turned away, muttering to himself, then broke off and turned back abruptly. "Wait a minute! They'll know who we are and I'm already on their radar."

"Good God, we're not going to go in wearing jerseys with our names on them," John said impatiently. "There's a reason criminals love balaclavas."

"You know they stink really bad," I offered. "Not balaclavas, Hunters, I mean. Well, that's what I've been told. Read, actually."

Ken chimed in. "Boy is that ever true. The one I examined was disgusting. I thought some of that was because the body was decaying. So they smell like that all the time?"

"I guess. That's what the books say."

"So do we add a breathing mask to our balaclavas?" Syd asked in a wry tone.

"Vicks under the nose. I used it when I watched autopsies back when I was a cop. Not perfect, but it helps. Cigarettes help too," John added.

"And how are we going to subdue and control this critter?" the ever-practical Syd asked.

"I'll figure that out," John said.

"Not what I wanted to hear," Syd replied.

John's single eye scanned us all again. "So are we agreed?"

Everyone nodded, even though I was the last and the most reluctant. "Okay, I don't like it, but I'll wait by the phone to bail you all out if this goes pear shaped."

"Wait," Ken said. "How do we know they even have these things near here? Or even in the U.S.? They could be breeding them in . . . in Siberia or Mongolia, someplace remote."

"When Chip got killed my dad was afraid they'd bring in a Hunter," I replied. "Which implies they're somewhere close."

"A bigger question is why your dad was worried about a Hunter," Syd said. My stomach clamped down into a hard, tight ball and I remembered the last time my father and I had talked. Syd stared at me, a frown on his bulldog face. "Unless he knew," he added softly.

I shook my head, unable to process, much less face, what the old lawyer was suggesting. John headed for the office door. "Hey, where are you going?" I called, grateful for the distraction.

"To locate a Hunter kennel. And get a van."

"In the Hamptons? Seriously?" I muttered to myself. I was parked on a winding street lined with electronic gates leading to large and very expensive houses and using a large rhododendron hedge for cover. The large shrub was just starting to show buds on this early spring day.

The police van was parked on the side of the road some hundred feet ahead of me. The paddy wagon had Philadelphia plates so I figured John and maybe even his human dad had pulled in favors from the PPD, where they had both worked, to get a loaner. I had known I didn't have the skill to follow John and not be detected, so I used deceit and guile instead. I managed to get Ken to tell me the location of the Hunter kennel. I had phrased it as needing to know where to send a rescue party or a bail bondsman and that had made Ken nervous enough that he spilled the address. John or Syd would have seen right through me, but Ken didn't know me well enough to know I could be very, very wily and that I didn't always play fair.

I felt very exposed under the bright sun. Who the hell did a heist in broad daylight? Answer: people invading a vampire compound. I knew it made sense, but it was still disconcerting. There was a crawling sensation between my shoulder blades and the left side of my chest was aching. Heart attack? Or just tension? John had set the trio up with radio headsets. I had thought about hitting Radio Shack and buying a set for myself, then trying to scan for their frequency, but I wasn't exactly sure how to do that and I feared I might inadvertently give away my presence. I was just going to hang nearby in case they needed me. I gave a silent prayer that they wouldn't need me.

I knew the basic plan. Step the first, park the police van. Step the second, John takes himself and Ken into Fey. They walk onto the property then return to our world. That would be step number three. Step four, they search for a Hunter. Step five, they subdue a Hunter. (They had been more than a little vague on that aspect of the plan and so had a number of possible approaches ranging from Tasers to sedatives.) Step six, they haul the Hunter back through Fey to the van. Step seven, they reenter the human world. Step eight, they drive back to New York. Step nine, they show Linnet to the Hunter. Step ten—Linnet dies. I pushed that final thought firmly aside, and instead reflected that there were a lot of damn steps that needed to go perfectly for this to work.

In the twenty-some minutes I had been in this ritzy area I had noticed one thing; there wasn't a lot of traffic. A UPS truck had driven past. A couple of expensive cars driven by women. My battered van had come in for a hard look, and I'd worried that someone would call the cops on me, but the presence of the police van seemed to have kept that from happening. The only sounds were the pop and ping of my cooling engine, the occasional bark of a dog, and frantic spring birdsong. It was warm in the van and I was starting to doze when whooping alarms had me bashing my thighs into the steering wheel and brushing my head on the roof of the van, so violent was my start.

As I watched, Syd opened the door of the police van and climbed out. The air near the van shimmered and John and Ken appeared dragging a limp, pasty white, unclothed body between them. Syd was fumbling with the back doors of the van. John dropped his side of the Hunter and quickly opened the door. The Hunter was flung into the back of the van, the doors locked. Ken was bent over, hands resting on his knees retching. John grabbed the young scientist and dragged him to the cab of the van. I heard the creaking and squeaking of the property gates sliding open. The police van was pulling away, gaining speed, but slowly.

I turned the key, the engine caught with a roar, and I drove forward as a long, fast black car with darkly tinted windows rushed toward the exit from the driveway. I stopped the van directly in front of the gates, blocking the way. The car jerked to a stop, and a pair of vampires jumped out. They didn't look like any vampires of my acquaintance. They weren't tailored and suave and handsome. Their faces were pushed in, their noses more like slits in their heavy-boned faces, and their fangs hung over their lower lips. Their skin was starting to blister and peel under the bright noon sun, but they weren't retreating. Instead, they were charging me. Their nails were elongating, and they didn't look like they wanted to have a conversation.

Terror fluttered in my gut, and I put my foot to the gas. At the same time, there was a howl of tortured metal and the gates started to close, but far faster than normal. The vampires reacted, and then had to leap to the side when their car jerked out of park and went racing forward to crash into the closing gates. *Thank you, little mystery power.* With luck, it would take a while to untangle the car from the bent and warped gates, I thought as I drove away. Still, I was glad I had thought to cover both my license plates with mud. On the other hand, the vampires probably wouldn't call the police to report a kidnapping or a theft of a creature whose existence they tried very hard to downplay.

As I made my way back toward Queens I replayed that chaotic scene at the entrance to the estate. How had my power closed the gate and made the car pop into drive? It seemed to be getting stronger and more potent. Why? And then I worried that the answer might be more unsettling than the power.

I tried to beat the boys back. I was supposed to be waiting for them at an empty warehouse that was tied up in an ugly divorce that Syd was handling. He had keys to the building so an appraisal could be done, and it seemed the perfect place to dangle Linnet in front of a Hunter like a minnow on a hook. As so often happens with best laid plans, that didn't work out. I hit bad traffic and an accident, and by the time I reached the building the police van was already parked out front.

I killed the engine and called John on the cell he had given me. "You followed us, didn't you?" the Álfar demanded.

"Yes, and you should be glad I did. I blocked some really creepy-looking vampires from catching you."

"You drive me crazy."

"Love you too. Are you ready for me?"

"Yeah, the thing is still unconscious. I've got a collar and chain on it, and the taser ready. That worked really well."

"Glad to hear it. Keep it handy."

I stepped onto the oil-stained pavement of the parking lot and headed for the door. We weren't all that far from the coast and the smell of brine and seaweed was carried on the wind. I opened the door into the big brick building and a new scent assaulted my nostrils. It was the smell of rotting flesh coupled with vomit and truly horrible body odor. I gagged, choked, and darted back outside. The bile that had risen up into the back of my throat burned as it went back down. I stood and panted for a few minutes. I took off my cardigan sweater, tied it around my nose and mouth, and entered once again.

The enormous space was empty, so the sound of my footfalls bounced off the walls and the extremely high ceiling. Sunlight poured in through high windows set up under the eaves, and chains dangled from ceiling-mounted cranes. I breathed shallowly through my mouth and tried to hold my rising gorge at bay.

The men were gathered around the prone, slug-white body of the Hunter. I had only seen the Roger Corman movies and their idea of a Hunter. Now that I was this close I could see the dead white skin was stippled with very faint markings similar to scales. I wondered if they were the pheromone-sensing structures that Ken had talked about? John had a Taser in his left hand, and the chain wrapped around his right hand. He was braced, staring down at the creature. Syd started toward me, and Ken was using a small camera held in one hand to snap pictures while the other hand held his phone. I could hear him speaking, but the echo made it difficult to distinguish words.

"I hope you're recording and not calling somebody," I said.

"I am," Ken replied.

"We're gonna put you in the control box for the . . ." Syd was saying as he approached.

Several things happened at once. The Hunter sprang up like a hopping spider, its long arms and legs coiled around its flaccid body. Ken let out a yell of fear and stumbled backward. Syd was cursing. John jammed the Taser against the creature's neck. There was a chittering like an electronic cricket, but it had no effect on the Hunter. The thing was on its feet and, despite the lack of eyes, the long undulating fingers reached toward me, writhing like disturbed worms. The moist, horribly red mouth was working, producing sucking sounds that were almost worse than the stink coming in waves off the monster. John dropped the Taser, grabbed the chain with both hands, and yanked, but instead of pulling the Hunter back he was pulled forward, lost his footing, and went down on his stomach on the concrete floor. The Hunter was dragging him effortlessly as it sprang toward me.

I saw the fingers stiffen until they resembled ten sharp white talons. I whirled and started to run. I was sobbing with terror, the sweater fell down around my neck, and the smell of the Hunter hit me full force, leaving me lightheaded. The pain in the left side of my chest was excruciating, and there seemed to be an overlay of another's panic over my own. This sense of *another* was also terrifying. This thing was real. I knew it now. It was as if it were clawing to be free, trying to burst out of my chest like the alien in the *Alien* movies.

I waited for the improbable to occur. It had worked against werewolves and Álfar and a vampire. It would save me now. As if in answer to my thought, the windows set high up beneath the eaves began to blow out as I ran. Glass rained down behind me. I risked a glance behind. The Hunter was still coming. Whatever the vampires had done to protect their monster they had done it well for there seemed to be a bubble defending it. None of the glass shards struck the creature. Not so my friends. I saw John grab Ken and Syd and drag them into cover.

I felt the sharp prick of those talons against my back. From overhead came the screaming cry of an enraged vampire. I had heard it only once before; when David had placed himself between me and a rampaging werewolf. A figure launched itself through one of the broken windows and came hurtling toward the floor. A broad-brimmed hat was swept from its head by the speed of the fall. I expected to see David because he had always been there. Instead I saw the female vampire.

Her feet struck the outstretched arms of the Hunter. I waited for the crack of broken bones, but the creature was adaptable. The arms were once again loose and sagging. The blank oval face was turned toward the vampire and the disgusting mouth was sucking at the air like a baby groping for a breast.

The screaming war cry ceased and she made a low crooning sound that had the hair on the back of my neck lifting. She pulled off her sweater, revealing a pretty lavender-colored and lace-covered bra. Her smooth ivory skin was showing blisters from the sun. She cut her chest with a nail, and the pale vampire blood flowed down, staining the material. *So that part of Dracula was true*, I thought inanely. A long whip-like tongue uncoiled from the little red mouth, questing for the dripping blood. The female vampire grabbed it and pulled like an angler landing a fish. A sound grotesque and terrifying emerged from the Hunter and it jerked and flopped as more and more of the tongue was pulled out of its maw. What appeared to be the innards of the monster were dragged out of its mouth to land with a wet splat on the concrete. The Hunter collapsed like a deflated balloon.

I lost it and threw up. I faintly heard Ken saying "That was really gross but also amazing!"

Syd's reaction was more in line with mine. "No, that was just gross! And damn it, I'm going to have to get this place fumigated."

And finally, John's ironic tones, "Well, this went well."

My throat burned, my mouth tasted of sour bile and the oatmeal I'd had for breakfast. My heart was pounding and my chest hurt. I staggered away from the puddle of vomit. I only made it a few feet before my knees went out and I collapsed. An arm snaked around my waist and kept me from hitting the floor. I smelled perfume and long dark hair brushed the side of my face. The female vampire was holding me. I tried to summon panic, but I was all panicked out.

"There, there, it's over now," she said gently. Her voice was softly accented in a way I couldn't identify. She helped me over to a metal ladder that led up to the catwalks. I perched on a rung and swallowed a few times to try and get the taste out of my mouth. My rescuer whirled to face the men.

"Are you all totally out of your ever-loving minds?" She didn't wait for an answer. "Obviously, yes. These creatures are so dangerous. Particularly to one such as her." She looked down at me, then added, "And why on earth did you ever agree to this?"

I tried to summon glib, but glib had abandoned me too. I settled on the truth. "I had to know. The truth. About what I am."

"If you hadn't run away from me you would have had your answer two days ago," she huffed.

"You attacked Jolyon Bryce!" I flared.

"Attacked? What? No, I didn't. My arrival kept him from being kidnapped or worse."

"Well . . . well, you attacked David. I thought you were a bad guy."

"It seems we both drew the wrong conclusions. I thought *you* were the people who had attacked Jolly coming back to finish the job," the vampire said.

"Jolly. Nice play trying to convince me you actually know him," I didn't make any effort to hide my skepticism.

She smiled, but not the normal closed-lipped vampire smile. Her fangs were there in all their glory. "But I do know him, very well. We've worked together for many years."

"Yeah? Doing what? And how do you even exist? You're not supposed to."

"Could somebody clue the rest of us in to *what the fuck is going on*?" Syd demanded.

I looked to my companions. Syd looked like a pugnacious bull-dog. John had his arms folded across his chest and was studying us, his face devoid of all emotion. Ken was on his knees by the entrails of the Hunter, poking at them with a ballpoint pen. I gagged and looked away.

"Maybe we should take this conversation to a more comfortable locale," John said. "Preferably a place that has alcohol. Lots and lots of alcohol."

"I'll second that," Syd said.

John came to my side and helped me to my feet. He put himself between me and the female vampire. She paused to pick up her hat and everyone started for the doors except Ken.

"Can we take it with us?" he asked plaintively.

There was a chorus of *No!*

"It stinks too bad," John said.

"Please. It's for science," the parasitologist begged.

"I'll take it in my car," said the vampire. "I don't have to breathe."

"Thank you, thank you, thank you," Ken said. "Anybody got anything I can put the entrails in?"

"I'll pull the car in. We'll just pitch it all in the trunk," she answered.

"You both better wash your hands before you join us," Syd grumbled.

"And sell the car," John added dryly.

15

We gathered at John's office. He had a bottle of good scotch stashed there and he poured out drinks for the three of us. The vampire turned up almost thirty minutes later, which had me staring at her suspiciously again. She seemed to read my thoughts because she explained before any of us said anything.

"I dropped off the beamish boy and his aromatic prize at a lab I know," the vampire said.

"Christ, that's one weird kid," Syd said.

The woman's dark eyes raked across us. "And you three aren't?"

"I think we've had enough of your lectures," John said. "It was a dumb play, okay? We all acknowledge that. But we've got real problems here. She . . ." He pointed at me. "Is . . . well, I don't know what she is. What the hell is she?"

"Predator. Destroyer. Scourge. Slaughterer."

I felt myself drooping at each word. "Gee, thanks," I muttered. Syd sensed my distress, moved to me, and dropped a comforting arm over my shoulders. I appreciated the kindness but really wished it had been John. Of course, that would never occur to him in his present state.

"Really? This little tiny thing?" Syd asked. His skepticism was evident.

"A virus is small but can still kill," the vampire said.

"And what, exactly, is she going to kill?" Syd asked.

"All the vampires and the werewolves."

That shut us all up for the space of several long heartbeats. "You're kidding," John finally said.

"Nope."

"*I'm* the thing that's going to kill them?" I didn't recognize my own voice.

"No, the parasite you carry is going to do that. But I think we have a lot to cover. You have questions. I have answers. And then we've got to make some decisions."

Now that things were calmer I could study her features more carefully. She looked like a woman in her late teens or early twenties. I searched the dark eyes looking for something, anything to indicate her true age, but they were bright, eager, and very present, unlike some vampires, who seemed distant. I realized I was tired of thinking of her as *the female vampire*. "Hey, what's your name?" I asked.

"Hetepheres, but you can call me Hettie."

"Hetepheres," I said. "That sounds Middle Eastern."

"It's Egyptian."

"Kind of a funny name. Aren't you all, like, named 'Fatima' or something?" Syd asked.

She smiled at him. "No. Egyptian names often honor our past, but I came by mine honestly. I was born in the reign of Khufu, you probably know him as Cheops, and named for his daughter. My father was a painter, my mother a perfumer. He worked for the court. She sold to the court. It was a good life until it ended."

"And when was that?" I asked faintly.

"Calendars change, you know, so I'm going to have to guess a bit, but probably around 2567 . . . B.C."

I went tottering off to a chair and collapsed into it. "You're . . . you're . . . you're . . ."

"Over four thousand years old. Yeah, I get that a lot." She sounded like a chirpy college kid.

John was staring at her with an almost frightening intensity. "How do you do it? I dread the coming years, and my lifespan is peanuts compared to yours," he said referring to the Álfar lifespan, which was much longer than a human's but not virtually immortal like a vampire's.

"Stay connected. We can talk more about it later. Right now we've got a lot of problems to solve."

I raised my aching head, which I had been cradling in my hands. "Starting with Jolly. I've caught on that I made the wrong assumption, but if you didn't attack him, who did?"

"The Black Masons."

"Oh, of course. *Has* to be the masons. Yeah, right," Syd snorted. "You know that's like a cliché for every crazy conspiracy nut on the planet. And by the way, *I'm* a mason. I suppose I should just be grateful it's not the Jews this time."

"Well, there are Masons, and then there are *Masons*." Hettie pinned Syd with a look. "As Shriners are to you guys, so you are to us. Among our members and the black lodge's members there are actually . . . well, let's call them wizards for lack of a better word, and they have mystic powers. I'm a member of the White Masons—"

"We don't take women," Syd interrupted.

John spoke up. "That's true. My captain down in Philly was one. I dated his daughter. She was like a Daughter of the Nile or something."

"Well, whether you believe it or not, I really am a member of a Masonic lodge," Hettie said.

"So did it really start in Egypt or was it medieval bullshit?" Syd asked.

"Oh it really started with us—"

Anger, fear, and resentment were a toxic mix roiling in my chest. Bolting out of the chair, I balled my fists at my sides and screamed out, "STOP IT! Why are we having this inane conversation? Who cares about any of this? I'm some kind of Typhoid Linnet, and I've got a *thing* inside me. I've been all brave and noble, but this damn well needs to start being about *me* now."

Syd looked embarrassed. John had his pissed-off-camel look. Hettie's look was pure compassion. She crossed to me and gathered me in a hug. The chill off her undead body didn't make it all that comforting.

"You're scared and rightly so. If the vampires or the werewolves find out, they'll kill you and the Black Masons are searching for you, and if they have to they'll kill all your friends to get to you. They will. Then they'll keep you prisoner until they can trigger the predator."

"What does this thing do?" I whispered.

"Well, I don't exactly know. None of us do. Obviously this thing has never really gotten rolling or I and my fellow Spooks wouldn't be here." She paused and added thoughtfully, "Though it came close once and destroyed the Hittite Empire, but they managed to kill the woman and all those affected before it could spread. That's when the prohibition against women was put in place." She looked thoughtful for a moment. "I'm probably the last woman ever Made." She waved it off. "But that's all ancient history. Anyway, that hasn't stopped the Black Masons from continuing to try, and if they manage to trigger this thing all the vampires and werewolves die."

"So Jolly knew that I . . . well, about the predator?"

"Yes."

"Is that why he came to the States and got close to Linnet?" John asked.

"Yes."

"What alerted you guys?" Syd asked and then added, "Assuming any of this is true."

"You've just established it's true and very nearly got her killed in the process, but to answer your question, we had word that a predator had been nursed to the point of implantation. We knew it was one of a handful of girls." Hettie looked back at me. "Then there was the murder at the firm and your escape and it was pretty clear it was you. We sent Jolly to keep watch and to verify. We probably should have acted before you went off to California. After the events out there . . . well, all doubt was removed."

"And Jolly was going to tell me?"

"Yes."

John, seated behind his desk, beat out a tattoo on the surface with a ballpoint pen. "So why all the aliases?"

Hettie frowned at him. "You shouldn't have been able to find those."

"I'm good."

"I guess you are. I'm going to have to alert our security department. And yes, Jolly has had a lot of identities tracking the activities of our enemy."

"Those being these Black Masons who want to kill all the Powers?" Syd asked.

"Those would be the ones."

"This just sounds crazy," the lawyer muttered.

Hettie grinned at him. "Crazier than the world we live in?"

"Point."

I rubbed at my aching forehead. "So, Jolly was attacked to keep him from telling me that I had this . . . thing inside me?"

"Yes." She forced extra air into her lungs so she could sigh. "I arrived in time to keep him alive, but not fast enough to prevent the attack."

There was the clink of glass on glass as John poured himself another drink. "So where were the bodies of the bad guys? You're a vampire. You could easily have smoked them all."

"We do try not to kill people. We like to think of ourselves as the good guys. I settled for driving them off. Also, I didn't want to draw any more attention to Linnet. If another person closely associated with her fetched up dead it might have begun to penetrate that she should be looked at more closely." She paused and studied me for a moment. "In some ways the events in California helped us. They pulled the attention away from you and onto the Álfar. And since my kind are suspicious of Álfar magic, and distrust the Álfar on general principles, it had them looking at the elves and not at you."

"So why didn't the hounds twig when so many of them were getting croaked whenever they tried to attack her?" Syd asked.

"It's my kind that breeds the Hunters and has the potentially infinite lifespan. The werewolves are mutated so they're stronger and tougher but not appreciably longer-lived than the average human, so they lack our sense of . . . perspective."

"And you're secretive," I said.

"Knowledge is power." Hettie grinned. "Vampires hoard both."

I gave her a hard look. "Why are you so concerned with protecting me? Isn't your real interest keeping the vampires and werewolves, and bluntly, *yourself,* alive? Why not alert the vampires and let a Hunter kill me? Problem solved, right?"

"We want to study the creature. Figure out how to either destroy the parasite or at least neutralize its effects. We need it alive and, by extension, we need you alive too."

"Gee, thanks."

"If it's any comfort, it quickly became a lot more personal for Jolly. He likes you."

"Well, that's nice." I hoped I didn't sound too sarcastic and ungrateful.

"So are we done? May I take both you and Ken to a safe place where he can work and you can be studied?" Hettie asked.

"There is one more thing," I said. "Was it these Black Mason guys who stopped the train?"

"No, that was one of ours. After you called the lodge in London we were able to make the trace. And by the way, what made you dump your phone? Jolly had paired to it so we could keep track of you."

"John did that."

She looked over at the Álfar. "Good call, though it made my job a whole lot harder."

"That was the idea. It was clear after the break-in at her apartment that somebody was after her."

Hettie turned back to me. "Anyway, your call to London put us back on your trail and that's when we realized you were on a train heading to Newport. We had to stop you. Fortunately, Fusashi was watching your father and was able to react in time."

"My father," I said faintly. Outrage gathered in a burning pain behind my breastbone. "He is *not* part of this. How dare you even suggest—"

"Yes, he is."

I gave another vehement head shake. "Bullshit! I don't believe you!"

Syd spoke up. "I think you ought to listen, Lynnie. You said yourself your dad was real upset at the idea they might bring in a Hunter after Chip was killed."

"No." I couldn't muster up anything else. I just clung to stubborn negation as if it were a floating spar and I was a shipwreck survivor.

"I'm sorry, but lying to yourself really isn't the best plan," the vampire said.

I stormed away and threw back, "I wish David had managed to cut your damn head off!"

"Killing the messenger also doesn't change the facts," John said.

Hettie came after me. Pushed into my personal space to the point we were almost nose to nose. "Listen to me! The parasites are fragile outside of a body. They have to be bred and nurtured, and they don't come to maturity easily. When they do they have to be implanted in an infant. The members of the lodge that have raised the creature draw lots, or throw dice, or play some other game of chance to determine which of their members will offer up their infant daughter. This could not have been done without his knowledge and consent."

"My mother would never—" I began, but I broke off. I had always felt like children were just an accessory she had picked up. I could totally picture her paying no attention when my father said he wanted to take me for an evening. I raised another objection.

"So, your group has actually witnessed this, and more to the point, didn't try to stop it if you did?"

"No, we've found it difficult to place agents inside their lodges. Our guys always get caught."

"Then you don't know!"

"But we do. We do get the occasional defector, a man who can't bear to be part of this cabal any longer. We're certain about this."

"If my dad had been involved he would never have let me be fostered! It would have been crazy to put me in a vampire household if I actually . . . well, I guess I do actually have it, so it was stupid and my father is anything but stupid, which proves he didn't know." It was a convoluted sentence, but Hettie seemed to follow my inchoate thoughts.

"No, what it proves was they were ingenious. It was frankly brilliant, and a big change from their previous pattern. Before they had always tried to hide the predator in isolated spots. There was a pattern and the vampires exploited it, but someone in the Black lodge understood that normal vampires are disgusted by Hunters. That they don't want them anywhere near them. The cabal decided to take the risk and go for the big throw, anticipating the vampires would never think someone would try something so ballsy as to hide you in plain sight."

My father's face seemed to float in the air before me. Smiling, smoothing his mustache, the gold Masonic ring catching the light. She had just described my father. He had always been a risk taker and loved to gamble. I shivered.

"My kind are rather risk adverse, to put it mildly, so such a move would never have occurred to them. And the ploy even fooled us in the White lodge. It wasn't until the news of the murder at IMG and your escape surfaced that we realized a new Destroyer had arrived on the scene."

"But the vampires missed it," John mused.

"Pride. Pride can blind a person." She cast a glance at me. "Just like love."

I sank down into a chair. We filled the room with silence for a long, long time.

"What can I do to convince you?" she asked gently. "Or maybe I can't. You don't know me. Would you believe Jolly?"

"What are you talking about? He's in a coma," I said.

She gave me a flash of the fangs again. "I expect Jolly's not just lying in the hospital waiting for the body to recover. I'm betting he put his consciousness in the horse."

I swallowed hard a few times. "The . . . horse. You mean Vento?"

Hettie nodded. "That'd be the one."

"What, he's like, fuckin' Mr. Ed?" Syd broke in.

"Sort of, though he can't actually talk. Jolly is one of our masters and can place his mind, soul, spirit, whatever you want to call it, in the body of another creature. He and Vento are very closely bonded."

Heat suffused my face, and I banged my forehead several times on the edge of John's desk. The idea that all those times I had been riding the Lusitano stallion Jolly had been riding along too, was really, really creepy. I thought about the way I used my seat to cue the horse, and the way my legs rested against his sides.

"Uh, just how aware of me was Jolly while I was . . . uh, riding?"

"Oh, completely."

I dropped my face into my hands and mumbled, "This is like some kind of Freudian nightmare." Syd guffawed and even John showed a flicker of reaction.

"He did save your life in California," Hettie pointed out.

"Yeah, true, but all the times I stroked him and hugged him and kissed him on the nose. The horse, I mean." I shook off the embarrassment.

"So, shall we go to the horse?" Hettie asked. "Get the answer and then get you someplace safe."

"Sure. He should be back from California by now, but let me call and make sure," I added. "Oh, and there's no way in hell I'm going anywhere alone with you. I want John to come with us."

"She can be taught," he murmured more to himself than to the rest of us and stepped to my side.

It was very easy for her to say they were the good guys, but aside from saving me from the Hunter I had no proof that that was actually true. What was abundantly clear was that I was just a pawn in everyone's game, and I hated it.

Hettie pointed out that the vampires had seen my van and while I might have covered up the license plates, it was fairly distinctive with its bashed-in front end so we were going to take her car. It was a high-powered BMW with darkly tinted windows. It had been double-parked on a side street. An NYPD card on the dash meant it didn't have a ticket or hadn't been towed. I stopped and stared at it suspiciously. Once again, the vampire seemed telepathic.

"Don't worry. Different car. I dumped the other one."

"Money must not be an issue for you guys," John remarked.

"It's not." She pressed the starter, the car roared to life, and we pulled out into traffic. She gave me a sideways glance. "You must have questions, but you're not saying much."

"I'm still trying to wrap my head around all of this."

"The if-I-don't-talk-about-it-it-won't-be-real approach?" Hettie suggested.

"Yeah, something like that."

"So what is going to happen to her?" John asked.

"Well, hopefully we're going to find a way to remove or at least neutralize the predator. That's why we were hoping to fund Dr. Zhèng's research."

"Yeah, 'cause that's worked out so well in the past," John said.

"True."

"So, who kills the scientists? The vampires or these . . . these Black Masons?" I asked.

"The vampires and the werewolves. They don't want it widely known that there's a way to destroy them." She reacted to my expression. "I've shocked you. I'm sorry, but they're not really all that nice."

"And does that go for you too? Makes me wonder if I can really trust you."

"I hope you do since I'm the only thing standing between you and certain death right now."

"Don't discount my friends. I'm not alone in this," I countered.

"No, you're not. And your capacity to inspire loyalty is admirable, but most of your allies are merely human."

"I've got a mess of Álfar on my side." She gave me a wry look, one eyebrow climbing toward her hairline. "Okay, so they're not the most . . . *focused* of allies, but they've got powers too."

"And ADD."

John, in the backseat, gave a snort. "Ain't that the truth."

Talking about Álfar raised an interesting question and another opportunity to avoid thinking about my father. I posed it. "I know this isn't all that important in the grand scheme of things," I said. "But do you think this predator parasite affects choices the Álfar make too?"

"Hmm, interesting notion. I don't know. Why? What are you thinking?"

"Well, there have been legends of elvish abductions going back hundreds of years, but as I recall most of them were about *men* being stolen away." I cranked around so I could look at John. "And the times I have been in Fey it seemed like most of the human servants were men. So why is that? Álfar can glamour anybody—"

"Except you," John said.

"Yeah, good point." I remembered Qwendar's confusion when he had been unable to take control of my mind and force me to commit suicide. I also remembered how Ryan had tried to use vampire powers to mesmerize me the night I'd been stupid enough to go home with him. It hadn't worked that time either. I shivered and hugged myself. We drove in silence for a few minutes then I asked, "So, why doesn't the predator kill Álfar too?"

"They're a different species. Our best guess is that the predator targets the changes in human DNA when a person becomes a vampire or a werewolf and reacts to that."

John leaned forward and rested his folded arms on the back of my seat. "It just seems strange that if these Black Masons have a hard-on about the Powers, why aren't they pissed at the Álfar too? Why wouldn't they try to find a way to kill them . . . us too?"

Hettie shrugged. "Maybe they are. As I said, we haven't had a lot of luck infiltrating."

Something had been niggling at the back of my mind and it finally came into focus. "I get why you don't want the parasite released—it's personal for you. You'll die along with all the male vampires but the rest of your group, they're human. So why all the concern for the Spooks?"

She glanced over at me. "Parasites don't kill just for the hell of it. Like any other living creature their primary purpose is to survive and propagate. There aren't a lot of vampires and werewolves. So what happens after the parasite has run its course and killed all the hosts?"

"It will try to evolve," I whispered.

"Yes. And at base we're human so it might not be all that hard for it to make the jump from the Powers to normal humans. And the one thing we do know is that this thing kills."

"A world without humans," I murmured.

"Hmm, sounds like an Álfar wet dream," Hettie mused.

"No way," John replied. "They're like cats, and cats need something to torment."

"Sounds like you need therapy. Self-loathing, much?" Hettie shot back.

"What he needs is to get the ice out of his eye," I said.

"Ice? What are you talking about?"

"What he needs is for everybody to shut up about him," John grunted.

16

Thirty (silent) minutes later Hettie made the turn to the riding facility. The afterschool jump class was busy circling the arena, and popping over the brightly colored fences. As usual it was all little girls. I found myself longing for the days when I was twelve with nothing more pressing on my mind than which horse I would get to ride and whether I could stay late to help feed rather than having to hurry home to the Bainbridge house and do my homework. I tried to remember those days, but the featureless face of the Hunter kept rising up.

"Why is that?" I asked abruptly as we rolled past the arena, heading for the barn.

"Why is what?"

"Sorry, guess you're not telepathic after all. Why do the vampires . . . real vampires . . . well, not creepy vampires . . . hate the Hunters so much?"

"Because the Hunters are mutated vampires. They are the men who broke the rules."

"Rules like loving a woman?" I asked slowly.

Hettie nodded. "Or who have Made a woman or even considered Making a woman, for that matter."

I thought of the creature's blank face and sucking mouth. Then I saw David, pictured him twisted into one of those things. Cold washed through me and I began to shake uncontrollably. I sat shivering, thinking how close David had come.

"I thought they were just killed."

"It would be kinder."

We pulled up in front of the barn and entered. Dust and bits of wood shavings danced gold and silver in the gleam of the westering sun. Inquiring nickers greeted us. As we paced down the length of the breezeway the horses hung their heads over the stall doors. I bestowed pats as I walked past and an admonition.

"It's not dinnertime yet, guys."

Vento's gleaming white head was thrust out of the stall. He watched us intently as we walked to his large stall at the end of the barn. Before I would have taken this as just an example of his affable nature and his fondness for me. Now it took on a whole different meaning that still struck me as sort of creepy. We reached the stall and I stared into his large dark eyes with the unusual blue ring around the iris. Hettie and I exchanged a glance.

"I really wish Syd hadn't made that crack about Mr. Ed," I muttered. "I feel like an idiot." I took a deep breath and asked hesitantly, "Jolly? You in there?"

The mobile pricked ears swiveled between Hettie and me, then the head went up and down as if he was nodding yes.

Hettie glanced over at me. "Told you."

"That's a common action in horses. They do that naturally," I countered.

Vento whiffed and spun away from the door, paced his stall, and then pawed at the wood shavings near the automatic waterer. He then returned to the stall door and gave a trumpeting whinny that had all the other horses in the barn calling. He once again paced away and pawed at the particular spot.

I pulled back the handle, pulled open the stall door, and slipped inside. Vento placed his head against my back and shoved me toward the corner where the waterer stood. It was hard enough that it almost knocked me off my feet.

"Hey, watch it!" I said, not certain who I was addressing.

I studied the wooden walls of the stall. There were places where the wood was scarred from a bored stallion's teeth being dragged across the panels. Were any of them more regular and deliberate? It was too dim to tell. "There's a flashlight in the office. Would you get it, please?"

"Use this." She pulled out her cell phone and cued up the flashlight app. I shined the light on the stall walls. The marks were all around, most of them random, but on the wall next to the automatic waterer the lines crossed each other.

"Check this out," I called. Hettie and John joined me in the stall and we bent down to peer at the marks. It was rough and crude, but it was a shape Hettie and I recognized. We both straightened and stared at each other while Vento watched us, his ears flicking between us.

"I take it that means something to the two of you," John drawled.

"Yeah, it's the Masonic symbol, the square and the compass," I replied. I looked into the horse's eyes. "Okay, I guess you really are in there." There was a fervent nod of agreement. "You know this is really weird, right?" The head went up and down again.

Hettie stepped around so she could look in the horse's eyes. "Linnet doesn't believe that her father is involved in this. Can you set her straight?" Vento/Jolly nodded again.

"Was my father among the people who attacked you?" Vento shook his head.

"I could have told you that," Hettie said.

"But you didn't," I countered. "Maybe because it undermined your narrative?"

"No, that's not why. I just didn't think of it."

John stepped in. "Was he with the people who broke into Linnet's apartment?" A vigorous nod.

"Did *you* actually see him?"

The long equine head swung over to Hettie as if seeking guidance. "Jolly wouldn't have. It was Fusashi who was watching your father."

"Well, that's convenient since this Fusashi guy isn't here and can't tell me this himself," I said snidely.

"You're right," Hettie said. "I should have called him in, but we didn't want to take our eyes off your father and the other Black Masons. There's too much at stake."

"Which is just another glib excuse."

"I can get him here."

John stepped in. "It won't help. She won't believe his unsupported word."

I folded my arms. "Yep, that's true. I need proof."

"And I might be able to get it," John said. "There are traffic cameras all over town, security cameras on nearby businesses, that kind of thing. I just need to find a cop willing to help."

"I've got one," I said. "Lucius Washington at the 19th."

"Great, I'll talk to him."

It had been weird leaving Vento's stall. Hettie was unperturbed. She hugged his neck and said farewell to Jolly as if his soul and consciousness wasn't living inside the skin of a horse. I nodded, gave an awkward wave. John just left. In this particular instance I envied his lack of emotion.

This time I took the backseat of the car. I wanted to be alone with my tumultuous thoughts. Hettie tried to elicit polite chitchat from John and found him to be an unresponsive participant, so the drive back to Manhattan was made in total silence. As we neared Manhattan John thrust his hand at me.

"Phone," he ordered.

"What?"

"I need to call this cop."

"Let me prime him first." John looked sour, but nodded and handed me his phone. I called the detective. "Hi, Lucius, it's me."

"Hey, Lynnie, how are you?"

"Fine. I'm fine—"

"You don't sound fine."

I rolled my eyes, hating the fact that everyone around me seemed to be a damn psychic. "I'm okay. I probably sound funny because I need another favor."

"What do you need?"

"My friend can probably explain it better." I handed the phone to John.

"Hey, Detective, this is John O'Shea. I work for IMG as their investigator. I was with the Philly PD." John paused, listening then said, "Yeah, I know Lieutenant Heine. Hell of a gal." Another pause. "Yeah, that doesn't surprise me. Look, I need to take a look at any surveillance cameras up around Linnet's apartment. Can you get me access? Tomorrow morning? That'll be great. See you then." He snapped shut the phone and handed it back to me. "Tomorrow," he said unnecessarily.

Another night without knowing, I thought, but I didn't voice that. I just nodded.

"So, what now?" Hettie asked. "May I please take you someplace safe?"

I drew in a deep breath. "Soon." I leaned forward and tapped John on the shoulder. "We need to go to the bank first."

"Why?"

"So I can check the messages on my real phone."

Hettie shook her head. "I don't think that's a good—"

I cut her off. "*My* decision."

Hettie and I waited in one of the small privacy rooms at the bank. We had made it with only fifteen minutes to spare, and the staff wasn't happy about us wanting to get into the safety deposit box, but complied. John entered carrying the box and set it on the counter. I pulled out my phone. It came to life and the icon appeared indicating I had twenty-three messages. I scrolled the list. Most were from my father. The last one was from my mother. I set the phone on speaker and cued it to play. Her odd speaking pattern where she emphasized the wrong word and her overly loud delivery filled the room.

"*Oh* dearest. It's so *terrible. Charlie's* been hurt. He's in *the* hospital. You *need* to *come* home. *Right* away." A knot of fear formed in the center of my chest, but doubt and suspicion were just as strong. I tapped on the final message from my father.

"I know you won't believe me, but maybe you'll listen to your mother. She'll be calling you. Your brother was frantic. He started driving to New York and he was in an accident. He's in the hospital. That's the truth. You need to come to Newport." Then his voice sounded a bit distant. "You need to call her, Cathy, right now." The message ended.

"Do you want me to check the papers about a wreck? Call the local hospitals?" John asked.

I shook my head. "This was two days ago. Another few minutes isn't going to make a difference."

I ran through the rest of the messages in reverse order. After the message about Charlie there were a lot of angry ones from my dad. What was I thinking? I was worrying my mother sick. My brother was frantic. How could I behave this way? Then the first six messages. They were contrite. He begged my pardon. He loved me. He had overreacted. He didn't want me to ruin my life. He was just thinking of me.

John and Hettie were staring intently at me. "You're not think-ing of going—"

I interrupted the vampire. "Jesus, how stupid does he think I am?"

"He doesn't actually know you very well," John pointed out.

I didn't answer. I wanted to pace, to run, to flee from the situa-tion, but the space was tiny and we were jammed together. I breathed hard and tried to analyze my chaotic emotions. I should have been devastated, but in some ways not much had changed. I had been living with this sense of abandonment since I was eight years old. For years a kernel of doubt and fear and hurt had lived inside me. I had been certain I had been sent away to live with our vampire liege, Meredith Bainbridge, because my family hadn't wanted me once my brother was born.

The truth was much, much worse. This horror could not have been inflicted on me without my father's knowledge, and worse, his consent. And my mother? Had she known too? All the pain, rage, and sorrow of my childhood came rushing back. My father had gambled with my life first as an infant and then all through my childhood. He hadn't protected me, his allegiance to this group had been stronger than his love for his child. I wasn't his daughter. I was a tool. I had been twisted and changed to deal death to his enemies.

Hettie's cold hand landed lightly on my shoulder. "What can I do? How can I help?"

"You can't. I have to deal with this. With him."

"And do what?"

"I don't know yet. I have to accept that he's my enemy. He turned me into a weapon. Well, he would do well to remember that a weapon can always be turned against its maker." I dashed a hand across my eyes, wiping away the betraying tears, and looked at John. "We don't have to bother with the surveillance."

"Yeah, we do," John said. "What you're saying now—it's nothing but brag and bravado. This is your dad. You have to be absolutely convinced. If you're not you'll hesitate at a time when hesitating could ruin everything. They're going to try to grab you again. We . . . *you* have to keep that from happening since we have no idea how this thing manifests. It might kill you when it goes active. You really want to take that chance?"

We were back in the car. Hettie looked back at me. "*Now* may I take you someplace safe?"

"Not yet. I want to talk to Ken," I said. "I have questions."

"Well, I'm going to keep the two of you together so I guess that's okay."

"They need to stay with me," John said abruptly. "I can take us all into Fey if anybody comes after them."

Hettie glanced over at him. "Why don't you just take them there now?"

"I can do that."

"Not without dinner first!" I protested.

"I could eat," Hettie said.

"You're really going to go into a restaurant and order off the sipping menu?" I asked. "You're not supposed to exist."

"No, we're going to a Starbucks and John will order for me. Grande Premium blend. No one will know it's not coffee."

"They will if you get blood mustache on your upper lip," John said.

"I'll be careful."

John tugged thoughtfully at his upper lip. "We'll go someplace where the service sucks because they don't pay any attention to the customers. I know just the place," he concluded.

Hettie laughed. "Well, that's a hell of a recommendation."

It wasn't easy prying Ken away from his specimen, and he was very pungent when he climbed into the backseat with me. He was also babbling,

"The tongue is fascinating. It seems to serve as an olfactory organ, which suggests the parasite has a distinctive odor."

"Speaking of odor," I said, which was hard since I was trying to breathe through my mouth.

John said to Hettie, "Swing by my apartment so he can shower and we can burn his clothes."

"Hey, what am I supposed to wear?" Ken objected.

"We're about the same size."

"Why can't I just go to my apartment?" We all gave him an incredulous look. "Oh, yeah, right. Forgot. Oh, and I think the tongue and those faint scales also throw off sonic signals so they don't run into objects despite being blind." I shivered and looked away. Ken noticed. "Oh, sorry, too soon? I guess it must be upsetting since it nearly killed you."

"You don't know the half of it," I answered.

It took another hour, but eventually we were settled at a hole-in-the-wall Chinese restaurant. John had taken me to dinner there. It had been the first meal we had ever shared. It was the same bored teenager waiting on us, and he had an earbud in one ear connected to the iPod in his hip pocket. It was also pushing nine o'clock so the place was empty aside from us. John started to order, then stopped and looked at Ken.

"I realized you might be better at this than me," he said to the Chinese scientist.

"Not really. I'm third generation."

"Okay then."

Food began arriving and we ate. Hettie draped herself in a chair and sipped her Starbucks blood. I took a look around, but the waiter was back in the kitchen. I said in a low tone, "My boss always hated the blood from Starbucks," I said. "He said they were collecting from homeless people."

"This whole connoisseur thing is just silly," Hettie said.

"So there isn't a difference in flavor?" Ken asked.

"Sure there is, but having us act like wine snobs makes us even more obnoxious than we already are. Acting all superior isn't going to endear us to people."

"Hettie, there's nothing you can do that would endear you to normal people," I said. "You're predators. You scare us."

"Are we more frightening than werewolves?"

I thought about it for a moment while I dragged a handful of chow mien noodles through sweet and sour dipping sauce and slowly chewed on them. "Yeah, I think you are. You're not only predators you're dead predators."

"The Dead Predators. That'd be an awesome name for a rock band," Ken said.

I found myself chuckling and I blessed him for the momentary release from worry, fear, and grief.

"We'll start it. Does it matter that I can't sing?" I asked.

"We'll put you on drums or something." Ken grinned at me.

"Assuming either of you survive," John said.

Ken gulped. I glared and Hettie's brows climbed toward her hairline. "Wow, you're a real asshole," she said.

I went to John's defense. "He can't help it. His mother did something to him. It killed his emotions."

"Magic?" Hettie asked, genuinely interested.

"Yeah." He indicated his blind eye. "She stuck a sliver of ice in my eye."

"Ah, so that's what you were talking about in the car. Well, as you've seen with Jolly, we have people who are magic wielders. We might be able to help."

"Sounds good." John pointed at me. "But keep the focus on her for now. She's the one in real trouble."

Everybody stared at me. It made me nervous and I dropped my handful of noodles into the sauce. I tried to fish them out with my chopsticks which just made things worse. John pulled over the bowl and picked them out.

"You did say you had questions," Hettie said.

I looked to Ken. "So we've established that I carry this parasite that can kill vampires and werewolves, but I worked at a vampire law firm and no vampire died there. And Hettie's been hanging around me and she's not dead or dying. So what triggers this thing?"

The bored teenager and his mother arrived with trays of food, and we paused while people scooped food onto their plates.

Ken mumbled around a mouthful of kung pao chicken. "Parasites don't kill just for the sake of killing. Death might be a by-product of their activities, but those activities are dictated by one thing and one thing only—procreation." His voice had taken on the cadences of my professors at Yale. "The evolutionary drive to spread the species. The vector is the question. How does the parasite move from host to host?"

John beat out a nervous tattoo on the edge of his plate with the end of a chopstick. "Werewolves eat normal human food. They're tougher and live longer than a normal human, but not significantly longer, and they're sure not functionally immortal like a vampire. I don't see any overlap between the two."

"Blood," Hettie said quietly. "It requires an exchange of blood in order to Make a werewolf or Make a vampire. A woman's blood has to be the vector."

"'Cause menstruation wasn't enough reason for women to be suspected and despised," I said and I didn't care if I sounded bitter.

Ken paused for a sip of tea. "What I don't understand is how the creature can stay dormant for so long. Reproduction is a powerful motivator and only creatures with higher faculties are able to postpone procreation."

"The ancients figured that out and put in place the prohibition about feeding on women or Making women," Hettie mused. "Which implies you have to get a vampire or a werewolf to bite a woman."

"The prohibition is deeply ingrained," I said. "Even a shithead like Ryan—a vampire at my office," I explained in response to Hettie's puzzled look. "Anyway, even Ryan, who was playing dominance sex games with female associates, never risked even a nibble."

"There's another thing about parasites," Ken said. "They evolve and adapt. If one avenue to pursue the prime directive—reproduction— is closed off they'll find another path." He turned to me. "Which is why I really need to do a full physical workup on you. If I can locate the thing in your body I might be able to remove the creature so I can study it more effectively."

"I'd vote to destroy it," John said.

I drew patterns in my rice with a chopstick and debated how much to say. I realized I had to trust the people around me or I was doomed. I cleared my throat and they all looked at me.

"Well, as to that. I think it's more than a tapeworm or a fluke. It's aware. It can affect its surroundings, and that ability seems to be getting stronger. And . . . and . . . I can sense it. What it's feeling, if not what it's thinking. So maybe ixnay on the estroyday ingthay," I concluded.

"Huh?" Ken queried.

"Big brain doesn't know pig Latin?" John asked.

Ken looked haughty. "No, I know *real* Latin."

"Bully for you. Step aside and I'll translate."

The two men left the table. I glanced over at Hettie. "You think I'm crazy."

"No." Her expression was grim. "I think this just got a lot scarier and more complicated. If this thing is intelligent, sentient, however you want to say it, that presents us with a dilemma both moral and tactical."

"One parasite measured against thousands of vampires and werewolves?" I asked.

"Testing me, are you?" Hettie asked. I just raised my eyebrows at her. "Well, I turn it back on you. One father measured against thousands of vampires and werewolves."

17

Once we reached the Dakota, Parlan had demanded to be told the latest. Ken listened with interest as John and I went through everything that had happened since my last stay. Parlan's brow was knotted and his eyes stormy when I told him about my father. Ken looked shocked.

"Your dad? Wow, that's brutal . . . and kind of . . . twisted."

"He's a villain. Shall I deal with him for you?" Parlan asked.

"No. I'll fight my own battles, thank you," I flashed at him.

John brought me back to Earth. "And just how do you plan to do that?"

"I'm working on it. The most important thing right now is making sure this thing doesn't trigger." I turned to Ken. "So yeah, some medical tests would be a good thing."

"I can't do it from here, but we'll get something set up. I've got a lot of contacts at various hospitals because of my werewolf research," Ken said.

"Good."

"Dealing with the one in you is important," John said. "But is there more that can or should be done?"

"What do you mean?" Ken asked.

"Maybe this is something, like small pox, that doesn't need to exist in the world any longer," John answered.

"We could learn a lot studying the creature," Ken objected.

I rubbed a hand across my brow. "Let's table this until morning. I'm really exhausted, so I'm going to bed."

As I left the room Ken asked Parlan if he could gather samples in Fey, because maybe in Fey there were different kinds of worms and flukes and wouldn't that be cool? Parlan was looking grossed out and poleaxed all at the same time.

If I slept I didn't recall it. Instead I lay there staring at the intricately carved branches that formed the canopy on what had become my bedroom in Fey and trying to analyze the situation. If I stayed in the human world these Black Masons would try to use me and the Powers would try to kill me and probably succeed. If I stayed in Fey I might be safe, but I was functionally a prisoner in a gilded cage, unable to live a normal life. Being a victim or a pawn wasn't my style and I sure didn't want to die so we had to find a solution. I was twenty-eight years old and I had a life stretching out before me. Perhaps a husband, children, a law practice with cases that made a difference (I had always wanted to argue a case before the Supreme Court), and many more horses to ride.

I gave up on sleep and got up around six and found Parlan drinking coffee and reading through handwritten pages. "You're up early."

"I have a domain to manage." He waved the pages at me. "Reports from my staff."

"God, even in fairyland there's bureaucracy."

"But no lawyers," he said brightly.

"Yeah, you handle things with duels. Not seeing that as an improvement."

"Generates less paper," he said.

"True."

"I expect it will be a while before John gets here. Why don't you go for a ride?"

It had never occurred to me that I could ride in Fey and I hadn't been on a horse in several weeks. I was overcome by the desire to swing a leg over a horse. I reluctantly shook my head. "No boots, no clothes."

"We can handle that."

Thirty minutes later I was mounted on a chestnut mare that shone like a polished copper penny. The clothes they had found for me weren't much different than my normal riding attire except the cuffs of the boots were softer and they extended above my knees. What I really missed was my safety helmet, but no one in Fey seemed to worry about traumatic brain injury.

Parlan rode a glossy black stallion with a single white star. Ladlaw rode with us as bodyguard. His mount was a cream-colored mare with a golden mane and tail. Parlan caught me studying him with a horseman's critical eye.

"Well, do I pass muster?" he asked with a smile.

His horse was plunging, prancing in place. Parlan was relaxed, swaying in the saddle, matching each crow hop and buck. He was an excellent horseman.

"You ride very well." I wanted to add that he looked better in the clean lines of tall boots, skintight breeches, and a neat coat than he did in all the lace and frogging that he usually affected, but for once I managed to control my tongue and not be rude.

We left the courtyard of the Dakota. Ladlaw moved ahead and stopped the few cars so we could pass. Across the narrow road the Fey version of Central Park was pale spring green. Dew trembled on cobwebs that hung like pale lace on bushes. Ladlaw had a bow slung on his back and a sword at his side. Parlan also had a sword. We trotted down dirt paths, and our passing would occasionally release a shower of dew from the branches overhead. It was bracing cold against the skin on the back of my neck. My mare was a bit fresh and occasionally grabbed the bit and tugged, trying to rip the reins from between my fingers. The third time she rooted on me I tapped her with the spurs and gave her a sharp half-halt. After that she stopped testing me and went nicely on the bit. The trees gave way to an open meadow, a long swath of green heading down toward the lake.

"Shall we gallop?" Parlan asked.

I nodded and lightly closed my legs on her sides. She exploded into a gallop, and I gave a whoop of delight. She caught my mood, gathered her hindquarters beneath her, and increased her speed. The head of the cream mare was at my left knee. Parlan's stallion overtook us in five large bounds. My ears were filled with the rush of air and the pounding of hoofbeats. The stallion's head snaked over toward the neck of my mare, preparing to nip her. Parlan leaned forward and smacked him lightly on the muzzle. The stallion snorted his displeasure and Parlan laughed. The horses began to slow and we pulled up at the edge of the trees on the far side of the meadow.

Horses and riders alike were breathing hard. "There, now, don't you feel better?" Parlan asked me.

"I do. Thank you."

He looked at me and his gaze was serious. "Whatever comes, know that you can survive it, Linnet. You are strong in ways you can't even imagine."

"Well, thank you. I just hope that won't have to be tested."

We took a circuitous route back to the Dakota. We startled a small group of deer nibbling on the tender spring leaves. A young buck was rubbing his newly budded antlers on a tree trunk, leaving shreds of velvet behind. The herd leaped away with a flash of white tails as we rode by. There was a colony of bunnies out on the grass eating and hopping about. Ladlaw went to unlimber his bow, and I put a hand on his arm.

"Please, don't. I'm kind of squeamish about things getting killed. I've seen too much of it."

"Of course, my lady," the tall Álfar said.

"Oh, please, call me Linnet. And most people would argue I'm not at all ladylike."

We returned to the Dakota and walked up the stairs to Parlan's quarters. John was waiting for us. He thrust a McDonald's bag into my hands. "Washington has the video. Since electronics don't work so good in this place we'll have to go to the 19th to view them."

I stuck the Egg McMuffin back in the bag. My appetite was gone. I knew John was right and I really did need to see this, but I really didn't want to. I stood, just breathing hard for a few moments.

Parlan touched me gently on the elbow. "Do you wish me to accompany you? Stand at your side as your friend?"

"No. Thanks, but no."

"And what of Ken?" Parlan asked.

I nodded toward the bag. "Give him my Egg McMuffin and tell him I'll be back later."

Parlan looked heavenward. "I will give him a satchel and let him go off to collect bugs, or fungus, or whatever other disgusting thing that takes his fancy."

"Actually I was hoping I could get some fecal samples from a random sampling of your people," Ken said.

None of us had noticed him entering the room. Parlan's look was so horrified it was comical and I found myself giving a short laugh despite my inner turmoil.

"*Hilal!* No!" Parlan said. Ken looked crestfallen.

"And, as much as I want to collect, I should probably get those tests set up," the scientist continued.

"Good idea." John turned to his changeling brother. "Parlan, can you get Ladlaw to transit him between worlds and stand guard?"

"Absolutely."

"And this guy can bring me back?" Ken asked.

"Yes."

"Cool. Then I'll be able to collect too."

"How . . . nice," Parlan said hollowly.

Lucius had things set up in an interrogation room. The expression in his warm brown eyes was concerned, caring. It was a welcome change from the flat gaze from John's one good eye. I sat down in front of the laptop.

"The first image is from a bank on the corner. The second is from a traffic camera," the cop said. "You ready?"

I gave a tense nod and Lucius set the images to scrolling. Then, in an act of sensitivity that I deeply appreciated, he moved to the far side of the room and took John with him. I watched the images flick past. They were grainy, black-and-white, the perspective was off, but one image came through with devastating clarity. I saw my father with two other men walking past. The traffic camera showed them crossing the street. I recognized the background; they were across the street from my apartment building. I grabbed the top of the laptop and slammed it shut. For a few seconds I just sat, trying to breathe, trying to organize my chaotic and frantic thoughts. Eventually I succeeded.

I continued to just sit at the table. I heard the door open and close then open and close again. A plastic cup of water was set at my elbow. I looked up into Lucius's concerned face. "I don't understand why, but it's clear you're really upset. Will you tell me what's going on?"

I looked up into the cop's handsome face and realized that if I didn't fix this he would die too. Telling him might elicit a reaction that I didn't want. I feared his rejection. "Uh, not yet. I'm sorry." I took a sip of the water, then stood. "Thank you for getting this for me. It's . . . clarified things. Come on, John."

The two men exchanged a glance over the top of my head. I could almost hear their thoughts. *Poor girl. She's very upset. Keep an eye on her, won't you?* It infuriated me, but I let it go. I had bigger battles to fight.

"Back to Fey," John said once we were on the sidewalk outside the precinct.

"No. Back to the bank. I need my phone. It's time I hear what he has to say."

We ended up with the same clerk, and she gave us an exasperated look as she took down the box. John and I hurried into a privacy room, and I took out my phone. While it powered up I felt his eyes on me. I looked up. "What?"

"You seem oddly calm."

"I'm not the same woman I was last summer. I've been through a lot."

"And you're okay with that?"

"No. But I have to accept it. Some things you just can't change." I stared down at the face of the phone, filled with colorful, cheerful apps. Pity there wasn't an app for a shrink. "I think I began to suspect things weren't what they seemed back when Chip got killed. Back when my dad was nowhere to be found on that first day. I needed him and he wasn't there." I shook it off and squared my shoulders.

There was a message from Caroline.

"Linnet, I thought you'd want to know since you worked so closely with him. David Sullivan is missing. The partners have been keeping it quiet, but the Terrible Bruce—though he's been a little better recently—anyway, he told me in confidence and wanted me to tell you. I think he's hedging his bets by not calling you himself. That way he can say it didn't go outside the walls of the office. Yeah, maybe he still is a little shit. Anyway, I thought you should know. Bye. Call me. I miss you."

The message ended. I stared at the screen. "Oh . . . shit."

"What? What's happened now?"

"Why didn't you tell me David Sullivan was missing?"

"I didn't know he was. You might have noticed—I haven't been spending a lot of time at IMG. *You've* been occupying all of my time."

I didn't answer John. Instead I dialed my father's cell number. He answered on the first ring. "Lynnie, thank God! Where have you been? Doesn't matter. You got our messages about—"

"What have you done with David?"

"Why do you thi—"

"Oh please! How stupid do you think I am? First Charlie and now this. What? Do you think I'm just going to turn myself over to you and your group because of David?"

"My group. So you know," he asked.

"Yeah, pretty much everything."

There was a long moment of silence, then a sigh. "I told them the Charlie ploy wouldn't work."

"Huh, well, I'm oddly relieved that you didn't come up with that plan yourself. At least you knew me that well."

"What about your friend?"

"That's not going to work either, Daddy."

"They'll kill him."

"Meaningless threats? Really? Oh please. Let me see if I've got this right. I let you freaks get control of me to save David except then you trigger this thing and David dies. Along with Meredith and Shade and Lucius and all the other vampires and werewolves

I know. No thanks. Let me say it again—I am not an idiot. And I'm going to stop you. I've got people working on how to neutralize this thing. So you may as well let David go."

"You don't understand what's at stake." I could hear the frustration and impatience in his voice. "You won't be harmed, but you'd be freeing the world. Making it safe for normal people again. Giving us back control."

"And killing thousands and thousands of people—"

"Monsters!"

I was amazed and appalled. "You've smiled and interacted with them. Given me into their keeping, but you hate them this much? God, you must be a psychopath."

"I'm a patriot! A humanist."

"Who might be endangering all of humanity! The other group says this could jump from vampires and werewolves to ordinary people. Putting aside the morality of what you're doing, think about the risk to the rest of us. To Charlie and Mom and you. Everybody!"

John laid a hand on my wrist. "That's enough. We don't want to give them time to find you."

"Who's that? Who's talking?" my father demanded.

I ended the call and turned off the phone. John put it back in the safety deposit box, and we left, handing it back to the bank employee who locked it away again.

18

I was discovering I had claustrophobia issues. I had always known that crowds bothered me. When you're five feet tall and surrounded by people it starts to feel like the world consists of belt buckles and that somehow they're sucking up all the air and none of it ever gets down to you. As the table began to slide into the tube of the MRI, I started to feel a bit breathless. An earmuff style of headphones was clamped tightly over my ears. I was glad the rules of MRIs dictated that I remove my earrings. They would have been uncomfortable under the heavy headphones. I had also been forced to take off my bra because it had an underwire. I had been offered a selection of music and had gone with the pop choice. Kelly Clarkson was currently singing about catching her breath and letting it go. She stopped singing and I heard Ken's voice: "It's going to get really noisy now, Linnet, but you need to hold still. This is going to take a while since we're doing a full body scan. Okay, we're starting now."

Kelly returned mid-word, and then this horrendous banging began, as if a thousand dwarves were beating on sheet metal with iron hammers. It was muffled by the headphones, but it still penetrated even through the music. I tensed then wondered if that qualified as "moving," so I forced myself to relax. Hours went by filled with whirrs and bangs and clicks. I knew it wasn't really hours, but it felt like it. I wished I could see what Ken and John were looking at in the tiny control room off to the side.

Do you know we're looking for you? I thought to the creature residing somewhere inside of me. *Do you know we're going to destroy you? Can you read my mind? I suppose I owe you, you've saved my life, but I can't let you kill my foster father and my friends, and even all the vampires and werewolves I've never met and will never know.*

The music cut off again—Britney singing about being toxic—and John's voice came through. He was yelling. "Linnet, get out of there. *Run!* Ken, what the hell?" Then a crash and the sounds of a struggle.

I began frantically wriggling my way out of the metal and ceramic tube, using the curving sides to help propel my body down the length of the machine. I tore off the headphones, dropped onto the floor, and spared a glance toward the control booth. Ken had his back against the glass. Just past him I could see John fighting with a big man dressed in a suit. I didn't recognize John's attacker. I ran for the door that led into the hospital. It was flung open and another large male, also dressed in a suit, plunged in. He grabbed at me. I used the slick linoleum floor to my advantage and went into a slide like a runner stealing a base. I passed under his outstretched arms.

Despite his size he was fast. He had checked and whirled as I was regaining my feet, and he grabbed me around the waist. I started screaming, and he clapped his hand over my mouth. I bit him so hard that I tasted blood, and he roared in pain. I rolled a desperate eye toward the control booth. The man locked in combat with John was suddenly holding air. He looked confused. Ken grabbed him by the shoulder and my hopes soared only to be dashed when the scientist yelled, "Come on! He's gone into Fey. He could turn up anywhere!"

Ken and the man left through the door and joined me and my assailant in the MRI room. The man who had been fighting John drew a gun. Ken looked alarmed. "Hey, there's no need—"

The air shimmered and John reappeared. His expression still had that preternatural calm, but he moved with blinding speed as he punched the man holding me in the temple, then twisted his arm until I heard a loud crack. The man screamed at the same time I yelled "The other one's got a gun!"

John tried to spin the big man so he could be cover for him, but the slick floor betrayed him, and he overcompensated and spun the man too far. The other man had a clear shot and he took it, firing over and over again. Gunfire roared in the confined space and bounced off the hard surfaces. The MRI was still banging and whirring, and the strong magnetic field played merry hell with the bullets, but there were more than enough for the man's murderous purpose. John jerked and looked down as blood blossomed on the front of his shirt. He raised his eyes to mine and I saw *John*, the man I had known. The bullets that had struck his body had somehow shattered the ice. Another bullet took him in the thigh, and he collapsed. Blood frothed at his lips, and he held out a hand to me, mouthed my name. Blood flowed across the white floor.

I was screaming, the sound a file across the soft tissue of my throat. Rage and grief turned me from a human into a maddened animal. I threw myself at the shooter, screaming. I wasn't sure if there were words or if it was just a primal shriek. He fended me off, then closed and grabbed me in an armlock. I struggled, but his size and strength were too much even for my rage. And my little companion stayed mute because these were humans, and the parasite had no interest in protecting me from my own kind.

Ken stood staring in horror at John lying in an ever-widening pool of blood. "We've got to *go!*" the man with the broken arm bellowed, and gave Ken a shove with his good arm.

"Shut her up!" my captor ordered, and Ken, moving like a man caught in a slow-motion nightmare, pulled a syringe out of his pocket and jammed it into my neck.

I tried to resist, to fight the effects, but circulation trumped will. Within a few seconds I had gone down into darkness.

My head hurt. I fought the lethargy weighing down all my limbs and struggled to sit up. I was lying on a cot with a thin blanket thrown over me. The cotton that filled my mouth had also invaded my brain, making it hard to think and remember. And then I remembered. *John.* The pool of blood. The eyes-wide death gaze. A wrenching sob tore across my sore throat, and I huddled over my knees, crying and screaming "John! No!" as if words would banish reality. The tears came so fast and hard I couldn't draw breath and I began to gag. I leaned over and vomited. The bile washed across my raw throat, and the smell kept the spasms coming.

I realized someone was hoarsely calling my name. "Linnet. Linnet. Linnet. Lynnie, dearest, listen."

I looked up and pushed my hair off my sweat-damp face. It was David. He was naked and chained in a bright circle of light. There were two chains, one around his waist and another attached to shackles on his ankles, and they ran to a heavy steel ring that had been driven deep into the stone floor. They were short enough that he couldn't stand. He could only crouch or sit on the hard stone floor. His skin was a mass of oozing blisters, his features sunken and drawn so the fangs hung over his wizened lips.

I fought down the nausea, ran to him, and hugged him tight. A quivering sense of anticipation rippled through my body at the same time he pushed me away. "No, Lynnie, stay away. I might . . . I can't . . . I'm famished," he admitted, shamefaced.

I backed off. Understanding came in a flash. Starving vampire/predator host—lock them in the same space. Wait for nature to take its course. I moved to the far side of the room and took a moment to survey our prison. It looked like an old ale or wine cellar constructed out of heavy stone, and probably dug into the hard granite of New England. I moved to the door. It was solid steel and looked new. A chemical toilet stood in one corner. There was no sign of a sink. Long fluorescent tubes lined the ceiling, illuminating the space. There were security cameras in two of the corners, which gave me some hope there were a few dead zones. I wondered if there were microphones as well and decided that any conversations would be conducted in whispers. Which would make it hard to stay well away from David and keep from becoming a vampire entree. I decided that being overheard was probably safer, in the grand scheme of things.

I returned to the cot, used the case off the pillow to mop up the vomit, and threw it in the toilet. I then returned to the cot and sat down. David and I stared at each other. "How long have you been here?" I asked.

He forced air to make a sigh and shifted, but there was no escape from the unrelenting light. "Six days. Maybe eight. I was trying to keep track," he looked down at scratches on the stone. "But then it just got too hard. I'm having a hard time concentrating, thinking."

"You're stronger than a human, can't you pull out that hook?"

"Whoever they are, they're damn clever. My body is using all its strength to repair the damage from the light—"

"We're underground, how can there be light?"

"I think the bastards have set up the lights you'd use for a tanning bed. I'm getting beat to hell by UV rays." His head drooped.

"I've got nothing left, and the longer I go without food the harder my body has to work to heal itself."

"So no clouding men's minds or breaking chains." I forced myself to take a light tone though my heart felt like it was slowly cracking.

John killed. David facing the true death in a particularly grue-some way, and both of them brought to this because of me. I wanted to die. I paused, considering that. If I died, the parasite, the predator would die with me. Maybe that was the solution. But not yet. We weren't there yet. Perhaps there was still a way to escape, and once I did escape—by God they were going to pay. There was a brief mo-ment when I wondered if the creature would allow me to harm myself. As much as I hated Ken and truly wanted to kill him for his betrayal, I wished I could talk to him and learn about the parasite.

" 'Fraid not."

I looked up at the grating far above his head. The ceiling was a good twenty feet over our heads. "How did they get you?"

"I walked right into it. I got a call to represent an elderly man who was bedridden."

"I'm betting he was a very rich old man," I said dryly.

"Yeah, he wanted me to draft his trust and IMG to have admin-ister it—for a very nice fee. It was catnip to the firm. I got to the house and got locked in a room and bombarded with UV rays. Hurt like hell, I collapsed, and then they had me." He stared at me. "Linnet, why the hell are *you* here?"

I stared back. I didn't want to tell him. If I'd felt grotesque be-fore, now I felt like a total monster but he needed to know because it was imperative that he not feed on me. But could training and conditioning trump starvation? He admitted he was having trouble focusing. Would hunger drive him to madness? Or course he couldn't reach me as long as I stayed on the other side of the room.

Hands tightly clasped, I hunched over, drew in a shaky breath, and began. "Remember all those legends and bad movies about the predator? Well . . . you're looking at her." The David sneer appeared. I didn't argue. I just kept talking, detailing everything that had happened since my departure from the firm and slowly the sneer faded. I wound down to the dismal conclusion, and silence swallowed the room.

"I'm so sorry, Linnet. I know you . . . cared for him."

A boulder lodged itself in my throat. I blinked hard, fighting the tears, fighting the overwhelming desire to just lay down and wail. John was gone. I still had a chance to save David. I just had to find the means.

David went on, "And I promise. I won't touch you. I'll die first."

"No! Nobody else is dying because of me!" I was on my feet, fists clenched at my sides.

A sudden rattling from the door startled us both. I whirled. Three men entered. There was Ken carrying what I recognized as a portable ultrasound machine, another carrying a tray with food. A filet mignon so rare it left a pool of bloom on the plate, spinach, a glass of red wine—food designed to build the red blood cells—a glass of water. The final member of the trio was muscle, and muscle I recognized. He was the shooter who killed John. He carried a pistol, probably the same gun, and he also had a long kukri strapped to his hip just in case a vampire needed beheading. The tray carrier was also armed. I flew at John's killer, shrieking, "You bastard! You bastard! You're going to pay for what you did!" He stiff-armed me in the chest, knocking me back into the cot. The cot tipped over and I went down hard on the stone floor.

Ken extended his arm to block the man and said, "Hey, hey, take it easy on her."

"Yeah, fuck you and your concern. Now you're worried about me?" I glared at Ken and he had the grace to duck his head and look embarrassed. "So how much did they pay you to sell me out?" I asked, and I didn't disguise my hate and contempt.

"Nothing! You and your friends were going to destroy it. I couldn't let that happen. I did this for science."

"Oh bullshit! You did this because it's your research, and you couldn't stand to lose it. To hell with the people who are going to die . . . have already died." I choked on a sob and turned away.

"I didn't mean . . . I didn't want that . . ."

I turned on him. "He protected you. Kept you safe, and you repaid him by getting him killed!"

"And the vampires and werewolves were going to kill me. Why should I care? Why shouldn't I protect myself?"

"Talk about a non sequitur and a deflection! It wasn't a member of the Powers who killed John. It was that asshole." I pointed at the impassive guard. "If this thing gets loose thousands are going to die, and it will be *your* fault."

"Look, I need to be involved. Even if I refused this group would keep trying. Isn't it better that I'm here to study the creature and make sure it can't jump species to regular humans?"

"Yeah, you just keep telling yourself that. I'm sure the Nazi scientists thought they were doing valuable work too."

I had gone too far and saw it when his expression hardened. He turned to the two men. "Put that down," he instructed. "And hold her."

The tray was set aside, and the big men advanced on me. I backed away, thought about running to David, but I couldn't decide and then they had me. They held my arms. I struggled, kicking, trying to reach them to scratch, flinging my head back and forth trying to bite them.

"I can't get a reading with her moving around like that," Ken snapped.

They forced me to the stone floor and none too gently, then held my ankles and shoulders. They were big and strong and I could barely move. Ken pulled up my sweater, revealing my bare breasts, rubbed gel on the ultrasound wand, and began running it across the left side of my chest.

David was roaring with fury. "Let her go! You fucking bastards! I'll kill you! I will fucking kill you!" He was yanking at the chains, the clash of metal punctuating each word.

I could see the screen if I looked to the left. I'd watched a lot of ultrasounds of horse's legs so I had a pretty good eye. I could see the hazy lines of my ribs, my breastbone, and the left lung, a gray shape beneath the bones. And perched on the top lobe was a dark shape with two tendrils extruding from it. My skin went cold and a clammy sweat broke out across my body. So that was my little friend. It was horrifying. Ken followed the lines of the tendrils, and it showed they were heading for my jugular vein. Panic yammered behind my eyes. There was a slow pulse from the dark blob, and the tendrils waved as if moved by a slow current and extended a bit farther.

Ken was taking screenshots and muttering to himself. "Good . . . yes . . . my initial analysis is being borne out. It appears a pathogen is going to be injected into the host's bloodstream. And the subject seems aware of the proximity of a vampire and is preparing for eventual transfer."

The scientist stood up and wiped the wand clean. He then packed up the portable ultrasound machine. "You can let her go now," he said offhandedly. The men backed off. I rolled onto my knees and turned my back to them as I pulled down my sweater. I was blinking back tears of shame and fear.

"I want to see my father," I said.

"I don't think the senior warden or the master will let him in. This is upsetting for him too," Ken said.

I turned to face him. "You've seen him?"

"Yeah, he's the one I called. And he's here."

"Tell him I want to see him." I hesitated then added, "Please." I hated that my voice had a catch in it, but it seemed to affect Ken. He looked at me a bit shamefaced and nodded.

"I'll tell him. It's the least I can do." He and the men headed for the door.

"Yeah, no kidding," I muttered under my breath.

I picked up the tray of food and carried it to the chemical toilet. "Wait. Don't." David's voice stopped me.

"I'm not going to eat."

"They won't let you starve. They'll force-feed you. They've got too much invested in this. Keep up your strength. An opportunity might present itself and you won't be able to take advantage if you're weak from hunger."

They were good points. I hated to give my captors the satisfaction. I wanted to be strong and refuse, but David was right. A vampire slowly burning alive and starving and a starving five-foot-tall woman weren't going to be able to accomplish much. I retreated back to my cot, sat down, and ate the meal. I drank half the water, but left the rest for later. I looked at the residue of beef blood staining the plastic.

"You want to lick the plate?" I offered.

David shook his head. "It won't help, and it'll just undermine my resistance. And I won't touch you, Linnet. I swear I won't."

I drew a bit closer to the circle of light and the suffering man and said quietly, "If you did feed how fast would you regain strength?"

"Pretty damn fast. I wouldn't worry about looking pretty." He gestured at his blister-covered body with one equally blistered hand. "I'd use it all to regain my strength."

"This thing." I touched my breast. "Hasn't reached the jugular yet. Maybe you could feed before it had a chance to infect you?"

"A sip from you isn't going to do it, Linnet. I would need to drain someone and that would kill them."

I sat struggling with what I had to say and feared to say. I cleared the sudden obstruction in my throat. "Look, I'm probably going to die anyway. Nobody knows what this thing will do. It could be like the Facehugger in *Aliens* and bust out of my chest or something. If you could get free you could maybe stop them—"

"No!" So loud and explosive was the word that I jumped. "I will not ever harm you. I will die first. And if we miscalculate and I actually do get infected, then thousands are going to die. No." He shook his head.

"So I guess there's no hope for either of us." My head drooped and grief for John, for myself, and for David fell over me, an avalanche of shadows.

"Probably not."

19

It was hard to tell how much time was passing. I didn't wear a watch. Like most people of my generation I just used my phone to check the time, my email, Instagram, and Twitter. And even if I had worn a watch I would have had to take it off for the MRI. I paced, I tried to sleep. The lights were never turned off, which made it hard, but eventually exhaustion won out and I slept despite the glare. David and I talked, but talking exhausted him as his body fought its losing battle against burns and starvation. Meals arrived and trays were taken away. Based on the number of meals it seemed like three days, but I couldn't be sure.

I looked for things in our prison that could be used to help us escape. I had read a book once about a girl who had used the under-wire in her bra to pick a lock, but I didn't have my bra on and even if I had, I had no idea how to pick a lock. I upturned the cot and inspected the springs that laced across the bottom. I tried to remove one. Perhaps I could use it like a metal whip or something, but my hands weren't strong enough to break it loose from the frame. The frame was welded together too, and couldn't be broken apart to become a baton.

When the tray arrived I studied the two guards who accompanied it and wondered if I could shove one of them into David's arms so he could feed. They were both over six feet tall and probably weighed in at two hundred pounds, which made it pretty damn unlikely.

Ken turned up with his ultrasound and checked the progress of the parasite's tentacles. They were getting perilously close to my jugular vein. I had stopped fighting the exam because I was going to lose, and that made it more humiliating somehow.

David was starting to look more and more like a scrawny corpse, and he was muttering to himself. I stopped approaching the circle of light. I knew this was David and my friend, but he was turning into something inhuman and really scary.

I thought about Hettie and Parlan and Lucius. They must be looking for me. They knew the identity of at least some of the Black Masons. Couldn't this guy Fusashi have followed my dad and figured out where we were being held? Unless of course Fushashi was dead too. This crowd had shown itself more than willing to commit murder. Which made me think of John and that laid me out on the cot crying until I was too exhausted to cry or think any longer.

After the second exam on the fourth day Ken gave a grunt of satisfaction. I could see why. The tips of the tendrils were resting against my jugular vein.

"So, it's time?" one of the guards asked.

"It's time."

They all exchanged significant looks and left.

"David!" I called loudly. He slowly raised his head. "I think they're going to try something. Something to get you to drink."

"Don't worry," he croaked, and dropped his chin back onto his chest.

Time crawled past. I paced and ran my fingers through my limp and dirty hair. The door opened and six men entered. Three of them were my guards and Ken. The other three were older. One of them seemed familiar. Had I met him at the country club or one of my father's business gatherings? All of them seemed to be deferring to the oldest guy. I made the guess that he was the master.

The oldest man looked at Ken. "You're certain?"

"As certain as I can be since we have no relevant data," the scientist replied.

"Will it kill her?" The emotionless tone of the question shook me and also angered me.

"I don't know. It's clear the parasite is going to puncture the wall of her jugular. I can't predict the effect it will have on her."

The oldest man gave an annoyed grunt. "It's taken so much effort to get to this point. If she dies the predator dies, and it will take years to bring another one to maturity and try again."

Ken hunched one shoulder. "I'm sorry, but I can't be more precise. If one of your group had ever succeeded before we wouldn't be guessing now."

"If one of my group had succeeded we wouldn't be here today," came the dry response. "And the Powers would be gone."

I was sick of being ignored and talked about like a thing. I thrust myself into the conversation. "The Powers, wow, I'm surprised. I would have thought a hate group like yourselves would call them Spooks. You know, go for the pejorative."

The master approached me. I tensed and fought down fear. In an effort not to flinch, I focused on silly details—that he wore a Jaeger-LeCoultre watch and his cuff links were platinum and gold with the Masonic symbol on them, his Italian tie of fine silk. He took my chin in his hand and looked down at me.

"Your father said you had—"

"Spirit, right? You were going to say spirit, which would make you even more like a cliché movie villain." I didn't have to force the contempt. It just flowed out of me.

He released me and stepped back. "I was, but I'll amend that now to cunt."

It hit me harder than I expected. Only once before in my life had that particular slur been thrown at me, and it had been used by a low-life criminal who had helped kidnap me, and it had come in a particularly fraught moment. Coming now from an elegantly attired older man with a clipped Boston accent, a man who was a friend and colleague of my father's, it had weight and power beyond being just a word. I had once again been reduced from person to thing.

"We've watched you interact with that thing." He indicated David. "You're a traitor to your own kind." He gave me a smile. "But now you're going to be the instrument to rid the world of them and the Hounds. Future generations will remember you as a heroine."

"Funny, I don't remember people who caused genocides being called heroes."

"Take her," the master ordered.

The guards grabbed me. This time I fought because I knew something bad was about to happen. Since I hadn't been resisting the ultrasound exams they were a bit lax, and I actually broke free from one of them and managed to scratch his face before he grabbed me again. He was cussing and dabbing at his bleeding cheek with the back of his free hand.

"Forget that," the master ordered, gesturing at the scratch mark. "Bitch drew blood."

"She'll soon have hers drawn. Hold her now, and stay out of his reach."

The two men just lifted me off the ground and carried me over to David. Then, using me as a shield, they thrust me into the circle of light. One man put a hand on the back of my head and forced my head and neck to within inches of David's fangs. Groaning with pain he scooted away, retreating as far as his chains would allow. They once again pushed me in close. There was a wild fluttering in my chest and it wasn't my heart. A sense of excitement washed through me, and it wasn't my emotion. I was terrified, horrified, and crying. My little friend was ecstatic. Seconds ticking past measured by my thundering heart. Seconds into minutes. David was trembling, but his jaw was clamped shut, his lips an invisible line so tightly were they pressed together. There was also an unholy light burning in his eyes. We stayed like that for an agonizingly long time. The guards' grip on my upper arms hurt like hell as their fingers dug into my muscles.

Then, whimpering and groaning, David rose as far as his chains would allow. He stared over my head at the watching men.

"I won't touch her. Nothing you do will change that. My training is too strong." He paused then added, "So go fuck yourselves."

They tried four more times. Each time prolonging the exposure. Far from eroding David's control the repeated attempts seemed to be stiffening his resolve not to touch me, much less feed on me.

Finally the master uttered a curse and ordered them all out of the room. I raced to David, ready to hug him, but a sharp command froze me in my tracks.

"Don't! Do not *touch* me. Don't come near me."

I retreated to my cot. "But . . . but, you did so well."

"I was damned if I was going to give them any satisfaction," David grated. "But, Lynnie, I don't know . . . how much longer I can hold on . . ." He collapsed and wiped the seeping moisture from bursting blisters out of his eyes. "I'm so hungry, and it hurts so much. It's getting harder and harder to think. I'm becoming an animal, the monster they think I am." He rolled onto his side and tried to shield his face with an arm. "I wish . . . I wish I could just die. Really die."

"No, don't talk that way. We're going to get out of this. There has to be some way out of this. People are looking for us." I laid a hand over the place where the parasite resided. "This thing is also pushing me. It's excited and frustrated and it's pushing me to approach you."

"Then we're fucked."

"I won't give in either," I said.

"This thing has unnatural abilities. It might do something."

"It's not going to turn me into a meat puppet. If it could have it would have done it already." I frowned. "Why didn't it act like this before? When I was living in Meredith's house or working at the firm?"

"Because none of us were hungry?" David suggested, and he perked up a bit and seemed more interested.

"That makes a certain amount of sense. All I can say is thank God they grabbed you instead of Ryan. He was playing those dangerous sex games with human women. Once he got a bit peckish he would have had *no* control. Oh shit," I muttered. "They're probably listening. I shouldn't have said that."

"No, you shouldn't have," David said grimly.

Panic seized me. The thought of being in Ryan's power, knowing that he hated me for outing him and causing him to be demoted, knowing he wouldn't hesitate to drink and kill me sent me flying to the door. It was crazy, useless, and illogical, but I yanked frenziedly at the door, beat on it with my fists until my hands were bruised, the knuckles grazed and bloody. I sucked at them and noticed David forcing air and sniffing. There was a wild light in his eyes.

"I'm sorry. I'm sorry. I'm doing everything wrong," I cried. I returned to the cot, rolled myself up in the blanket, and turned my back on David. I could feel his stare as I tried to sleep. It was my only refuge.

The rattling of the lock pulled me awake. I sat up expecting Ken and the goons, but it was my father. I stared at him and felt joy and hope bubbling up, but two seconds of consideration had it crashing into despair and anger.

"I know you're not here to help me . . . us. So why are you here?" I demanded.

"I wanted to see you . . . before. And to beg you to stop fighting. I wanted to make you understand that we're not monsters. We're humanists, patriots. These things have been running us, controlling us for centuries. We had to be free and that takes sacrifice."

"Sacrifice? I didn't agree to this. You're acting like this is some noble act, but I'm just the goat or the lamb waiting to get its throat cut."

"This is hard for me too!" he cried. I guess my expression conveyed my utter scorn because he rushed on. "Look, the longer you wait the more chance there is he'll kill you." My father's eyes slid toward David, and I saw the hate and fear.

"You should have thought of that when I was a baby, before you put this thing inside me," I spat back. "And how could you have done that? How can you do this now? Did you feel anything for me?"

The answer surprised and hurt me. "I couldn't let myself. When I lost the throw, I knew I'd lost you. I couldn't allow myself to care for you."

"So you came up with the fostering idea. Not only to hide me in plain sight, but to get me out of your sight?"

"Yeah, pretty much. Even if we hadn't fostered you, you would have been taken away from us and hidden. But that hadn't worked the previous three times we tried. The Spooks always found our hosts and killed them."

"And you were always a gambler so you bet it all," I said.

"Yeah." His shoulders slumped. "I trusted to luck. Just like I did when you were a baby. I didn't think I'd lose the throw. There were five of us with baby girls. The odds favored me and I'd always been lucky. But . . ." His voice trailed away and he shook his head. "And fostering you meant I got to see you occasionally. If they'd taken you away to hide you I would never have seen you again."

"Why bother when you didn't care about me? Or maybe that's not completely true." I left the cot and crossed to him. Laid a hand on his arm. "If you have any affection for me at all . . . help me. Please, Daddy." That choking lump was back in my throat, and I blinked hard.

For the briefest moment I thought I had won. I saw the struggle, the love when he looked down at me, then he shook his head. "They've told me they'll kill Charlie if I do anything to help you. I can't lose you both. It's a fucking Sophie's Choice. One child for another."

Bitterness engulfed me. I was done with pleading. I stepped back, contempt rather than tears were now choking me. "Yeah, and lucky for you it's the boy you get to save. I'm sure that makes it easier."

"That's unfair!"

"Really? And by the way, you may lose him anyway. The other group says this thing might jump species. Move to humans. Kill us too."

"Ken doesn't think that's likely."

"And of course you'll take that bet too, because the other one worked out so well. Get out of here."

"You hate me."

"Yeah. I really do."

There were more attempts to place me in close proximity with David and they also failed. David was no longer hurling proud taunts at our captors. We had passed the point where he could form words. Instead he had gone to animal-like growls, but the training was holding. I could hear his teeth gnashing together, but he never touched my throat.

The frustration was reaching the boiling point among the cabal and my little companion was a physical flutter in my chest that was both uncomfortable and terrifying. The ultrasounds were over. The next time Ken came he drew blood. He was looking worried and harried and nervous.

"Your new friends losing patience with you?" I asked sweetly.

"I don't think anyone expected the conditioning to be this strong," he said.

"It isn't just that. David is my friend. You don't hurt your friends." He got my point and a dull flush rose up in his cheeks. It was also a conversation killer, and he and the guards left immediately after.

A few hours later I awoke from a doze. A lot of people came into the room. Ken, the guards, the honchos, and this time my father was with them. They all gathered around the cot and stared down at me. I sat up. My body felt strange, all the muscles were aching, and even my bones felt sore.

"So?" the master demanded of Ken.

"The parasite has released a pathogen into her bloodstream, there is also evidence of minute forms of the parasite itself. Without a subject to test I'm not sure precisely how it kills vampires and werewolves or the purpose of the cellular duplicates. Watching the effects on an infected subject would tell us a great deal about whether it's acting on the genetic—"

"Yes, yes, if anyone's interested they can read your paper when this is all over," one of the men said.

"But we can't tell anything if we can't get the vampire to ingest her blood," another complained.

"Could we take a pint or two from her and force it down his throat?" a third asked.

"You want to get close enough to hold that thing?" my father asked, and nodded toward David, who was lying on his side, plucking at the blisters on his face and growling and moaning. "If he grabs one of us and manages to feed . . . well." He shrugged. "It won't be pretty."

"Look at him," one of the men scoffed. "He's a mess."

"They can recuperate pretty damn fast," my father warned.

The master gave the sharp nod of a man who's reached a decision. "Then we take that other vampire. The one she mentioned. This Ryan."

"So, we don't need this one anymore?" one of my guards asked.

"No. You can kill it."

"No!" I shouted. At the same time my father said, "Hold on. First rule of wing walking: Don't let go of one wing until you have a grip on another. Let's not dump this one until we have our hands on the other. And I'm not too comfortable with kidnapping another vampire out of Ishmael, McGillary and Gold. Shade's no fool, and if two of his junior partners disappear he and the Convocation may start asking questions."

The tension leached out of my shoulders, and I heaved a sigh of relief.

"If this Ryan has fewer scruples than that one," the guard said, with another dismissive gesture toward David, "he won't be missing for long, and by the time the Convocation convenes, much less moves, it will be too late for any of them."

The thought of being at the mercy of a hungry, angry Ryan Winchester had me gulping with fear. On the other hand, my companions knew about David's disappearance. If another vampire were kidnapped that might alert them, and they would follow and find us. Or was I grasping at straws blowing past in a hurricane? The safer and more likely bet was that they'd grab Ryan, starve him for a few days, and he would kill me, but maybe I could bluff.

"My friends knew about David. They'll be watching. You take Ryan and they'll know, and they'll find you. And then you'll have not only this other Masonic group coming down on you, you'll have the NYPD too!"

The master of the order gave me that look men get when observing a woman, particularly a younger woman, the *isn't she adorable* look. "We're rich and respectable men. Men like us own the levers of power. No one is going to be allowed to search this house."

So I now knew this was a private residence, but the rest of the statement had me shaking my head. "God, you people are so illogical. If you're so wealthy and successful and control the levers of power, why in the hell are you so upset about the Powers? Or is it that you can't bear to share?"

"It's a false front," my father said. "Honey, think about it. It doesn't make any sense that creatures that have so much power and are superior to normal humans would be willing to just live among us and accept our rules. At some point their real agenda is going to come out, and it won't be good for our kind."

"It's been fifty years. Kind of a slow coup," I argued.

"Not for vampires that are functionally immortal or werewolves that live longer than normal people."

The master waved his hand impatiently. "Why are we engaging in this pointless discussion? We know what we have to do."

They headed for the door. I fought down the urge to throw myself at my father, beg for help. It would have been pointless, and I might not have had anything else, but I still had my pride.

20

Pain screamed through my body and ripped an actual scream from my throat. I sat up on my cot and hunched over my knees, groaning in agony. The ceiling lights were fluttering, a maddened blinking that sent pain stabbing through my eyes. I could feel bones moving beneath the surface of my skin, and I screamed again. Total darkness engulfed the room as the lights, even the UV lights over David, failed. Some of the overhead bulbs burst, sending glass showering down on me. Despite the darkness I was still seeing flashes and streaks of red as all the nerves in my body were lit on fire. It went on and on, and then I passed out.

Shouts and pounding footsteps from beyond our prison door pulled me back to awareness. A trembling ran through all the muscles in my body, and I was shuddering and shaking. My body seemed alien and unfamiliar. I rolled onto my side and vomited.

"Lynnie?" David's voice, thread-like out of the darkness. I was perversely relieved. He hadn't spoken or made any kind of sound for almost a day, and I had feared he was truly dying.

"Oh, thank God, David—" I clapped a hand over my mouth. An alien voice had emerged.

"Lynnie?" Then he added fearfully, "Who are you? Who's there?"

I wanted to call back, *David, it's me,* but I wasn't sure I *was* me. I hesitantly touched my throat. Cold air washed across my midriff and I realized my sweater was riding up above my waist and there were tears at the shoulders. My pants were also uncomfortably tight.

The door flew open, and beams of light from flashlights being held by shaky hands went bouncing around the room. I shaded my aching eyes with a hand. The guards, the master, Ken, and several other of the top officials. They all froze and words tumbled over each other.

"Jesus Christ!"

"What the hell?"

"How?"

Ken cut through the babble. "Oh, this is wonderful!" He even clapped his hands, which made me long to rip his face off.

The master turned on him. "What? What are you talking about?"

"You've just watched evolutionary science in action. The parasite can't propagate until it's ingested by a vampire or werewolf, and it can only survive and grow in a human female. The Powers respond by setting an absolute ban on Making a human female, so they put in place a strictly enforced ban on a vampire or werewolf ever even *biting* a woman. So the parasite evolves, changes. It's like the Wolbachia bacteria that affects wasps, but in reverse. Instead of turning males into females it turns females into males."

Horror washed through me. I looked down. My breasts were gone, my chest was wider, hence the torn sweater. Now that the pain was receding I could think again, could notice that my pants were way too short in the rise and far too tight as well as too short. I was clearly taller, though I had no idea how that happened. It was all too much. John, and now this horror. I had been violated as an infant and now it had happened again. Helpless, a pawn in the hands of evil men. Conflicting emotions warred in my chest—devastating, numbing grief and murderous rage. Which would win out? I decided on rage. Somehow these people would pay and pay and pay.

The unbroken lights came back on, and the UV light once again washed over David. I looked at him. He was sitting up, his eyes wide with shock, but even the brief respite from the burning rays had given his body a chance to heal. Our asshole captors might not have noticed, but I knew that beloved face very well, and I could see that the skin was less ravaged by blisters. I stood and found it hard to find my balance. My body had become a stranger.

"She's bigger, taller," one of the men said. Wonder and disgust were equally blended.

"How is that possible?" the master asked. "Conservation of mass should have made that impossible."

Ken glanced around at the shattered glass on the stone floor. "I didn't really accept the idea of magic until now, but I think it's a mix . . . of science and magic. I think the creature used raw energy to fuel the change. Hence the power failure. I'd be interested to see how far it extended. Was it just this house or the neighborhood? I'd love to calculate what was required to effect this change."

"Yeah, study this, you son-of-a-bitch," I yelped, and tried to charge him. I was desperate to batter at him, beat him to the ground.

I was shocked by the level of rage and the pulsing need for violence that beat through my veins. That, together with my unfamiliar form, betrayed me. I lost my balance, my feet tangled up, and I fell hard.

My captors all laughed, amusement yes, but a sense of relief. The master expressed it. "This is going to work, gentlemen." They exchanged smiles and nods and even a few handshakes.

One of the guards stepped forward. "Should we try it now?"

"No, let's starve this bastard for one more day. Then offer him this tasty morsel." They laughed again and started to leave.

Ken held back. "I'd really like to examine her. See how much the internal structure has been changed or if this is mostly just cosmetic. Monitor hormone levels, that sort of thing."

"Later, after it's done, and the Spook has been released to spread the infection," the master said.

"I might be examining a corpse," Ken objected.

"Don't be greedy, Doctor. We gave you an opportunity to study the predator, but our objective is the priority. Your research is a curiosity that won't have a lot of relevance after we return the world to human control."

"Can I at least do an external exam now?" the scientist asked.

The masons exchanged glances, reached an agreement. "I don't see why not."

They left. Ken was eyeing me. I backed away. I knew what was coming was going to be incredibly humiliating. The guards closed in on me.

It had been humiliating as hell to submit to my privates being inspected. Creepy as hell to accept that my privates had changed. I had considered trying to struggle, but unfamiliarity with my changed body would have made that difficult, and a wild thought had occurred to me during the inspection. My guards were as disturbed and weirded out by what had happened as I was, but I noticed they handled me exactly as they had before the change. It gave me an idea.

After they left I straightened my clothes as best I could. The zipper on my pants made it partway, but there was no chance I could close the top button. I then sidled over to where David lay cooking in the circle of light. I knelt down on the floor next to him. He pried open his eyelids, which were gummed shut by the weeping blisters that covered his face.

"Don't," he croaked. I could barely distinguish the word.

I backed off a bit, but not much because I needed him to hear. "Why not?"

"You smell . . . different. Right. Not sure . . . can . . . control myself. So hungry."

"David, once you feed how fast will you regain some strength?"

"We've discussed—"

"Just answer the question, damn it!"

"Quickly." His eyes reddened as if flames were dancing deep in the irises and he suddenly growled and grabbed at me.

I gave a squeak of alarm, which sounded ludicrous in my new baritone, fell back on my butt, and scooted away from him. A rough spot on the stone caught on the material of my wool slacks and ripped the seat. For some reason that bothered me worse than any of the rest of the horror I'd endured. It was deflection, as any shrink could have told me, but it was the final indignity to have my butt cheek hanging out. I burst into tears.

"Lynnie, Lynnie. I'm sorry . . ."

"It wasn't you," I snorted and sobbed. "I tore my pants."

"Oh . . . uh . . . okay. I'm sorry . . . scared you."

" 'S okay . . ." I mopped at my cheeks.

He groaned. "Want you."

"Well you can't have me. Look, just be ready, okay?" I whispered. "And . . . uh . . . don't hold back."

I retreated, and began pacing the cellar, circling David, but keeping close to the walls. I was testing out my balance, finding the center of gravity for this unfamiliar body. Years of dressage had given me incredible isometric control over different muscles groups. I applied that now, locating muscles and flexing them. I was only going to have one chance.

The key rattled in the lock, and the guards came in with my dinner tray. I bit the inside of my cheek bringing tears to my eyes, but it wasn't enough to really set me to bawling. In the past, I would have remembered when my father left me on the pier when he'd taken me at age eight to live with Meredith and that would have gotten the waterworks flowing. Now that memory just brought rage, not sorrow. I thought of John, but that too, brought rage and the promise of vengeance. I was desperate, I needed them to see weakness. My brain was flitting from memory to memory and then I recalled the night when my first horse had died and the tears came.

The men exchanged glances as I turned to face them with tears running down my face.

"Come and eat," the dark-haired one said. "I think this will be over soon," he added and his tone was kind.

And one of you will be dead soon, I thought.

A few hours later the leaders of the cabal arrived. Both Ken and my father were with them. He stared at me in horror and fascination, extended a hand, and said with a mix of wonder and doubt, "Lynnie?"

"Yeah, Daddy, it's me. Happy? You've got two sons now." He flinched at my tone. "Of course, I'm probably going to be dead soon."

My father looked like he wanted to say something, but the master pushed him back. "Enough. Let's finish this."

The men's attitude seemed calmer, more confident. The guards took my arms and frog-marched me to David, who was twitching, rolling from side to side as his flesh continued to burn away layer by layer. I resisted, but only a little. Close enough now to see that the blazing light was back in his eyes. David's hands were flexing, reaching for me, and those terrifying nails were extruding from his fingertips.

"Look at that," Ken said excitedly. "The attraction is overwhelming now that the impediment of the host being female has been removed."

"We know from the ancient texts we're supposed to release the vampire after it's fed to spread the contagion, but how can we be sure that will happen?" another officer asked.

"Look at him." Ken gestured at David. "He's beside himself, completely attracted to the host. Once he drinks I'm pretty sure the pheromones that are attracting him to the host will propagate in his body, along with the pathogens that are going to kill him. But before he dies he'll become a lure to both Suckers and Hounds. A regularly little honeypot." I hated hearing those pejorative words coming out of Ken's mouth. "Just make sure you release him in a target-rich environment."

"But will they? Bite him, I mean," my dad asked.

Ken shrugged. "There's no prohibition against Hounds and Vamps biting each other since they're all male. That one"—another nod toward David—"is going to be irresistible. I'm also going to bet he'll be driven to attack. The parasite is going to force him to spread the infection. He'll be bitten, the pathogen and the pheromones will propagate in the next one, and it will spread out exponentially from there."

"He'll warn them!" I yelled. Since David was growling and howling and jerking at his chains that seemed like a rather faint hope. Or maybe he would act so crazy he'd just get locked up before he ran across another of the Powers.

Ken gave me a condescending and pitying look. "Have you ever seen a host under the control of a parasite? It can force creatures to kill themselves if that's in the interest of the parasite. He'll follow the evolutionary imperative set by the parasite."

"Enough," the master snapped. "While that's all very fascinating, we're not in a biology class."

I was forced onto my knees, head jerked to the side, throat offered. We were all in our familiar positions. The guards were pinioning my arms and using me as a human shield. David, his mouth

opening and closing like a baby's seeking a tit, teeth clashing together. Me, heart thundering, knowing if he dug those fangs into my
throat we were both doomed. He wouldn't sip. He would rend and
tear, and that was, perversely, what I was counting on. David lunged
at me. I tensed every muscle, and spun my body hard to the right.
The man holding my left arm was taken by surprise at my strength
and leverage. He lost his footing, stumbled on the rough flagstone
floor, and fell against David. Everyone was shouting. David let out a
shriek like a hunting cat.

With my left arm now free I was able to reach across my body
and scrabble at the gun in the holster at the other guard's waist. He
tried to push me away, but his partner screamed, distracting him. It
was a horrible animal sound, and a gout of blood, warm and sticky,
splashed across the side of my face. The fountain of gore struck the
other guard full in the face. He yelled in horror.

I had the gun. I glanced down quickly, the safety was on. I
thumbed it off and did as Meredith had taught me all those years
ago when I'd turned fourteen. I clutched the grip with both hands,
braced, and aimed for his body mass. Somewhere deep in my con-
science a little voice was yammering at me that this was murder, and
I couldn't do this, but fear, fury, desperation, and meticulous training were stronger than the little voice. This was also the man who
killed John. That added to my resolve and rage. I pulled the trigger
twice. Once again, the strength in my upper body and arms took
me by surprise. In the past the recoil would have had the barrel
climbing to the sky and I would have had to pull the gun back down
level. This time it scarcely moved.

The guard was bending over the bleeding wounds in his chest and
belly, collapsing in segments, a broken puppet. I risked a glance at
David. He held the body of the first guard between his hands. The
guard's throat had been torn out, and David had his face buried in the
gaping wound. Blood coated his face, and his throat was working.

I was rather glad the report of the gun had deafened me so I couldn't hear what I was sure were horrible slurping sounds. I leaped to my feet and whirled to face the leaders of the cabal. My father, never a fool, was already bolting through the door. The rest were fleeing after him.

From behind me came the muffled sound of snapping metal and the clash of chains falling on stone. Then David was at my side, naked, bloody, his face filled with rage. He leaped toward the men. He hesitated, looking hungrily at me. I took a step back and snatched the kukri off the dead guard's belt. I held it out menacingly. "Hungry," he grated.

"I'm off limits, but . . ." I gestured at the stampeding crowd. "Buffet's open."

David whirled and ran across the cellar. Most of them were through the door, but the guy bringing up the rear wasn't so lucky. David fell on his back, grabbed him by the hair, and jerked his head back. David buried his fangs in the man's neck, tore open the jugular, and drank deep.

One of the Masonic officers paused to try and shut the door. I fired twice to discourage that behavior. One shot grazed his shoulder. His mouth worked, though I couldn't hear the yell through my ringing ears, and he bolted. David dropped his latest meal with the air of a man discarding a melon rind. His belly was hugely distended, filled with the blood of two humans. Even as I watched, the swelling began to slowly recede as, bit by bit, the blisters that covered his body began to heal.

He was staring at me. I wanted to think it was admiration and appreciation of our daring escape, or at least the first step in our daring escape, but it wasn't that. He was forcing air through his nose and mouth. "I smell you. More than just blood. It's maddening. I want you."

I once again brandished the big knife at him.

"You'd kill me?"

"To keep you from killing the rest of your kind and the werewolves as well. Yeah, I'd kill you. And you'd do the same if you were thinking straight." It was bravado. Only the desperate knowledge that my life and David's life depended on me pulling that trigger had allowed me to shoot the guard. There was no way I was going to find the strength to kill my friend.

"Once I'm back to full strength you wouldn't be able to stop me."

I stiffened. "Oh yeah? Well, you can . . ." I broke off, thrown off balance by my challenging stance and aggressive tone. I wiped the back of my hand across my forehead and relaxed from my stiff-legged pose. "Wow," I muttered. "Testosterone really is poison, isn't it?"

David gave a shout of laughter. "Oh, Linnet, my dear."

I pointed at him. "And that's the other reason you won't do it. You do care for me and you wouldn't violate me that way." Tears flooded my eyes. "I've already been violated . . . so . . . much."

"Oh my dear heart. No, but the desire is overwhelming. I'll fight it, but I've got to get away from you and soon."

"Right, yeah. We need to get the hell out of here before they come back with chain saws or torches and gasoline. You lead," I added with an abundance of caution.

David started for the door. I paused to drop the clip and check my ammunition. Five bullets remained. I ran back to the body of the other guard and took his pistol too. Another thought occurred and I riffled through his pockets and held up a cell phone with a cry of delight.

It was awkward with a gun in each hand, but I started to dial 911. "And you're going to tell them to come . . . where?" David asked in his smoothest and snottiest vampire tone.

"Good point," I muttered, and shoved the phone in my pocket.

We headed out the door and up the stairs out of the cellar.

21

"Wonder what time of day it is," I panted as I ran up the stairs after David.

"We'll know soon enough."

"I hope it's night."

"Not as much as I do."

The top of the stairs dumped us out in a hallway. The lights were on, which I at first thought was encouraging, then realized there were no windows so of course the lights were on. As we ran down the hall David growled, "I want some clothes."

"Not our number-one priority," I shot back as we entered a large country-style kitchen with state-of-the-art appliances. A huge Sub-Zero refrigerator dominated one wall, a massive Wolf cooktop and double ovens were against another. There were windows and it was dark outside. "We need to find Ken—"

"Also not a top priority."

"Yes, he is. We have to take him with us. He seems to understand what happened to me. Maybe he can fix it."

"You want to drag along a reluctant prisoner? Slow us down? Risk getting caught again?"

"But—" I began feebly.

"We're in way over our heads. We've got to get out of the deep water first. We'll find him, Linnet, I promise, but not right now."

I saw the logic in what he was saying and gave a reluctant nod.

David grabbed up a big butcher knife off the center island, then laid it back down and snapped, "Give me one of those guns." I handed over the one with only five rounds. Based on the way he'd handled that sawed-off BAR back a million years ago, I had a feeling he knew how to make each bullet count.

I checked the windows, wondering if we could just leave this party, but they were mullioned and rather small. There was no way we were going to fit through them. If I were still myself I might have made it, but—I broke off that train of thought. If I went down that rabbit hole I would plop down on the floor and noisily give way to hysterics. There had to be some way to fix this. Ken seemed to understand this horror.

I grabbed David before he could leave the kitchen. "One last thing. Whatever you do, don't kill Ken."

"I'll try, but if someone is trying to kill me I'm going to kill them first."

"I don't think Ken is the killing type." David looked at me and I realized how stupid that sounded because of course if David had been infected the predator *was* going to kill him. "Okay, point. Let's just say I don't think he's the hands-on kind of killer."

We left the kitchen and found ourselves in a large formal dining room. An elaborate crystal chandelier hung over a polished mahogany table complete with a two-foot-high silver centerpiece. Whoever owned this house was rich. Really rich. We moved on and found the living room. There were shouts from behind a closed door to our left.

"We can't call the police." I recognized the voice of the master.

"Damn it, we've got bodies. What are we going to do with those?" My father's voice.

Another person spoke up. "Greg needs a doctor. He's bleeding bad. That bitch kid of yours—"

My father. "Don't even—"

"Enough!" The master again. "Any gunshot wound that comes into a hospital has to be reported to the police."

"But he needs a doctor!"

"We'll try to find someone to come here. Someone discreet."

"Come here? Are you out of your fucking mind?" my dad yelled. "We've got to get out of here! That vampire's going to be here any minute."

"And here he is," David muttered and began to stride toward the door. I grabbed him around the waist and got dragged along. The parasite was quivering in my chest.

"Are you nucking futs?" I whispered, my tone stretched and urgent. "We have to get *out* of here!" He plowed on, with me an anchor weight. "That's my father, please stop."

"Don't you want me to kill him for you?"

"*No.*" The voices beyond the door fell silent. "Oh shit, they heard us. Let's *go!*"

He gave the door one last regretful look and then he turned away. I released him because his eyes were getting that weird glow again. A vestibule beckoned. We ran toward it and I heard the door behind us open. I ran harder, heart thundering a heavy rhythm in my chest, breaths loud in my ears.

"Lynnie, stop!" my father called. I ran harder.

David and I hit the entryway. David's bare feet slapping on the marble, and my stocking feet slipping on the polished black and white parquet floor. Carved wood double doors rose up before us with delicate stained-glass windows in each panel. David threw the bolt and yanked open the door. We raced outside, down a set of flagstone steps, and found ourselves on a curving driveway. A man was walking sentry duty in the grass on the other side of the drive. His left arm was in a cast and I recognized him from the hospital. He was the man whose arm had been broken by John.

"Damn it, stop her!" the master yelled from the top of the steps. The sentry stared at us and looked puzzled. "Him! Him! The little one!"

But the man's confusion had given us a precious few seconds. David leaped the intervening distance and punched the guard in the face. I heard bone crunch. We ran across the grass, heading for a tall stone wall. I leaned against the wall and wheezed, clamping an elbow against the stitch in my side. My feet were going numb, the toes burning from the cold. Same with my fingers.

"Can you climb?" David asked.

"I don't think so."

"Okay, I'm going to toss you up. Don't mess it up."

"Don't throw too hard," I countered.

I tossed the kukri over the wall. David cupped his hands and I gave him my knee. My little *friend* gave that shiver of delight when David touched me. I growled at it mentally, and the sensation subsided. *Just like getting a leg up onto a horse,* I thought, *if the horse was twelve feet tall,* and then I was airborne. I saw the top of the wall passing beneath me. Shards of glass sparkled in the moonlight. I decided not to grab for the wall. It was only twelve feet. How bad could it be? I tucked and pulled my head down, trying to orient myself so I would hit on my left shoulder and be able to roll. There was a bush to help cushion my landing, but I heard and felt the *crack* as my collarbone broke. The breath got knocked out of me, which was the only reason I didn't scream. My broken ribs were screaming. Apparently when it changed me into a male the predator hadn't bothered to fix my broken bones.

Bare, white feet flashed past my eyes, and David landed next to me, taking the shock on bent knees. He didn't even lose his balance, the bastard. "I can see why you avoided the top of the wall," he said as he dragged me to my feet. Thank God, he grabbed my right arm, but once again the damn parasite got happy. I pulled away from him. "You okay?" I just nodded because I still didn't have any breath for words. Tears of pain and shock and probably grief spattered as I moved my head, but I didn't have time to process their cause. "Still got that phone?" I nodded and fished it out. "Hope you haven't broken it," he complained.

I glared at him, but the question had made me nervous, so I checked. "It's okay."

"Then let's go." He started off down the street. I paused to recover the kukri.

We started limping down the street. Well, I was limping. The damn vampire was fine even if he was naked and barefooted. There were house numbers in wrought iron and tile set in impressive walls next to equally impressive gates, and it was a long way between gates. Wherever we were, it was a ritzy neighborhood. But numbers did us little good without a street name, and a street name was useless without some idea what town we were in. We reached a corner and were at the intersection of Oak and Maple. Street names that could be found in almost any northeastern city.

"We've got to find somebody, find out where we are," David said, looking indecisively in both directions. "Maybe it's time to ring a bell."

"We'll terrify them," I said. "And they'll call the cops."

"Cops are what we need now."

"Then let's get one that's on our side," I said through chattering teeth. I pulled out the cell phone and dialed Lucius's number.

David gave me a look of admiration. "You actually learn phone numbers? That's impressive. I thought all you kids just relied on pictures."

"Oh, shut up, and they're called icons, not pictures," I said through gritted teeth while the phone rang.

Lucius answered, "Washington."

"Lucius, it's me, Linnet, I need help." I was now shuddering rather than just shivering from the cold. The false spring was gone and winter had returned.

"What the hell? Is this some kind of sick joke?" His tone was hard and suspicious. "Who is this?"

I started to cry. "It's me. Really. I just . . . Things . . ."

"Give me that." David snatched away the phone. "Detective, this is David Sullivan, I'm an attorney at IMG—"

"Yes, I remember, I met you—"

"No time for pleasantries, Detective. That really was Linnet—"

"How?"

"Focus, Detective, we're in trouble and we need help."

"Where are you?"

"Well that's the problem—"

I grabbed back the phone. "We're on a stolen cell. If I give you the number and the carrier can you trace it?"

"Yeah, I can." He sounded weird. I didn't blame him. I went to the settings page and read off the number and the carrier. "Hang tight. Once I've got you located I'll send the authorities. Then I'll grab Hettie and head there."

"How did you . . . ?"

"She contacted me the minute you disappeared. Even though it was out of my jurisdiction I was able to get assigned to the investigation since I had relevant information on both you and John. Okay, I've got to hang up and contact Verizon. Help is coming."

I wrapped my arms across my chest, trying to hold in any trace of warmth. A cold wind blew through the tears in my sweater. David moved toward me, arms open to hug and hold me. I backed hurriedly away. "No, don't come too close."

"You're cold," he objected.

"And you touching me won't help! You vampires are freakin' *cold*.

And you just want to get close because you want to bite me, and the damn thing wants you to," I snapped. He had the grace to look ashamed. "You stay over there." I gestured across the street with my kukri.

"Across the street?"

"Yes. Go."

Headlights came around a bend in the road and washed us in their glare. It was a small white Ford with a fat-faced young man behind the wheel, and the first car we'd seen, suggesting it was very late at night. I squinted through the glare and was able to make out the driver's gawking expression. The car screeched to a stop, the door was flung open, and the man got out and hunched down behind the open door, a gun in his wavering hand. I could see a sort of faux uniform with patches on the sleeve and breast of his coat.

"Oh, great," David said. "A rent-a-cop. Just what we need."

"Put your hands up," the young man quavered. The gun was shifting between me and David in a most alarming way.

"It's okay," I said in my most soothing voice. "We're *so* relieved to see you. We really need your help." My soothing had the opposite effect. He looked even more alarmed and the gun was waving dangerously.

"You . . . You back off, you perv!"

And that's when I realized that the sugary, helpless, breathless tone I had taken worked great when it came out of a five-foot-tall female, but coming from me in my present form was just creepy.

"I'm calling the police!" the rent-a-cop shrilled.

Approaching sirens cut the night. "You're a little late," David said in his best snotty vampire tone.

Two squad cars and an unmarked car pulled up. Uniformed cops and a pair of detectives, one white male and one African-American female, boiled out of the various vehicles. "David Sullivan?" the male plainclothes cop asked as he eyed us warily. I could see why. David was buck naked and holding a pistol. My clothing was torn, the sweater now too short and revealing my midriff, and I was holding a mucking big knife, had a cell phone clutched in my other hand, and a pistol struck in the waistband of my slacks. I noticed every cop's hand drifting toward their holstered weapon.

David didn't miss it, and he threw down the gun and raised his hands. "I'm David Sullivan," he said with the air of a prince acknowledging his subjects. His nakedness was clearly no embarrassment to him. "We were kidnapped and have been held in that house for a number of days." He indicated the shadowy bulk of the roof of the big house visible over the high stone wall.

"Check it," the male detective ordered one of the uniforms, who moved back to his patrol car.

"And who's that?" the other detective asked as she hooked a thumb at me. I opened and closed my mouth several times and really wished that David and I had worked out our story before the police arrived.

"My . . . assistant," David said and dropped an arm over my shoulders. Once again, a wash of expectation ran through my body.

The remaining uniform looked from David in his magnificent nakedness to me, shoeless, dressed in my now too-short sweater that exposed my midriff, with the tears at the shoulders, and my ripped pants. "Yeah, and how exactly does he assist you?" he snorted.

I shrugged off David's grasp and stepped away from him.

"Shut up, Stevens. These are the people that detective down in Manhattan called about," the woman detective snapped.

"Okay, but how come he's buck na—"

"Perhaps we could continue these discussions at your station house. My associate is freezing." David was once again stepping closer to me. I edged away from him.

The uniform returned from the car. "House belongs to Reginald Halcomb the Fourth. Ran a quick Google search. He's some kind of big hedge-fund guy."

The male detective's stance changed and he almost sneered. "And that's who kidnapped you? Really?"

David drew himself up and looked down his nose at the man. "Yes." Typical vampire. No explanation, no effort to get the guy on our side. Just a single snotty word. I did a face palm.

The two detectives exchanged glances. "Okay," the woman said. "We'll send Boggs up to the house—"

"Please, get us away from here!" I begged.

"Yeah, we will absolutely do that," said the male detective and gestured toward their car.

"Uh, could we ride in separate cars?" I asked.

David's jaw and hands clenched. The uniformed cop, Stevens, gave the woman detective a triumphant *told you so* look. I hunched my shoulders against David's stare and moved quickly to one of the black-and-whites. The detectives escorted David to their car. I settled into the backseat. I was not familiar with the back of cop cars. The grate between me and the two policemen in the front seat, the lack of door handles on the back doors, and the smell of old vomit and body odor that seemed to have seeped into the seats left me nervous and jumpy even though I was guilty of no crime. *Apart from murder*, a nasty little voice whispered. I had a sudden flash of the guard collapsing after I shot him. It was more than cold that had me shivering now. I hugged myself and ventured a question.

"Excuse me," I said hesitantly.

"Yeah?" the cop in the passenger seat said.

"Where am I?"

"In a cop car." Yeah, he was quite the wag. I clung to my rapidly fraying patience.

"I'm sorry, that wasn't what I meant, I mean, what city? What state?"

"Fairfield, Connecticut," said the driver.

"Oh, thank you."

I leaned back and considered my situation. I had no ID. It was in my purse, which was sitting in a locker at the hospital. And even if I had it, what the hell good would it be? My license said Linnet Ellery, female, and showed my height at five feet with black hair and gray eyes. Well, I guessed I still had the hair and eyes, but everything else . . . not so much. Now I wished I had stuck with David. We needed to come up with a story, be on the same page. He had said I was his assistant. Who was I? What name would he give? I thought about having hysterics so no one could question me, but I was afraid if I opened that door even a crack, full-blown real hysterics would come rampaging through. As it was, I was only hanging on by a thread.

22

David ended up in an orange jumpsuit, which brought on a vampire temper tantrum of epic proportions. The cops got a little testy too, pointing out that no one wanted to give up their civvies to this guy. "Vampirism doesn't rub off!" David said in his most condescending manner. I dropped my face into my hands again and muttered,

"Oh, shut up."

I realized my skin felt rough against my palms. I frantically explored my cheeks and chin with my fingers. It wasn't skin. It was stubble. That's when I started to cry, scratch that, I started to wail. Everyone in the precinct looked awkwardly at each other. Finally the woman detective grabbed my arm and pulled me to the bathrooms. I started through the door into the women's room only to get yanked back. I gave a yell of pain.

"What?" the woman asked.

"I think I broke my collarbone," I whimpered.

"Oh, sorry, but you want that door," she said and pointed across the hall.

Maybe she'll just think I was blinded by tears and pain and not weird, I thought.

It was a white-tiled room with a line of urinals against one wall.

(I avoided looking at them because of all that they implied.) Four stalls, a line of sinks with mirrors above them. I wanted to wash my face, but then I would *see* my face. What had been done to me. I continued to stand with my back against the bathroom door, reluctant to advance even one step.

"You die in there?" the detective waiting impatiently outside called.

Of course she was staying close. They didn't trust us. *I* wouldn't trust us; we were a riddle that made no sense and we had accused a rich white guy of kidnapping. I forced my unwilling legs to move and walked to the sink. I looked down at the porcelain basin, turned on the water, and while I waited for it to get hot I pumped a bunch of bright pink industrial soap into my palm. I then scrubbed and scrubbed my face. I was aware of the smell of sweat. The exertions of the past couple of days, and no shower or bath for days before that, had left their mark. I wanted to strip off the ill-fitting sweater and wash my underarms. I decided to wait for the cavalry to arrive. Get taken someplace safe and actually take a bath. Further delay was pointless and cowardly. Water dripping off my chin, I slowly raised my eyes and looked in the mirror.

A familiar stranger looked back. The shape of the face was roughly the same, my brows were thicker. A faint five o'clock shadow was forming. My pageboy haircut brushed at the edge of my chin. (Apparently, the predator didn't do hair). I gave a hollow laugh. As myself I had always been described as "cute" and "vivacious," even occasionally "charismatic," but this new Linnet, she . . . he was gorgeous. Real vampire and werewolf bait. Add to that the pheromones, which, according to David I was shedding like leaves in autumn, meant any vampire or werewolf who ran across me would instantly want to bite me. I was going to end up like the Bubble Boy living inside an environment suit, assuming the Powers let me live. There was no place I could go and be safe. Then I realized that wasn't exactly true. I could always go into Fey, spend the rest of my life among the Álfar. It was not an attractive proposition.

I left the bathroom and the detective escorted me through the bullpen. David was nowhere to be seen. "Uh, where's my boss?" I asked.

"Randal's getting his story. Why don't you and I have a talk?" she said. Her tone was warm and friendly.

"I'm sure my boss will answer all—"

"Let's have a talk." It was no longer a request and it was no longer quite so friendly.

She led me to an interrogation room and indicated a chair. I sat down. The straight-backed wooden chair was hard and I found it uncomfortable to cross my legs. I was starting to understand the actual importance of which direction a man "dressed." I eyed the detective warily. She rested her chin on her folded hands.

"I'm Wanda. What's your name?"

I swallowed a couple of times and wondered what name David had given me. I wondered if he would use the name of the receptionist on the seventy-fourth floor at IMG? Or just say Lynnie, which could also be a man's name? I just kept staring at her, and she finally said, "Okay . . . We'll leave that for the moment, though it seems like an easy one. Why don't you level with me about what's really going on? That's a woman's sweater you're wearing. I know 'cause I saw it on the rack at Macy's last week. And those pants don't fit you at all." She glanced down at my tightly clenched hands. "And nail polish. Now maybe those apes who are out there sniggering about gay vampire sex games can be fooled, but I'm not that credulous. Something strange is going on here."

I sighed and shook my head. "It's too crazy. No one would believe it. *I* don't believe it."

"What's clear is that you're scared of that vampire."

"Not for the reason you think. He really is . . . was my boss, and I'm more frightened that *I'll* hurt *him*."

"And just how would you manage that?"

I closed my eyes and tried to find the strength to explain. I didn't even know where to start. A knock at the door of the interrogation room saved me. Wanda left the table and opened the door. One of the uniforms said, "That New York cop who called us is here, and he ain't alone."

"Oh?"

"Just come and see. I can't begin to explain this."

Wanda gave a head jerk that I should accompany her. We stepped out into the bullpen to find Lucius, Hettie, and *Jolyon*. The Brit was wan and had a bandage on his head, but alive and awake. I gave a sob of joy and relief and rushed to him, knelt in front of his wheelchair, and laid my head in his lap.

"Oh, Jolly, Jolly, you're not dead. You didn't die. You're alive," I babbled.

For a moment the trio stood in stunned silence as they processed . . . me. Jolly rose to the occasion.

"There, there, *Leonard* my *lad*," he said as he softly stroked my hair. "No need to carry on so. I'm quite all right. And everything's going to be fine now."

"How?" I sobbed.

"Well, we'll talk about that once we get home."

He handed me his handkerchief, and I mopped my eyes and blew my nose and looked around. Lucius had gone into a huddle with his Connecticut counterparts. Hettie and David were studying each other. David had that stiff-legged stance of a dog faced with an interloper. Hettie was smiling, fangs exposed, clearly enjoying David's discomfort. She held out her hand.

"Hello, youngling, sorry we got off to such a bad start at our first meeting."

David looked confused, but he took Hettie's hand. "Aren't you concerned about exposing yourself like this?" he asked.

"I think we've got bigger problems than one little female vampire."

"The Convocation won't see it that way."

"Yes they will, when they know about the predator."

"I'm not going to let them kill Linnet!" David shouted.

"Neither are we, child, so no need to bluster."

Despite my own woes, I was finding it both amazing and rather delightful to see somebody treating David like a grubby brat.

"We'll go for the warrant in the morning," I heard Wanda say, and I turned my focus to the conversation between the police officers.

"So your guy didn't get into the house?" Lucius asked.

The male detective, Randal, spoke up. "No, he rang the bell at the gate. No answer."

"You had probable cause," Lucius objected. "Two people who said they were kidnapped and imprisoned—"

"Yeah, and we're a small community. We don't have a damn tank to take down those gates or go through the wall," Randal objected.

"And he's a really rich guy," Wanda offered. "We gotta have a judge on board with this. You understand that. You're in Manhattan." Lucius didn't like it, but he gave a reluctant nod.

Jolly took command of the situation. He pushed me gently aside and rolled his wheelchair forward to the Connecticut cops. "I'm going to take our friends home now. Here is my card. They'll be available for questioning when you need them. Thank you for your quick response and all your help. Come along," he said, the order encompassing Lucius, Hettie, and David.

I was walking at his side as he headed for the exit. "They're going to get away," I said quietly.

"Not for long. *We* know who they are," was the serene reply.

Once outside, Lucius ran an agitated hand through his hair. "Jesus Christ, what in the hell is going on? Is this really you, Linnet?"

"Yes," I whispered.

"What the hell happened?"

"It's a long story." I touched the left side of my chest. "It's this thing inside me. It's trying to make them"—I glanced at David and Hettie—"bite me. I assume this thing's affecting you too?"

"Not a bit, my dear, but judging from the looks David is giving you, you're like vampire catnip."

Hettie looked at Lucius's big Ford parked out front. "Which means we need another car," she said. "David and I can drive together and get to know each other. You and Jolly and Lucius should get going before those confused cops inside decide we're all rather dodgy and they need to keep us here."

"How are we going to get a car?" David asked. The fact that he'd ask such a dumb question indicated how exhausted and off-balance he had to be.

"Well, we could steal one, but since we're in the parking lot of a police station that probably isn't a very good idea," she said with another of her bright smiles. David gave her one of his patented grumpy, exasperated looks. She sailed serenely on. "And Enterprise Rent-A-Car does deliver, but I think I'll just call the Order and have someone bring us one." She patted his cheek. "We have a lot to talk about." She made shooing motions at us humans. "Now all of you . . . go."

Lucius helped Jolly into the backseat of his car and put the wheelchair in the trunk. I slid into the passenger seat. Lucius took the wheel and we pulled away. He kept giving me very nervous and uncomfortable sideways glances.

I sighed. "I know. It's weird. How do you think *I* feel?"

We drove in silence for quite a while. The eastern horizon was starting to show a faint line of silver. Lucius glanced over at me.

"I understand this won't be easy, but I still have a murder to clear. What can you tell me about what happened at that hospital?"

"The guy who killed John is dead," I said dully.

"How?"

"I shot him. When we were escaping. There was another guy at the hospital. John broke his arm. That guy was on the grounds of the house where we were held. David smashed him in the face. Maybe he lived. I don't know. We kept running." Jolly leaned forward and laid his hand on my shoulder. Gave it a squeeze. Unfortunately, he picked my left shoulder. My collarbone objected and I gave a hiss of pain.

"What's wrong?"

"I broke my collarbone going over the wall," I said.

Lucius met Jolly's eyes in the rearview mirror. "Hospital?" the detective said.

"Hospital," Jolly agreed.

"No," I said. "Too many questions we can't answer. I came off a horse jumping a few years ago and broke my collarbone. There's really not much they can do. There's a brace you can buy at the drugstore. Just get me one of those." I clutched at my filthy, oily hair. "Right now I just want a bath . . . and I want this *thing* out of my chest, but *not* until we make it fix me. "

Lucius reached for me again, and I shrank back against the passenger door. "No! Don't touch me. This thing is attracting you, too."

Lucius looked confused, then thoughtful, and finally, he nodded slowly. "You're right. It's a scent that's just maddening—"

"Can you control it or do I need to get out and hitch a ride?" I asked.

"I can handle it."

"You better!"

The silence returned. I watched the sun rise and looked at a life in ashes. I had been transformed and violated in the most shocking and basic way. I was also a threat to large numbers of people, some of whom were friends, colleagues, and my actual father. And a man I had cared deeply about was dead. I fought the tears. The time for tears was over. There were duties to be performed.

"Have John's parents been informed?" I asked, forcing myself to keep my voice level.

"Yeah, I called them," Lucius said. "They claimed the body three days ago."

My eyes stung. I grimly blinked away the moisture. "And his brother?"

"I assume the parents will have told him."

"No, not him. His changeling brother. The human he was swapped with."

Lucius looked over at me. "I didn't know about him. Where is he?"

"In Fey."

"They got phones there?"

"No. I'll handle it. I can get a message to him." I cranked around so I could look at Jolly. "You guys had a man following my dad. Since my dad was at the house I have to assume something happened to him."

"They ran him off the road when he was following your father."

"Is he . . . ?"

"He'll live." Jolly gave a rather grim little smile. "The other team plays rough." He gestured at his useless legs.

"Hettie indicated you were aware of this group, knew the members." Jolly nodded. "So why didn't you bust in and get us? Why did you leave us there?"

Lucius used the rearview mirror to look at Jolly. "Yeah, good question."

"If you check the police blotters in a number of cities you'll see that we *were* looking. We just hadn't gotten to Mr. Halcomb's third house yet."

"So the cavalry was on the way," I mused.

"Yes, but we would have gotten there too late. Fortunately, you had already effected your own rescue. How did you do that, by the way?"

I explained. Both of the men looked at me, and I saw the admiration there. "Talk about making lemonade out of lemons," Lucius said, his eyes drifting down my altered form.

"And you kept your friend from being contaminated, well done," Jolly said. "Because of course if you had failed he would have had to have been killed before he could spread the contagion."

"I knew that."

"And I expect would have done the deed yourself had it proved necessary," Jolly said.

"Not something I like to think about. When did I become the person who can kill other people?"

"When they were fucking trying to kill you," Lucius said firmly. "You've got nothing to feel guilty about, but saying that doesn't fix anything. That's why we send cops for counseling after a shoot. Even a righteous shoot. You should talk to somebody."

"If only shooting somebody was my biggest problem. Lucius, if I talk to somebody I'm afraid I'll completely go to pieces." I gritted my teeth against the pain and turned around to look at Jolly again. "Jolly, what is this thing? How could it do this?"

"Well, it's not from around here."

"And what the hell does that mean?" Lucius asked before I could.

"We think they're from another dimension."

"Fey?" I asked.

"There are more dimensions than just the world of the Álfar. That's the problem with magic. You muck about with reality and probability and you can cause big and very real problems. We think some ancient magus cast a line and hooked one of these things."

"Well, can a modern magus throw it back?" I asked rather acidly.

"That's what we need to figure out. And I think it's time we come out of the shadows and involve the Convocation as well as the Álfar. You have become the bridge between all these disparate groups, Linnet. Fostered by vampires, ruler of a territory in Fey, human but more."

"I'm probably not all that popular with the werewolves," I said.

"You might be surprised. You exposed a renegade," Lucius said. "Believe me, we don't love the reputation we get for being violent assholes."

"And you didn't have any problem with Stan Brubaker, that werewolf lawyer in Los Angeles," Jolly added.

"God, you really have been watching me," I exploded.

"Yes."

"Then why weren't you there when it counted?" I yelled through tears and rage. "You let them kill John and get me."

Jolly looked devastated and older than his forty-six years. "I'm sorry. We were so busy looking to the outside threats, we didn't think about a betrayal from within."

I fell silent, fighting for control. Eventually I said thickly, "I know I can't but, damn, that is somebody I wouldn't mind killing."

Jolly shook his head. "Unfortunately, we need Ken. His research on the predator is vital. Hopefully he has the brains to realize his new compatriots will view him as a liability now, and he'll run. We're looking for him and with luck we'll find him first."

23

Lucius dropped us off at Jolly's house at the riding stable. The stall cleaners were at work picking out the stalls while the horses ate. I didn't see Kim's car and I was relieved. I didn't want to see anybody I knew. Not for a while. Actually, maybe never again. I didn't want to be a bridge, the consolidating force to unite the Powers and humans. I just wanted to be Linnet again. I wanted to practice law. Argue a case before the Supreme Court and win. Love. Marry. My brain shied away from that line of thought like a terrified horse. That line took me to John. And to what had happened to me.

The front door lock was still broken. Jolly and I both studied it. "Well, let's hope the bad guys don't come calling," he said only half-humorously.

"We can put a chair under the knob," I suggested with more than a touch of irony.

"Well, at least we'd know they're coming," Jolly said.

"Do you have a gun?" I asked.

"You've changed," he said.

"No shit," I said.

There was a moment when we both stared at each other in a "*Doh*" moment, then the absurdity of it all hit both of us. I started to giggle.

Jolly began to snort with laughter and then we were both whooping. A few minutes later I caught my breath and mopped my streaming eyes. Jolly gave me a questioning look. I shrugged. "What else can you do?"

"You're going to be fine," Jolly said gently but firmly and pushed open the door. "And by the way, several of our members are keeping watch. We won't let them take you again."

Once inside, we discovered that someone (probably Kim) had made an effort to straighten up the mess left by the cabal. The furniture was still a wreck, but the cushion stuffing had been cleaned up. Jolly pointed me toward a guest room and the attached bathroom. I was relieved to see it had a big bathtub.

"My clothes will be too big, but I'll lay out some for you. Take your time. They did rather destroy my kitchen so we'll order delivery Thai. If that's okay?"

"Sounds wonderful," I said.

He rolled out of the bathroom. I closed the door and ran scalding hot water into the tub. I stripped off my tattered and filthy clothes, balled them up, and threw them into the trash. I kept my focus on the edge of the old claw-footed tub and the beckoning water and tried not to look down at my transformed body.

Step one—don't drown yourself out of desperation. Step two—get clean. Step three—find a solution.

And if you don't? a horrid little voice asked.

Accept, I answered firmly. These bastards had been damaging me from the time of my birth. I wasn't going to let them win now.

I slid into the water, took a deep breath, and studied my new taller, broader body. I was no virgin and certainly no prude, but it was hard to do. One thing I noticed right off—not only did the parasite not do hair, it apparently didn't do circumcisions either. I gave a strangled, embarrassed sound and after that kept my eyes focused firmly on the far wall as I got clean. As promised, there was underwear, including a pair of really thick wooly socks, jeans, and a sweater laying on the bed when I emerged from the bathroom. I was wrapped tightly in a towel and discovered that breasts really do help secure a towel. I dressed quickly and went in search of Jolly.

He was in the kitchen setting out plates on the small table. White cartons exuding delicious smells dotted the table. "You didn't have to rush," he said.

"Yeah, actually, I did," I replied as I started opening drawers until I found silverware. The last time I'd been in this room it had been a filthy mess of spilled flour and sugar, broken bottles. Now it was spanking clean and smelled of Lysol.

We dished out food and began wolfing down pad Thai. One thing hadn't changed—my penchant for wanting food after shocking experiences. After a few minutes I said, in what I hoped was a level tone, "I need to get to Manhattan, to the Dakota to leave word for Parlan, and can I use your phone?" I paused for a deep, steadying breath. "I need to call Big Red and Meg."

"Are you sure that's wise? The funeral has probably already occurred." I raised stricken eyes to meet Jolly's gentle gaze. "And who will you be? A friend of John's from New York?" he asked.

Appetite gone, I set aside my fork and pushed away the plate. The doorbell rang and I tensed. A few seconds' thought made me realize that kidnappers didn't normally announce their arrival, and I let my shoulders relax.

"Stay, eat," Jolly said, and rolled out of the kitchen. Instead I listened to the murmur of male voices from out in the hall. I didn't think much of it, figuring it was some of the White Masons come to report to Jolly, but when he returned his expression was very odd.

"Lynnie, I think you need to come into the front room."

"Okay." I followed after him and froze on the threshold of the living room. My father was there. And Ken. There were two other people, a man and a woman. Their attitude screamed guards, though they held no weapons.

"What the hell?" I said.

"We're here to help," my father said.

I struggled to decide how to respond. Conflicting emotions warred in my breast. A desire to seek help and comfort, press my cheek against the tweed of his jacket, smell the aftershave and pipe tobacco. An equally strong desire to smash in his face. Instead I whirled, snatched a bookend off a nearby case, and threw it into the fireplace, where it hit with a shattering crash. Ken looked alarmed and tried to make like a turtle, pulling his head down between his shoulders.

"I'm sorry," Ken gasped out. "I didn't know . . . I didn't realize . . . what would happen. I messed everything up."

"So, *fix* it!" I growled. That was one thing my deeper voice did very well.

"I don't know how." He hurried on at my probably violent expression. "But I'm going to try. I'll figure it out. I'll fix everything, I promise."

"Yeah, well, good luck with that, Ken, because there are some things you can't fix. Dead is dead," I said harshly and it gave me a bitter pleasure when he looked stricken.

Jolly stepped in before my rage derailed everything. "So what do you propose, Doctor?"

"First, a medical doctor to make a full examination of Lin . . . Linnet." He stumbled over my name.

"We can arrange that. We have physicians among our ranks," Jolly said.

"Can we get this thing out of me?" I asked. There was a subtle flutter inside my chest. *Yeah, fuck you,* I directed the thought at my little companion. *I want you to die . . . horribly.*

"Probably . . . possibly. I mean, we want to be sure it won't fight back and harm you. Well, any more than it already has," he added lamely.

Jolly shifted his chair so he could face my father. "What is your order planning?"

"Now that this has turned into a giant clusterfuck?" my dad asked. Jolly nodded. "They know they're busted. We've"—he waved his index finger between Jolly and himself—"always kept things . . . well, let's call it . . . civil. But now the Powers know. That bloodsucker got away. The Convocation's going to be coming after us . . . them." I noted the way he set himself apart from the Black Masons. "I think they intend to take the fight into the open since our plan's been busted."

"Start the revolution, eh?" Jolly asked. My dad nodded. "Not good." He tugged thoughtfully at his upper lip. "Are there any more larvae out there?"

"Couldn't say. That wasn't my task. My job was to get close to the Powers. Form relationships, get information. All this other stuff didn't interest and involve me until—" He broke off.

"Until you lost your daughter," I said dully.

"Yeah."

I looked over at Jolly. "I don't understand. Apparently you've been watching, tracing this other group for decades—"

"More like centuries," Jolly said placidly.

"So why didn't you deal with them permanently a long time ago?"

"Because we weren't certain what powers they possessed, and whether, if they had felt threatened, they might have used them in a way that would unbalance our reality. Also, it's not what we do." He gave me a quick smile. "We're the good guys. Or at least we like to think so."

"You should have told the vampires and the werewolves, they would have handled it for you."

"And killed humans indiscriminately trying to get to the cabal, since their very survival would have been at stake. Which would have led to the war that seems to be threatening to break out now. No, it was safer to foil them."

"You're not as pure as you claim," my dad said. "You didn't manage to save any of the other women who were infected. You let the Spooks kill them."

Suspicion bloomed and I stared at Jolly. "You really like to stir the pot, don't you, Mr. Ellery?" Jolly's kind smile was starting to look more like a grimace. Jolly met my gaze. "We didn't have the tools, technology, or understanding before now to actually try to cure someone. In the past we focused on destroying the larvae, but once it was implanted, we had to rely on the Powers to end the threat. The last time they"—he indicated my father—"got this close was in 1908. The Powers took a rather extreme and violent action." I frowned. There was something niggling in the back of my head about that date but I couldn't place it. "Tunguska," Jolly said quietly.

"Tunguska!" Ken yelped. "Jesus Christ! But wait, nobody was killed."

"That's the official story. One young woman and a predator were killed," Jolly said.

"Talk about swatting a fly with a bomb," I muttered.

"One assumes they were very close to releasing the predator. Rather like now." I couldn't help it, I cast a nervous glance at the ceiling. "Hettie has gone to the Convocation requesting a meeting. They won't act precipitously this time," he said soothingly.

"The vampires might not, but the werewolves?" My skepticism was evident.

"The world is a different place in the twenty-first century, and the Powers are in the open. They won't risk destroying the acceptance they have achieved. They'll hear us out."

"Well, I sure hope you're right," I said. "Let me know how that meeting goes so I can decide if I need to go on the run."

"Oh, you're going to be there," Jolly said serenely.

"Whaaaa?" was all I could manage.

I had fled after that, and returned to the kitchen, where I was in the process of furiously scraping my uneaten food into the garbage disposal. My father came in.

"May I talk with you?"

"No!"

"Look, I understand you're upset—"

"Upset! UPSET! Upset does not begin to express what I'm feeling."

"Look, I saved the scientist. The others wanted to kill him, but I rescued him because I thought he might be able to help you. I came here for you."

The plate hit the counter with more force than I'd intended and broke in half. I cringed. I was taking a real toll on Jolly's possessions because of a combination of rage and strength I still couldn't control.

"Oh damn," I said. I leaned on the edge of the sink for a moment, then turned to face him. He wasn't a tall man, but to me he had seemed tall. Now we stood eye-to-eye. "What do you want from me? Thanks? Forgiveness? What?"

"Maybe a bit of both."

"Well, you can forget the thanks. You've stolen my life from me on every level and in every way. I was pushed into my career. I thought I was pleasing you and making you proud by becoming a lawyer, but it was just to further your plans. A man I cared deeply about is dead because of you, and I can't even call his parents to offer my condolences because I've been violated in ways that are beyond description. How can I ever see Charlie again? Any of my friends?"

He studied my changed form. "I didn't realize that could happen—"

"No, you just thought I would die and apparently *that* would have been okay."

He fell silent and began spinning the salt shaker. The scratching sound of metal on wood filled the room. "You think I'm a monster," he finally said.

"I know you are. Your group talks about the Powers as monsters, but you're the real evil. You exemplify every hateful, xenophobic tendency that humans possess."

Another moment of silence. He traced his mustache with his little finger, then looked at me from beneath his lashes. "Okay, so thanks is a no-go . . . How do you think we'll do on the forgiveness front?" It was said with the light charm that exemplified his personality and smoothed his way through the world winning friends and contracts.

I made a choked sound and shook my head. Partly in wonder and amazement and partly in frustration. "Ask me in a few years." I headed out of the kitchen.

"Assuming we live that long," he called after me.

I woke in the gray light just before dawn. I got up, dressed, and slipped out of the house. Frost had turned the grass into white-tipped spears and it crunched beneath my feet. Hay had been thrown to the horses, and I could hear the engine of the John Deere Gator firing up over in the equipment shed. I went into the feed room and mixed up a bran mash for Vento, liberally sprinkled with carrots, and carried it to his stall.

His ears were flipping back and forth as he whuffled at me. Apparently he decided I was actually not a stranger, and he licked my hand. I slipped into the stall and poured the steaming mash into his feed tub. I wrapped my arms around his neck, pressed my face against his warm hair, and breathed in the dusty, grassy scent of horse while he ate.

"You should take him out for a ride." Jolly's voice behind me.

"And you're going to tell me I can use your clothes, right?" I gave Vento a slap on the neck and turned to face his owner.

"Yes."

"Are you going to come along?" I tapped first Vento on the forehead and then Jolly.

"Not if you don't want me to."

I left the stall and sat down on the blanket box in the breezeway. "Okay, now I can ask you. How did you happen to be there at just the right moment in California?"

"I always left a small part of my consciousness in the horse. Whenever you turned up I paid closer attention. And it didn't take a rocket scientist to know that when I got awakened at three in the morning to the sound of you crying, something was probably wrong. I took a look, realized what was happening, and called David while Vento worked that metal clasp."

"Thank you. You saved my life."

"Yes, I did rather." He smiled at me and I found myself smiling back. "Good," he said approvingly. "Now ride your horse and smile some more."

"Okay."

"May I watch?"

"Sure."

Like the regular clothes, Jolly's riding britches were too big, as were the boots, but I stuffed a sock in the toe of each boot and made it work. The day brightened and I worked on finding my balance point in the saddle.

"So, how is it?" he asked when I transitioned down from the canter and gave Vento a walk break.

"Different. Uncomfortable at points."

"I set out an athletic supporter for you."

"Yeah . . . and no." I hurriedly changed the subject. "It is nice having a longer leg. I can cue the lateral work so much more easily."

A BMW pulled up to Jolly's house and I recognized it as Hettie's. She and David climbed out, unfurled umbrellas against the sun, and hurried into the house.

"I think that is our cue to stop being equestrians," Jolly said. He opened the arena gate for me and we headed back toward the barn.

"I haven't seen Kim," I said.

"No, I told her to take a couple of days off. We didn't need any awkward questions right now."

I didn't like doing it, but I turned Vento over to one of the grooms. I preferred to tack and untack my own horse, but the real world had intruded and I couldn't take the time. Jolly and I returned to the house.

Hettie and David were in the living room, to-go cups of Starbucks' house-blend blood in their hands. All of the blisters were gone, but they had left faint scars as if he'd had a terrible case of acne in his youth. He had been a handsome man but, thanks to me, those good looks were being eroded.

"They've agreed to meet," Hettie said as we entered. "Given the gravity of the situation they want to call in representatives from Europe, Asia, Australia, and Africa so it's been set in three days' time."

"Good," Jolly said. "That gives us time to gather our own representatives."

"Looking to keep up appearances?" David asked sourly.

"Exactly. We know how much importance your kind in particular place on protocol."

While they talked, David had been edging toward me. Hettie reached out, grabbed the sleeve of his suit coat, and reeled him back. He gave her an irritated look. "I just wanted to say hello to Linnet."

"No you didn't. But nice try." She crossed to me and gave me a quick, chill-inducing hug.

"How can you do that and not be tempted?" David demanded.

Hettie shrugged. "Don't know. Just not interested." David made a growling noise and paced away. "We've got you lined up to be examined by Dr. Maness this afternoon," Hettie continued. She glanced at Jolly. "Ken should probably also be present."

"Absolutely."

David whirled. "Ken? How did you get him?"

"Linnet's father showed up with him last night." David reacted by crushing his cup, sending blood cascading over his fingers and onto the rug.

"Jeez, David, now you've wrecked Jolly's rug," I said.

"It's all right. Small loss," the Englishman said placidly.

"Is he still here?" David asked.

I didn't mistake who the *he* was David was talking about. "Yes, as far as I know my dad is still here and, no, you still can't kill him." There was another growly noise from my former boss.

24

It had been a long afternoon. I had been poked with needles and had enough blood drawn to fund a blood bank. There had been X-rays, a physical exam that was intrusive and embarrassing, and there had again been an MRI. That had been hard. I had stood in the middle of the room, staring at the metal tube and shivering. Only Jolly's quiet and calming presence had gotten me back into that machine. Ken had been present, standing at Dr. Maness's side as tests were run. We were careful to never look at each other or speak to each other.

I was also quivering with anxiety because I had yet to get a message to Parlan about John. Red and Meg probably really needed their firstborn son and he wasn't there because I was a terrible person, focused only on my problems, and hadn't told him. It was now nearly six o'clock. I was seated on an examination table in a small, stark-white and sterile room. Hettie had turned up a few minutes before and was now perched in a chair. Jolly was trying to maneuver his wheelchair out of the way of the door so Dr. Maness and, presumably, Ken would be able to get in when they finally finished reading the MRI and the X-rays and examining my blood and studying the entrails of a chicken for all I knew. I was not kindly disposed to any Masonic order right now—black or white.

"So, you'll take me to the Dakota after this?" I asked for probably the fifth time.

"We can't get into the inner courtyard, Lynnie," Jolly said. I detected less patience in the answer than there had been previously.

"There are Álfar guards out front too. They'll know me."

"Not as you are now," Hettie pointed out.

I opened and closed my mouth several times, trying to think of an answer to that, but came up blank. The door opened and the doctor entered with Ken trailing after him. The scientist was carrying a laptop. William Maness was a handsome man in his mid-forties with a neatly trimmed goatee and mustache and no gray in his brunette hair or beard. He was frowning down at the papers in a manila folder, but he smiled when he looked up at me. I looked back suspiciously, wondering if that was the patented "doctor smile," meant to be reassuring when they're about to give you horrible news.

"Well, Miss Linnet, you are an interesting conundrum. You have all the external indicators of a male, but you still have ovaries and a uterus, and your testosterone level, while elevated for a female, is still below what I would expect to find in a normal, healthy young male of twenty-eight." He glanced up from his notes. "And your sperm is not viable."

"Well, that's a relief, I was so worried I was going to knock somebody up," I said acerbically.

"So, you're not attracted—"

"To women? No," I answered before he could finish the question. "Look, all of this may be fascinating to you, but I only have one question. How do you turn me back?"

Now he had the serious doctor expression. "Well, that's a problem." He stuck X-rays up on a light panel, turned to Ken, and held out his hands, saying, "May I?" Ken handed him the laptop. Maness opened it and brought up the MRI scan.

"This is one hell of a critter. It's using your lymph channels as trails for sending out these filaments. A couple of them have punctured your jugular."

"Yes, I know," I said, and I glared at Ken.

"But it's also sent a tangle of these threads into your left atrium."

I stared at the image on the computer. There was my beating heart with what looked like roots growing inside one of the cavities. It was phantom pain, not real, but I pressed a hand hard against my chest, horrified by what I was seeing. "Wh . . ." I cleared my throat and tried again. "Why?" I managed to croak.

The three White Masons exchanged glances. "We think it's a protective move on the part of the parasite," the physician said.

"Meaning?" I asked.

"That if we try to surgically remove the creature from your chest it could throw you into refractory ventricular fibrillation. We might be able to do it if we had a heart to swap in for yours. And we'd have five minutes to do it if we want there to be a brain left," Maness added.

I couldn't sit still any longer. I slid off the table and paced the very small available space in the crowded room. The heart we had just been discussing was hammering against my ribs. I clenched and unclenched my fists and felt the nails biting into my palms. *Need to get off the polish and cut them short if I'm stuck like this*, I found myself thinking inanely.

I hate you, I directed to the creature.

Another thought. *It saved your life.*

No, it saved its own life. I was just along for the ride.

Everyone stayed silent, allowing me to process. I took a deep breath and looked around at all of them. "Well, that's it then." I started for the door, shoving Ken out of the way to get there.

Hettie spoke up. "Ken, what will likely happen to the parasite if a vampire does bite Linnet?"

The scientist frowned at the far wall. "Often the principal creature will die. It's met its evolutionary imperative."

"Thank you," she said.

I gave her a suspicious look. "Why? Why ask that?"

"Just trying to get a better understanding."

"Hettie, you rarely ask random questions," Jolly said. "What are you thinking?"

"We'll talk about it later, Jolly dear," she said as she patted his cheek.

"Even though we have an agreement with the Convocation I'd feel better if you were in Fey and out of the reach of any disgruntled vampires or werewolves."

I was sitting in darkness in the guest room at Jolly's house, gazing out the window at moonlight washing across the barn and arenas. It was Jolly's voice that emerged out of the gloom. I didn't answer. "Just tell me how and we'll leave a message for Parlan."

"No. I don't want to see him. I don't want to see anyone I used to know."

"We'll find a solution."

"You really believe that?" Silence. "Yeah, that's what I thought."

"Lynnie, we really are trying to help," he said gently.

I closed my burning eyes and tried to release the inchoate rage that held me in its corrosive grip. "I know. I'm sorry. I don't mean to be such a . . . bitch."

"It's all right."

"So what's the plan with the Convocation? Are you going to turn them loose on the other group? And what do you want me to say?"

"Since Dr. Maness was unable to remove the creature we've decided it's best you not attend. We wouldn't want anything to . . . er . . . happen."

"Yeah, guess it would kind of wreck the big powwow if werewolves and vampires started jumping on me." Once again, bitterness infused the words.

"It can't be denied you have a strong effect on Powers," Jolly said.

"Except Hettie."

"Yes, well, but Hettie is rather a unique case. Only female Power in the world, so far as we know."

A thought as fragile as mist and as fleeting as a falling star flickered through my mind and was gone before I could grasp it. I tried in vain to pull it back but it was gone, having left only the faintest residue, like the aftermath of a camera flash on the retina of an eye.

"Jolly, do me a favor. Call Red and Meg. Tell them you're a friend of mine, but please make sure that Parlan knows about . . . about John."

"They'll want to know about you," he pointed out.

"Tell them I died too. It's not all that far from the truth."

The look he gave me was both sad and frustrated. I knew he wanted to help and that his frustration was directed at himself, at his inability to fix this, but there was nothing he or anyone could do. I had been brave and resourceful and, for the most part, I had controlled my emotions, but now I was tired and devastated. I had nothing left emotionally, which translated into a physical exhaustion so profound that all I wanted to do was crawl into bed and pull the covers over my head.

"Do you want some dinner?" Jolly asked.

I shook my head. He turned his chair and left me alone in the bedroom. I vacillated between going to bed, walking over to the barn to see Vento, taking a bath, and reading a book. I decided to follow my first impulse. I shed Jolly's borrowed clothes and burrowed under the down comforter. I didn't so much fall asleep as plummet into a black abyss.

Unfortunately, there were monsters waiting there. I kept seeing

John, but often he was covered with oozing blisters as he and David became entwined. Blood, like rising floodwaters, lapped about me. Hands gripped the back of my neck, trying to force my head below those sticky red waters.

A touch on my bare shoulder had me fighting the covers. I struck out with a fist, a panicked reaction, and had my hand gripped in an icy vise.

"Lynnie, Lynnie, calm down, it's me." It was Hettie. I sat up, gasping for air. "I'm sorry. I didn't mean to scare you," she said

At the same time, I said, "I'm sorry, I didn't mean to hit you." My little rider was quivering with excitement again. I sent hateful thoughts in its direction, to which it reacted not at all.

Her face was in shadow, but her smile was a flash of ivory in the moonlight. "Needless to say, you didn't hurt me." She swept my sweat-matted hair out of my eyes. "Bad dreams?" she asked.

I nodded. "Very bad dreams."

The mattress sagged a bit as she sat down on the edge of the bed. I stuffed the pillow behind my back and leaned against the headboard. Frowning, I tried to read her expression, and finally gave up, leaned over, and snapped on the lamp on the bedside table. "You've got the look of a guilty puppy," I said.

There was a flash of offended vampire and then she laughed. "Yes, I suppose I probably do. Linnet, I think there is a way to end this for you." Suddenly breathless, I found myself cringing back against the pillow. She made an erasing gesture in the air between us. "No, wait, scratch that. That sounded ominous."

"Yeah, it kinda did."

"I mean, I think we can allow the predator to die so it can be safely removed. And I wonder, if it were no longer active in your body, if you wouldn't default back to your normal form? What?" she asked in response to my expression.

"I want that almost more than anything, but I dread it and I'm scared. It hurt so bad when it did this to me. Going through it again . . ." I shivered, then squared my jaw and took a breath. "But I'd do it if I could be me again. So, what are you thinking?"

"That I bite you." She held up a hand to forestall the reaction she saw coming. "I spent a few more hours with Ken and we looked over a lot of literature. I think this thing will die once it delivers its pathogen."

"But. But then you'll die!"

"Maybe, but maybe not. The fact I'm not being driven wild by you is interesting, and I'm a woman. These things have had several thousand years to adjust to only affecting males. It can only gestate in a female. What if it can only spread its DNA via males?"

"But we don't know that. You're risking your life."

"I'm very old, Linnet." She forced air out of her lungs to form a sigh. "And rather tired. Oh, I put up a good front, but sometimes the years lay on me with the weight of mountains."

"Hettie, I can't be responsible for your death too. I've already cost John his life. Please, don't—"

Her hands closed on my shoulders, pinning me against the head-board. I had as much chance of breaking free as a butterfly trying to escape a lepidopterist. I gasped as her fangs punctured the skin of my throat, then a warm lassitude washed through me and a sense of deep contentment. Her lips closed over the wounds and she sucked at the blood. She drank and I hovered on the edge of unconscious-ness. Eventually, she released me and lowered me onto the bed. That sense of presence that had been with me for so many months began to fade. There was pain again. Not as severe as what I'd endured in that cellar, but significant. Hettie held my hand, stroked my sweat-slick forehead. Eventually, it passed. I lay panting on the bed with my eyes tightly closed. Slowly, I reached up and touched my chest. I had breasts again and my hips felt right.

"It put me back," I said softly.

"I think it was forcibly holding you in that strange hermaphroditic state," Hettie said.

I opened my eyes and looked up at her. "I still don't feel one hundred percent like myself."

The vampire smiled. "Probably not. You're taller, Linnet. That didn't change back. Probably a good thing. If the energy that creature stole to affect the change had been released we might have blown out the wall of Jolly's house."

"Not to mention it probably wouldn't have been too good for us either."

She forced air out and chuckled. "Probably not."

"Speaking of . . . How do *you* feel?"

She cocked her head and smacked her lips. "Fine. Though I wouldn't expect any symptoms yet. I have to become irresistible to vampires and werewolves first and get bitten numerous times before it kills me." She gave me a smile. "We should get David over here and see if he finds me beguiling and tantalizing. Somehow I doubt that will happen."

"You have a theory."

"I think the creature will try to implant as if I'm a host rather than generate the killing pathogens. If it does, we can surgically remove it because it can do fuck all to my heart."

I stood up. I was a bit shaky and Hettie grabbed me to keep me upright. I looked down the length of my restored body. "Well, I'll be able to use my leg more effectively when I ride. That's a win." I paused. "On the sucky side—I have to buy a whole new wardrobe."

Hettie laughed again. "Well, you'll certainly need something to wear before we go to the Convocation. In Jolly's hand-me-downs you look rather like Chaplin's Little Tramp."

25

"What have you done? Oh, Hettie, what have you done?"

"Oh, for God's sake, Jolyon, stop having a glamour fit. I returned our girl to normal," she said proudly.

Jolly spun his chair to face me. "And you agreed to this?"

I opened my mouth, but Hettie ran over me. "Of course, she didn't. She tried to argue so I just attacked her."

Jolly moaned and dropped his face into his hands.

We were in the living room early the next morning. Jolly's expression when I'd come in wrapped in a frothy, lacy dressing gown that belonged to Hettie was first delighted, then comically dismayed. That's when he'd started yelling at Hettie.

"Linnet needs clothes so I'm going to go shopping and get her some."

"Where'd she get that?" he asked, pointing at the dressing gown.

"It's mine."

"You don't sleep."

"What has that to do with anything? It's pretty. And I'm still a girl."

"You're a nightmare is what you are," he muttered.

She leaned down and patted his cheek. "I'll be back in a few hours."

I finally managed to utter a few words. "Really, Hettie, you don't have to shop for me—"

"This is the closest I will ever come to having a daughter," she said. "So don't argue."

"Okay." She started for the door. "Don't forget shoes," I called after her.

"As if I would. Shoes are what I live for—so to speak." She gave us a jaunty wave and was gone.

I looked over at Jolly. "I'm sorry. If I could have stopped her, I would have. If it's any comfort, she doesn't think the parasite will . . . well . . . kill her."

"But she might still be able to infect others. She should have waited for our ruling council to arrive before taking such an action," he grumbled.

Hettie stuck her head back in the door. "Oh, forgot. I'm going to stop by IMG and see if anybody wants to bite me."

"What!" Jolly shouted, but she was gone again. "Damn the woman! You can't tell her a damn thing."

"She's four thousand years old, Jolly. Why would she listen to anything any of us tell her?"

He scratched his chin, where he was sporting a mix of silver and gold stubble, and gave me a rueful smile. "You're right." He paused and frowned at me. "You're taller."

"Yeah. I noticed."

"How do you feel otherwise?"

I touched the place on my breast where the predator had lurked. "I don't sense it any longer."

"Well, that's good. We'll get you to Dr. Maness as soon as possible."

"Good. I want this thing out of me." A new thought intruded. "Uh, where's my dad?"

"Being debriefed by our council."

"Ah. Okay." I tried to figure out how to phrase my question and finally gave up and decided to just say it. "Jolly, am I ever going to have my life back? A normal life? A boring life?"

"I don't think you've ever had a normal life. Fostered by a vampire, Ivy League educated, your first job was in a world-class law firm, ruler of a principality in Fey."

"How did you know about that?"

"Hettie told me."

"When you woke up?"

"No, she told Vento while I was residing there."

"I am never going to get used to that."

The doorbell rang. I tensed. Jolly held up a hand. "Probably Parlan. We reached him late last night."

He rolled out of the room, heading to the door. I wanted to rush to the door, but I also wanted to rush back to the bedroom and hide. I dreaded the coming meeting. At least I wouldn't have to face it as the wrong gender. Male voices in the hallway and then the two men entered. Parlan looked drawn and tired, but his expression lightened when he saw me. He crossed in three long strides and hugged me tight.

"Thank the Phase you are all right. I should never have let you leave. And I intend to kill that miserable scientist."

"Oh, please don't lay this big testosterone act on me," I said, more weary than angry. "Haven't enough people died already as a result of this clusterfuck?"

"My brother is dead and you were taken. Can I just let that go?"

"Yes, because I'm asking you to. And if that's not enough, I'll tell you." Parlan bowed his head in acquiescence.

"And we need Ken. If there are more of these creatures out there, we have to figure out how to neutralize them," Jolly added.

"All right, all right. I'll do as you wish, but I don't have to like it," Parlan said, then added, "Just don't expect me to be polite to the bastard."

"I can't manage that either, so no problem," I said. I took his hand and led him over to the battered couch. We sat down. "How did you find out what had happened? And were you there for Red and Meg?"

"Red contacted me. Left letters at the intersections. I was there for the funeral. Your Catholicism is rather beautiful, though I found the man nailed to a cross of wood to be rather disturbing. And I met my actual sister and brothers," he said with some wonder. "They . . . welcomed me."

"Of course they did. They're Red and Margret O'Shea's kids."

"I'm beginning to understand what that means," Parlan said. "I was raised to be heedless, proud, and self-indulgent. They all serve. And even while they grieved for John, their thoughts were on you. My father"—I realized that was the first time Parlan had ever called Red "father"—"called the Philly police and asked for help in searching for you."

The thought of that action warmed me and gave me some small hope that Red and Meg didn't hate me. I voiced that fear and Parlan shook his head. "No, they would never blame you. You were a victim too."

"I need to tell them that John regained his humanity right at the end."

"They'll be glad to hear that, and I'm glad for you too. So what do we do now? As a faithful member of your Scooby Gang"—he stood and bowed—"I stand ready to serve."

The juxtaposition of the formal Álfar presentation with mentions of Scooby-Doo had Jolly choking on a laugh. It made me smile too. "We find these Black Masons and put them out of business. First step, we enlist the aid of the Convocation that governs matters pertaining to werewolves and vampires."

"Yes, she is a lawyer," Jolly murmured.

"I will be at your side," Parlan said.

"Actually, it's just going to be Linnet, me, and the master of our order," Jolly said.

Something about that hit me wrong, and then I realized what. I shook my head. "No, Jolly, if I'm really the bridge, as you claim, then we need to broaden the membership." I stood up and began pacing excitedly. "We need David and Hettie and Parlan and Lucius and Ladlaw. Think about it, Jolly. It needs to be more than just three humans telling a council of Powers *Hey trust us, we'll take care of a human plot to kill you all.*"

Parlan was grinning and Jolly just shook his head. "She's quite correct," Parlan said.

"Yes, damn it, she is."

Parlan turned his smile on me. "By the way, you look quite fetching in that cloud of lace." He then frowned and looked puzzled. "Though there is something . . . different . . . Have you changed your hair?"

Jolly and I exchanged glances and I laughed. It felt good. Despite all the loss, pain, and sorrow it was a promise that life did get better and that I would survive.

Naturally, the Convocation met at the Cloisters because of *course* they did. Only the Powers would think they had the right to use the museum built from parts of five different European abbeys and funded by money from John D. Rockefeller as a place for their meetings.

"If they wanted old buildings why are they meeting in the United States?" I asked as we drove the winding road through Fort Tryon Park at the extreme north end of Manhattan.

"Because the U.S. is where power resides. We are the only super-power left," David said from the backseat.

We were a tiny convoy of two cars. Our car, driven by Lucius, led the way. We had the two vampires in the backseat. In the following car were Parlan, Ladlaw, Jolly, and the master of the White Masons, who had turned out to be a mistress. Madame Adrienne Pelletier was a tiny woman who looked to be in her seventies or eighties, but her dark eyes were piercing, missing nothing, and she had a motherly smile that was at odds with her clipped French accent. She exchanged air kisses with Hettie, patted Jolly on the cheek, reducing him to a boy with one gesture, shook hands with Parlan and declared he looked a fool in those clothes, told Ladlaw she wished she was ten years younger, and thanked Lucius for his service. She then took my chin in her gnarled hand and studied my face.

"You have suffered but survived," she said, and I had found myself blinking back tears. "Don't cry in front of the Convocation," she said. "Like all men, they can't handle a woman's tears. And they *always* assume they are a sign of female weakness. Poor fools," she added with that sparkling smile.

We pulled up to the front of the building. Moonlight washed the gray stone, turning it to silver, and made the tiles on the roof look like blood. There were guards who opened the doors and scanned each of us with frowning attention. They were more of the heavy-featured, brutal-looking vampires I had seen at the Hunter kennel. They bared their fangs at Hettie. David bared his in response. Hettie merely gave them a disdainful look and stalked past them with the air of a queen mingling with the hoi polloi. She then stood in front of the closed doors and gave the guards a pointed look. One of them actually hurried forward to open a door for her. She swept through and David gave a hoarse laugh and followed her into the building. A vampire was waiting for us just inside.

Within a few moments the rest of our party had joined us and the vampire led us deeper into the building. Our footsteps echoed off the stone walls, and the blank eyes of statues, paintings, and effigies seemed to follow us. It was unnerving, and I swallowed several times, trying to summon saliva from a suddenly dry mouth. At least I looked the part of brave rebel leader, or at least I hoped I did. Hettie had impeccable taste and had dressed me in a calf-length beige skirt cut on the bias so it hung at different lengths against my knee-high black boots. I wore a black silk shirt and a short black leather jacket finished the ensemble. Hettie was dressed in her usual shimmering peacock-colored silk blouse and black leather pants and boots. She looked very beautiful and very badass.

David couldn't keep his eyes off her. He might have been dead, but he wasn't dead-dead, I thought. I choked down a nervous giggle. His gaze held none of that red flicker he'd gotten when he'd wanted to bite me. He just seemed like a poleaxed ox, and I hoped he had started to transfer his affection for me to Hettie. She was certainly a more appropriate object for his affection. I just wondered if the age difference would prove to be a problem. There was again that giggle response. I bit the inside of my cheek to quell it.

We were taken into a long hallway lined on one side with windows inset with stained glass in some of the mullions. They looked out on the arches and columns of a cloister walk. The moonlight was bright enough I could make out the garden beyond. A dais had been set up at the far end with a table and chairs, forcing us to look up at the fourteen men seated there. It was all designed to make us feel very insignificant.

I started a bit when I saw my vampire liege, Meredith Bainbridge, among the fourteen. I shouldn't have been surprised. I knew he was very old and the fact that he took in fosterlings from human families should have given me a clue. Seven of the men were vampires, the other seven werewolves. I recognized one of the wolves as the head of Goldman Sachs and another was a member of the Joint Chiefs.

They were staring at all of us, but mostly at Hettie. She gave them the fang-baring smile. "Yes, boys, I'm not a unicorn, a griffin, or a dragon. Or any other kind of mythical creature you can name. I'm real."

"You run a risk coming here," said Meredith. "All of you."

I stepped forward. "No, actually, we don't. We've all got a problem, and you're going to need us—*all* of us—to help you solve it."

BORNI   FLT
Bornikova, Phillipa.
Publish and perish /

05/18